Kiss my PUCKING BASS

Sheridan Anne
Kiss My Pucking Bass - Kings of Denver (Book 3)

Copyright © 2023 Sheridan Anne
All rights reserved
First Published in 2023

Anne, Sheridan
Kings of Denver (Book 3) Kiss My Pucking Bass

This book is a work of fiction. Names, characters, places, and incidents are products of the author's imagination. Any resemblance to actual events or persons, living or dead, is entirely coincidental.

No part of this book may be reproduced, stored in a retrieval system, or transmitted in any form or by any means, without prior permission in writing of the publisher, nor be otherwise circulated in any form of the binding or cover other than in which it is published, and without a similar condition, including this condition, being imposed on the subsequent purchaser.

Cover Design: Sheridan Anne
Editing: Fox Proof Edits
Formatting: Sheridan Anne
Beta: Holly Swain-Harvey & Kat Uluave

DISCLAIMER

Kiss My Pucking Bass was previously published as Xander - Kings of Denver (Book 3) 2018-2022.

The content of Kiss My Pucking Bass remains the same with new edits and tightening up of each chapter. The story within has not changed. Simply received a facelift plus new interior formatting, title, and cover.

PROLOGUE

XANDER

10 YEARS EARLIER

My brows furrow as my father pulls into a parking space and cuts the engine outside Big Rex Gym. "What are we doing here?" I ask, watching as he gets out of the car.

Dad doesn't bother glancing back at me as he throws his orders over his shoulder. "Grab your training bag," he mutters, the loud slam of his door making me jump.

Reaching into the back and doing as I'm told, I haul my training bag off the seat before rushing out of the car and scrambling to catch up with him. It doesn't pay to be tardy with my father.

We walk in silence as he leads me toward the gym, every step confusing me further. I have no idea why we're here. Aren't gyms for adults who want to lose weight or turn themselves into big muscle men? It's possible my dad had the sudden urge for a workout, but he wouldn't have brought me along for that. And he could have just used our home gym. It doesn't make sense.

Reaching the door, Dad pulls it open and ushers me inside before striding through and letting it fall shut behind us. As we head deeper inside the gym, I take a good look around. The place is packed with men and women working their butts off, sweat drenching their clothes as grunts and groans fill the room, and I can guarantee there are no other kids in here. Just me.

I take in the sights. Women on treadmills jogging with their earphones in. Big, bulky men lifting heavy weights with strange belts locked tightly around their waists. A couple of different studios are in the middle of hosting classes, and another class is taking a break. The place is awesome, but it's no place for me.

An older man with bulging muscles approaches my father, his sharp gaze sailing over me with suspicion, and I do my best to stand up straight and pay attention. After all, I wouldn't want to make my father look bad. That never ends well.

"You must be Byron?" the man asks, sticking his hand out for my father to shake.

"Indeed, I am," my father responds with a curt nod, sparing me a small glance before turning back to the man. "Thank you for meeting with me on such short notice."

"No problem at all. My name's Rex," he says, his gaze falling to me. "You must be Xander?"

My gaze narrows suspiciously. How does he know who I am? My

brows furrow, and feeling the sharp, disapproving stare from my father, I straighten myself out, positive my delayed response has just earned me a one-way ticket to the back of his hand. "Yes, sir. I'm Xander."

"Good," my father cuts in as he checks his watch. "Now that we're all acquainted, he's all yours. I'll be back at seven to pick him up."

What the . . .? Seven? That's three hours away. I didn't just get my first job, did I? Nah, couldn't be that. My family is loaded and I'm only eleven. Surely there are rules against kids working, right? Don't get me wrong, I'd love a job if it meant getting out of that house, but this doesn't feel right.

I'm still lost in thought trying to figure out what the hell I'm doing here when Rex pulls me out of my head. "Right, you're with me," he says as he starts walking away, making me realize my father is already long gone.

Not sure what I've just gotten myself into, I scramble to catch up. I'm certain anything that happens here is going to get back to my father.

Rex strides through to a back office and I follow through his door, taking in my surroundings as I do so. He asks me to stand tall against his back wall and spread my arms out. I do as I'm asked, and he starts writing numbers down. It takes me a while to realize he's taking my measurements. "Um, excuse me, sir?" I ask. "What am I doing here?"

He looks up with a strange thoughtfulness, something that I don't tend to see from the other adults I'm usually surrounded by. "You don't know?" he questions, making something within me want to like him.

"No, sir."

He lets out a breath and astonishment flashes in his eyes. "First off, cut the *sir* bullshit," he warns, leaning back in his seat and watching me closely. "The name's Rex. Use it. Secondly, you're here to train. You'll be here every afternoon after school."

"What?" My eyes bug out of my head, not impressed with this revelation in the slightest. But hell, I should have expected some kind of messed up move from my father. This is hardly surprising.

Rex shrugs his shoulders. "Apparently you're some big ice hockey protégée and your father wants to ensure you stay that way."

Disappointment fires through my chest. I should have known this had something to do with hockey. Everything *always* has something to do with hockey. "Fine," I sigh, knowing without a doubt that I don't have a choice here. My father will do anything to make sure I make it to the NHL.

The day I showed just the tiniest bit of talent on the ice is the day it went downhill. My father not only saw money bags, but he saw his chance to become relevant in the hockey world again. He's a former star no one even remembers, and I'm his ticket back into the limelight. But I don't mind playing along for now. I'm sure Mom and Dad will eventually loosen the reins and let me try a few other sports one day.

"You don't seem too impressed," Rex murmurs, studying me with a sharp, curious gaze.

"Would you be? My friends are going to the movies this afternoon, and I'm stuck here training for a future in hockey," I scoff.

"What's with the tone?" he questions, crossing his big arms over his chest. "You're not keen about a future in hockey?"

"I mean, I don't know," I tell him with a shrug, having to look away from his intimidating stare. "I like to play."

"But you don't love it?"

I shake my head ever so slightly, feeling a strange betrayal settle in the pit of my stomach. Admitting after all these years that hockey isn't the love of my life like my father expects it to be, feels odd. Wrong, almost. But for some reason, I find myself trusting this guy. "No, I don't."

"What are you interested in?"

I shrug my shoulders again. "I don't know."

Rex considers me for a moment before standing up from his desk. "Alright, here's the plan. Whether you like it or not, you're here every afternoon until seven. So, you're going to take every class we offer until you figure out what you want to do, and then I'll train you after classes in agility and strength to keep your father off my back."

My eyes widen, feeling a ray of hope burning through my stomach. "Really?" I ask, my back straightening, somehow feeling taller.

"Sure thing, kid," he says, walking out to the gym. I follow behind and listen intently to the only person who has not only heard me, but is willing to do something about it. Rex looks down at his watch then back to me. "The mixed martial arts class starts in fifteen minutes. It's an adult class, but it'll have to do. Go and get warmed up."

I make my way deeper into the gym, trying out the treadmill, but I'm really not sure what I'm doing. I usually run outdoors to warm up, but I guess I'm trying new things today.

Fifteen minutes later, I walk into the martial arts room, unsure and nervous, then an hour later, I walk back out seeing my future so perfectly laid out. It's suddenly all too clear that I've been wasting my time with hockey.

Martial arts is it for me. I know it with everything I am.

I guess now all I have to do is tell my father.

CHAPTER 1

XANDER

New year, new me.

Yeah, fucking right.

It's my junior year of college, and my dick of a father pulled every damn string he could to get me transferred to Denver University so I could be a part of the team that took out the championship last season. Not to mention, the Denver Dragons just happen to be the same college team he played for.

How fucking sweet of him.

I get it. He was a Dragon, the team captain his senior year, and he got himself a one-way ticket into the NHL. I can't blame him for wanting the same for me. The only problem is that anything else that might be a viable option for me simply isn't an option at all. Not according to him.

Dad's plan has always been the same. Get into the NHL and make our name relevant again. What a fucking joke. He's put me through all of this shit just so he can have his two seconds of fame and show the world what a great job he's done raising his son. Fucking bullshit. If I could, I would have bailed years ago, but the fucker's got me by the balls—quit skating and lose everything. My trust fund, my living arrangement, my whole fucking life. I'd be out on the streets.

And what does my mother do about it? Fuck all.

Great parents I have.

So every day, I skate. Day in and day out. And despite how I feel about it, my years of training have ensured that I'm the fucking best. Well, apart from Jaxon. He's not so bad.

I've only been in Denver a few weeks, and I can already see it in Coach Harris' eyes. He wants to offer me the role of captain for next year. It's way too early in the season to be thinking about that shit, but I can feel it coming from a mile away. If only that's what I actually wanted.

Coach Harris knows who I am and who my father is. Hell, he trained my father twenty-odd years ago, and without a doubt, I know he expects me to be just like him. The shining star, the golden boy, the kid who's going to lead the Dragons to victory next season.

Not if I get a say in it. This isn't who I am, and it's not who I want to be.

My blades cut through the ice as we finish our morning training session, and I must admit, I'm already exhausted. Jaxon, this season's captain, has us up early running every fucking morning and then working out in a field before we head to classes or to our on-ice training sessions. Not to mention all the added gym time we've been politely asked to do, but it isn't a question at all. It's mandatory. My last team was nothing like this. We showed up for training, worked our asses off, and went home. It's no surprise Dad wanted me here, especially after the Dragon's epic win last year.

Jaxon is a great captain, and I have no doubt we'll be undefeated champions come the end of the season. Coach Harris and Jaxon together are a deadly team. It's admirable, really. I'm not saying it's going to be easy, but every senior on this team will have the attention of every scout across the country.

Being a part of this team sure has its perks, though. Everywhere I go, whether it be to Micky's Bar, a club, a house, or a frat party, there's a line of chicks just begging to suck my dick for bragging rights. And hell, who am I to deny them? Every party is the same. Drinks are thrown my way, dudes want to be me, chicks want to be with me. No matter how the season goes, it's going to be an epic year.

I step off the ice, dripping in sweat as I make my way back to the locker room. "Good job, boys," Jaxon says, clapping me on the back as he passes, being the first to push through the locker room door. We all murmur a quick thanks as we find our lockers and start stripping off our hockey gear.

After so many years, I have it down to a fine art. I throw my skates into my hockey bag, and as the boys talk shit around me, I grab a towel from my locker and head into the showers. My shirt sticks to my body, making it a pain in the ass to yank over my head, and I drop it to the narrow bench in the shower stall before working on my pants. Reaching into the shower, I turn on the water and wait a few agonizing moments for it to run warm.

The second I step into the hot water, instant relief washes through me. My feet burn from the ice while my muscles ache, and this hot shower is the one thing standing between that torture and sweet, sweet relief. But by now, I'm all too used to it. My body craves the agony of being pushed to its limits, of being the best and the fastest. Like they say, no pain, no gain.

Giving myself just a moment to breathe, I brace my arms against the shower stall and close my eyes as the hot water rushes over me, bringing life back to my cold feet. I take a few deep breaths when I hear the other guys moving into the showers around me, and with that, I pull my shit together and get my ass out of here.

Not one to hang around to talk shit, I grab my bag and head out of the locker room while quickly scanning the schedule pinned to our notice board. It hasn't changed since the start of the season, and I don't expect it to, but habit has me looking anyway. "Hey, kid," I hear from behind me.

Turning back, I find Coach Harris jogging to catch up to me, and I trail back a few steps, meeting him in the middle. "What's up, Coach?" I ask, hoping like fuck I haven't gotten myself in trouble.

"Wipe that look off your face. You're not in any trouble," he says, rolling his eyes. "I just wanted to check in with you. See how you're settling in?"

"Oh," I say, unsure why I feel so taken aback by such simple questions. Wanting to keep this short and sweet, I give him the response he's looking for. After all, he wouldn't be doing his job if he weren't checking in with his players. "Um, yeah. I'm doing fine, I guess."

"Good," he says with a slight nod, holding my stare as if trying to figure out if he needs to push for more details. "How's your independent training going? I've noticed you don't have many hours logged in the campus gym."

Shit. I should have known he would be checking up on that. "Yeah, about that," I say, hitting him with a generic response. "I actually prefer not to train in campus gyms. Gets a bit crowded, you know. Too many personalities."

"Right," he says with a scoff, clearly knowing exactly what I mean before narrowing his gaze. "But the training is still getting done?"

"Yes, Coach," I say with a firm nod, hoping he can see the honesty in my eyes. I may not love hockey as much as other things, but I've made a commitment to this team, and I won't be the reason they fall behind.

I see the moment he decides to give me the benefit of the doubt. After all, he has no reason to doubt me. If only he knew. "Okay, that's fine," he tells me, letting me off the hook. "But if you start to slacken off on the ice, you'll be back in the campus gym where the boys can keep an eye on you."

"Yes, Coach," I say, giving him a tight smile.

His lips press together as he continues studying me. "Alright, kid. Get out of here," he says after a short pause, finally dismissing me.

With pleasure.

Tightening my hold on my bag, I turn around and get my ass out of there before anyone else decides they need a moment of my time. After tossing my bag into the back of my truck, I get in and hit the gas.

It's a short drive back to the house my parents have rented from the University. I push through the door, thankful for Dad's strict rules about not having roommates to distract me from my goals. Don't get me wrong, it's a boring as fuck life with not nearly enough social aspects, but I can't completely blame my father for that. I like being alone and having my space respected. There's a reason they call me the black sheep everywhere I go.

After collapsing on my couch and having a nap, I wake up a few hours later and fix myself some lunch. When I check the time, I realize I'm almost late for my business lecture.

Scrambling for my things, I grab what I need and race out the door, making it just in time. The lecture is long and boring, but I do what I can to concentrate on my professor and soak in his wisdom. After all, if I plan on opening my own business one day, this is exactly the type of shit I need to know.

I get through two lectures before finally returning home, and despite my exhaustion, I push through to the small home gym set up in the spare room with a heavy sigh. I need to get another two hours logged before the day is out.

Heading straight for the weights, I work through my sets before moving on to cardio. I'm only halfway through when my gaze locks onto the punching bag in the corner, and a desperate need pulses through my veins. There's nothing quite like throwing a good punch, but I know I shouldn't. I need to concentrate on hockey training.

I've always hated training by myself. Since my father set me up with a trainer as a kid, I've always relied on having that person there to push me harder. While I've gained enough discipline to not need that extra push anymore, I can't deny how good it feels.

I clench my jaw, knowing I should ignore that nagging feeling within me, but fuck it. I'm done being my father's puppet. If I'm going to be here working toward a hockey career that I don't want, then it's going to be on my terms.

Abandoning the rest of my cardio requirements, I walk out of my home gym, grabbing my wallet, phone, and keys on the way out the door. I hop back in my truck and head downtown.

My gaze scans up and down the streets, searching for a gym I overheard a bunch of freshmen raving about. I go down backstreets, turning left then right, and left again until I finally find it. An old run-down gym with nothing but a sign above the door with a pair of boxing gloves, declaring the place as Rebels Advocate.

I eye the place down. This isn't exactly what I was expecting. But what the hell, I'm already here. I might as well check it out. Parking my truck in one of the few available spaces out front, I grab my shit and make my way to the door.

Pushing my way inside, I stand in the small foyer, looking completely dumbfounded as I take it all in. The gym is alive with activity. Punching bags swing under heavy fists while the sound of clashing metal reverberates loudly through the room. Weights clink along bars, and old-school boxing rings filled with fighters grunting and groaning line the back of the room.

My fucking dream come true.

Sun filters through the old windows, shining on the dust particles that float through the air, all but making the room fucking sparkle. It reminds me of all those fight movies I loved watching as a kid. It's clear that this is a gym dedicated to producing MMA fighters, and I realize without a doubt that Rebels Advocate just became my home. I don't care that it isn't traditional for a hockey player to train here. This is where I belong.

As I make my way deeper into the gym, my gaze locks on a fighter in one of the rings who looks like he has given his all for the trainer. The kid scrambles out of the ring, his face turning white as he grabs his water and races toward the bathroom, looking as though he's about to hurl.

A grin pulls at my lips, knowing the feeling all too well. "Can I help you?" the trainer bellows through the gym, casually making his way through the ropes of the ring before jumping down off the edge and watching me through a narrowed gaze.

"Yeah," I say with a slight lift of my chin. "What'll it take for me to train here?"

His gaze lowers to my shirt that declares me a player for the Denver Dragons, and I see the very second he decides I'm a piece of shit college athlete with nothing going for me but frat parties and pussy. "Look, kid, I think you're better off in the campus gym. This isn't the place for you," he says, dismissing me and starting to walk away. "See yourself out."

"You're wrong," I tell him, letting him hear the conviction in my tone, throwing every ounce of defiance I possess into it.

The trainer stops in his tracks and turns back to look at me, letting out a heavy sigh. He probably thinks I'm wasting his time. "Look around you, kid. We're an MMA gym. We train fighters, not college kids looking for a step up in their hockey training," he says with a scoff. "Let me guess, you're at the bottom of the barrel, and your coach has given you an ultimatum to improve or fuck off."

A smirk pulls at my lips as I ignore his comments and make my way up into the ring.

"What do you think you're doing?" he questions, standing back and watching me with his arms crossed over his wide chest.

I pull my shirt over my head and toss it in the corner of the ring, feeling more at home than I have in weeks. I look the guy in the eye, itching to fight. "Proving myself."

He considers me for a moment before shrugging his shoulders and making his way back into the ring. "Ahh, what the hell. You're lucky I'm in a good mood," he declares, positioning himself in front of me.

The familiar adrenaline pumps through my veins, and it feels glorious, like welcoming home an old friend. Then without hesitation, I get the show on the road. We begin circling each other, and I realize in order to prove myself, I need to make this quick and exciting. A fight he'll never forget.

As I notice a few guys in the gym stopping to watch the show, probably waiting for me to get my ass kicked, the need to prove myself only gets stronger. Springing into action, my fists strike out, narrowly getting through his defenses and nailing him in the shoulder. His eyes widen in shock, clearly having not expected such a move from me. He's suddenly on high alert now that he knows exactly what he's working with.

He immediately launches into a counterattack, but he only manages to get a hit to my forearm as I block his advance. I have to give it to him, he's fast. Incredible even, but no one is faster than me.

On and on it goes. This guy is well matched to my skill level, a fucking perfect match to train me. His punches are powerful, packing heat like I've never experienced, but I come fully loaded with speed and agility. Hell, I could even teach this motherfucker a thing or two.

I watch as he smirks at me, clearly impressed with what he's seeing, but the determination in his eyes warns me that he's not giving in. He's going to see this right to the end. Goddamn, I couldn't have asked for anything better.

Power pulses through my veins, my muscles rising to the challenge as I push myself harder.

A grin tears across my face, knowing I can finish this. I can see the trainer's eyes sparking with the thrill of it all, probably matching my own. I deliver a swift uppercut, followed by a combination of punches and kicks before I completely get through his defenses, slamming his back right to the ground and keeping him pinned as he gapes up at me in surprise.

"Well fuck," he says, breathless, tapping out in astonishment. "I give in."

A wide grin tears across my face as I release him before stepping back and offering my hand. He takes it, and I haul him to his feet as he continues watching me, clearly deep in thought. "I wasn't expecting that."

I resist grunting at him. "No shit."

"What's your name?" he asks, striding to the edge of the ring and grabbing a towel before wiping his face.

"Xander Phillips."

"I'm Cole. This is my gym. I own it with three of my friends, Caden, Luke, and Jace," he explains as he climbs out of the ring and jumps to the ground, our audience diminishing as they return to whatever it was they were doing before my little spectacle. "What's your story, Xander?"

Pulling my shirt back over my head, I follow him into what must be his office and take in the room. The back wall is lined with photographs of himself in competition with his students, each of them with their hand raised in victory. "I started training in MMA when I was a kid. Eleven, maybe twelve years old. I've been on my own since my trainer passed away a few years ago."

"So what's with ice hockey then?" he questions, indicating toward the logo across the front of my shirt.

I scoff, taking the seat opposite his desk. "Consider it a requirement of being my father's son."

"Right. So I'm assuming he doesn't know about this then?" he asks, gesturing to the gym around him.

"Nope. He doesn't need to, and neither does my team," I tell him. "If I get caught fighting, I'm off the team and lose my shot at signing with the NHL."

"Well, that explains why I've never seen you on the competition rounds," he muses before narrowing his gaze at me. "Correct me if I'm wrong, but I don't get the impression you're really interested in signing with the NHL."

"No, sir. I want to fight," I tell him, explaining my father and his conditions a little further.

He considers me for a moment. "You're serious about fighting?"

"I am," I tell him, letting him see the sincerity in my stare.

"Look, I think you're good. One of the best I've seen come through that door in a while, and with the right training, I think you could go all the way and sign with the pros," Cole says, but I shake my head, ready to remind him that competing isn't an option—at least not yet. "So, what the fuck am I supposed to do with you then?"

Hmm, good fucking question.

He studies me for a while, his lips pressing into a firm line before he leans toward me. "What if there were another way?"

My gaze narrows as my back stiffens, listening closely. "What do you mean another way?" I question, knowing damn well what lengths I'd go to in order to fight.

He nods toward his office door, indicating for me to close it, and I reach back, giving it a flick. The door shuts with a thud, and he focuses a heavy stare on me. "Ever heard of the Underground?" he questions, keeping his tone low despite the closed door. "New season starts in a few weeks. I wouldn't suggest it to my students in any other case, but you have the potential to take it out."

Leaning back in my seat, I consider his suggestion. Of course I've heard of the Underground. Anyone who fights has heard of it. You can earn a shitload of money, but it's dangerous and not to mention illegal. I've considered it before, but my old trainer would have come back from the dead to beat my ass. But desperate times call for desperate measures.

The Underground is an illegal fighting ring where anything can and will go wrong. It's complete with drugs, alcohol, dirty money, mob bosses, and of course there's always the risk of death. One nasty punch to the temple, and it's lights out.

If I fought in the Underground and actually succeeded, I'd be raking it in. It would be dirty money, but it's all the same to me. That money would be just what I need to get out from under my father's hold. I could finally break free. I could quit the team and get my own place. I could compete professionally and buy my own gym. But if I get caught before I'm ready, I'll be left with nothing.

It would be a massive risk. Extremely dangerous and incredibly stupid, but it's a risk I'm willing to take.

A grin stretches across my face as I look Cole in the eye. "I'm in."

CHAPTER 2

CHARLI

The rain pours down as I rush out the front door in the middle of the night, dragging my suitcase behind me, not bothering to close the door. What does it matter? She's drunk again, so fucking off her ass she passed out on the couch. With all that alcohol in her system, not even a hurricane could wake her.

The rain drenches my clothes in a matter of seconds, but I forge through it. I have no idea where I'm going or where I will end up, all I know is that I need to leave. I need to go somewhere she'll never find me.

Bypassing the mailbox and turning onto the sidewalk, I hurry past her old, beat-up car, and for a brief second, I consider taking it as my own. I could hotwire it like my daddy taught me before he died, but that will only give her another reason to come for me. And let's face it, my driving skills are nonexistent. She certainly made sure of that.

Dark strands of hair stick to the side of my face as I turn my eyes down, shielding myself from the heavy rain as I try to concentrate on the path before me. One step after another, I have to keep going. The street lights flicker above me, creating an eerie glow across the deserted road as I dodge puddles and try to remind myself that this will be worth it. Yeah, it's shit now and scary as fuck, but I have to do this. I have to be free from her.

Heading toward the city, my feet start to ache as I will a car to drive by and stop for me. I've never been one to take a ride from a stranger, but I'm freezing and wet with the rain pounding against my body, and goddamn this wind feels like a million tiny shards of glass hitting me at once. There's not a lot I wouldn't do right now. But I doubt anyone will be out this late at night, especially during this storm. I have to face it. I left on my own, and I'm going to see this through on my own.

A lump forms in my throat as I realize just how shitty this situation really is. But I have no choice. It was now or never. I hold back my tears, feeling more alone than ever as my hands violently shake from the chill seeping into my bones.

What the hell am I going to do? I have no family, no friends, and nowhere to go. It's going to be my first night sleeping on the street, and I scold myself for being so stupid. I should have waited for morning or at least until the storm had passed, but who knows what might have happened had she woken before I had a chance to leave.

If she knew what I'd done . . . fuck.

Reaching the peak of a hill, something has me looking up, and I gaze out at a view that's just as beautiful as it is haunting. The soft glow of the city light shines below as the storm rages around it. I must have been out here for hours. The view of the city has tears welling in my eyes, but I refuse to cry. I'm nearly there. So fucking close.

I can do this. I will not give up. My daddy didn't raise a quitter.

Picking up my pace despite my aching feet, I push myself toward the city, the determination drumming through my veins. I make my way down the hill, my feet pounding against the pavement, desperation spurring me on. I continue for another thirty minutes or so before the city streets finally appear before me, and I'm hit with a wave of undeniable relief. She won't find me here. It's too busy. She hates coming into the city. She always said she could never navigate her way around.

Making my way through the deserted streets, I look for any *help wanted* signs in store windows or adverts for places to stay I could check out come morning, but there's nothing. Nada. Zilch.

My feet begin dragging as my heavy eyes beg for sleep, and I know I need to stop. I look up and down the streets, desperately searching for somewhere safe enough to crash for the night, but everything is closed. I find some sheltered steps that lead up to a storefront and quickly dive into it, giving my feet a small break while relieved to be out of the heavy rain. Though the shelter can offer a small reprieve, it does nothing for the chill deep in my bones or the water soaked through my clothes.

Pulling my suitcase up beside me, I go about searching for a dry hoodie only to find everything inside the case is just as wet as I am.

Helplessness tears through me as a loud sob rips from the back of my throat. I've never felt so deflated in my life. I just need to make it through the night, and I'll be alright come morning. It's just a setback. Nothing I can't handle.

Needing a few minutes to wallow in self-pity, I drop my face into my hands and rest them on my knees as the tears stream from my eyes. Taking deep breaths, I try to get myself under control as I listen to the soothing sound of the rain against the road, hoping it can offer me just a moment of peace.

"What's a pretty little thing like you doing out here all by yourself?" a voice says from above me.

My head snaps up as my heart leaps out of my chest, racing a million miles an hour. Fear pounds through my veins as I find a man standing on the step below me, somehow still towering over me. He's looking at me like I'm his next meal, a predator come to play, and I scold myself for being so stupid.

With the sound of the heavy rain pouring down around me and the sharp claps of thunder, I hadn't noticed him sneaking up. Something dark lingers in his eyes as he looks me up and down, licking his lips, his intentions clear in his wicked stare.

He inches in closer, watching me as if he's trying to figure out how best to take me.

The pervert reaches for me, and I spring to my feet, my eyes wide with fear, my aching body now having more than enough energy to evade his advances. He wobbles on his feet, his brows arching in surprise. He clearly didn't expect me to have moved so fast, but the smirk on his face makes it obvious he's getting off on my fear. He lifts his foot to move up to the same step as me while leaning closer, the smell of rum wafting off of him. "That's more like it, baby," he slurs, reaching for his belt buckle and starting to free himself.

Oh, fuck no.

Bile rises in my throat as pure disgust fills my veins, then without hesitation, I spring into action. My fist slams out, and I punch the fucker square in the jaw, but with my lack of energy and strength, it only pisses him off. Pain tears through my hand, and I'm pretty sure it might be broken, but I don't have time to dwell on it. I need to step up my game, otherwise, this fucker will force himself between my legs, and that shit is not about to happen. Not now, not ever.

Anger burns through his stare, and he lunges for me, but I scurry back, his drunken state making him slow and sloppy. But that's not stopping him from trying again. "Come here, you little bitch."

Fuck no.

I have to get out of here, but his big body is blocking my way, and my gaze snaps from left to right, desperation slamming through my chest. With nowhere to go and nowhere to run, I do what any sane woman would do in my situation. I knee the fucker right in the balls and watch with triumph as he drops to the ground, gripping his balls as a loud, pained groan tears from deep in his chest. "Ahhh, fuck. You're going to pay for that, whore," he promises.

Yeah, not today, asshole.

Realizing this might be my only opportunity to escape, I look the fucker right in the eye and let him have it. My booted foot kicks up in a devastating blow to his face, and the sweet crunch of his nose breaking is like music to my fucking ears.

The fucker roars in pain, my blow sending him tumbling down the rest of the steps. He lands on the walkway with a heavy thud, the water on the pavement splashing up around him. Not wanting to hang around, I race down the stairs, not even daring to look back before bolting down the sidewalk and leaving the very last pieces of my belongings behind.

I don't look back, so I have no idea if the asshole is following me, but considering the blow to his balls, I'd dare say I'm safe. Either way, I don't stop. My aching feet pound against the sidewalk, dashing through walkways and back alleys, desperately trying to navigate my way to safety.

Spotting what looks like a bar, I race toward it, feeling just a sliver of hope blooming in my chest. The streetlights are out, and in the storming darkness, it's almost impossible to make out the name across the top, but this could be my only salvation.

There's a single light on inside the bar, and it's clear the place is closed for the night, but I don't care. I continue running right up until I'm standing at the locked front door. Raising my fists, I desperately pound on the door with what little energy I have left. "Help," I cry over and over, the tears streaming down my face. "Please. Someone, help me."

Clanging metal sounds on the opposite side of the door and hope surges through me, but I keep pounding, keep banging my fists.

A moment later, the door swings open, and I practically fall inside the empty bar. "What the hell's going on out here?" an older man grumbles, eyeing me with a narrowed stare.

I don't respond as I rush around him and hastily close the door behind me with a heavy thud, leaning against it as I try to catch my breath. My knees shake from exhaustion as I close my eyes, tipping my forehead against the wooden door as I desperately try to catch my breath. I feel the tears still streaming down my face, and I do my best to wipe them away, but after a moment, I realize they're here to stay.

"My God, child. What the hell is going on?" the man demands, repeating his question.

Opening my eyes, I spare a moment to take him in. He's a younger version of Santa Claus with white hair and a messy beard, looking at me with real, genuine concern that puts me at ease. "I'm sorry," I begin to say through my ragged breaths. "I just . . . I didn't have . . . there was a man . . . and he, he . . ." A big sob rips through me once again and the man stares at me blankly.

"Come on," he finally says, walking over to the bar and pulling out a chair for me. I take a seat, watching as he makes his way behind the bar and pulls out a box of tissues. I greedily pull out a few and attempt to dry my drenched face.

Santa Claus grabs a shot glass and places it down on the bar before grabbing a bottle of vodka and filling it almost to the brim. He pushes it in front of me before snatching it right back. "Wait, are you twenty-one?" he asks, his gaze narrowed on me.

I don't know why, but the question brings a smile to my face.

"Yes," I laugh before he pushes the shot glass back toward me, finally allowing me to drink it. It burns its way down my throat, and I try not to make a face. Vodka isn't exactly my drink of choice, but after the night I've had, anything will do.

"Right," Santa Claus says, pulling my attention back to him. "Start from the beginning."

I'm not particularly proud to tell him my story, but it's the least I can do for the man who's just saved me from being raped on the sidewalk. "Well, it sounds childish, but I ran away from home tonight. I couldn't stay there any longer. I just . . . it wasn't safe for me anymore. My stepmother had gotten so fucked up on drugs and alcohol and just . . . passed out on the couch, and so I packed my shit and just left. It's just my luck that it's pissing down with rain right now."

His gaze narrows, and I can see the questions forming in his mind, but he stays silent, allowing me to continue. "I walked for maybe three hours until I made it into the city and thought I could find a motel or something like that, but there's nothing. So I stopped to rest on this little storefront that offered a bit of shelter from the storm, and that's when this man just . . . appeared. I was so messed up about having to spend the night on the streets that I didn't even see him come up to me, and I—" I cut myself off and take a breath. I'm certain that if I allow myself to, I would get carried away and start sobbing on his bar. "This guy was wasted, and I could see it in his eyes. I knew exactly what he wanted from me, and when he tried to grab me, I just . . . reacted. I nailed him in the junk and when he fell to the ground, I kicked him in the face, and I'm pretty sure I broke his nose, and I just

". . . I ran, and now . . . now I'm here."

"*Pretty sure* you broke his nose?"

"No, I know I did," I admit with a cringe. "I heard a crunch."

"Well, shit," Santa Claus murmurs, grabbing my empty shot glass before refilling the little bastard. He passes it back as I nod in agreement, downing that shot too. "First of all. You're a damn fool for leaving in the middle of the night during a storm without a ride or a place to stay. I'm also betting that you haven't got any money. I'm not going to pretend like I know why you did it, but I'm sure you have your reasons," he says, sounding like a disappointed father scolding a daughter.

I don't know why, but the thought of disappointing this man does weird things to me. My head hangs, ashamed of how I've handled myself tonight. "Alright, darlin', what's your name?"

My eyes come back up to meet his. "I'm Charli."

"Nice to meet you, Charli. I'm Micky, and this is my bar."

I nod as I take the chance to have a quick look around and realize, even in the low lighting, that the place is pretty damn awesome. There are big tables in the back for large groups, little single tables for intimate dates, and a dance floor for the girls to shake their asses while their boyfriends drink beer and talk shit. The place looks well-worn and very loved, like it could be a popular hangout spot. "I like it," I tell him honestly.

"Thanks," he says with sincerity. "Now, down to business. You got any friends or family you can stay with? Hell, even a plan for what you're going to do now?"

I cringe, knowing he won't like my answer. "No. I have no one. No job, no money, no car, nothing," I sigh. "I thought I had a suitcase filled with clothes until I left it on that storefront with that asshole."

Micky considers me for a moment before coming to some sort of decision, determination and sincerity in his stare. "Alright, here's what we're going to do," he starts in a gruff tone. "I have an apartment upstairs that I crash in every now and then. Consider it yours. You'll work in the bar each night and you can start paying rent in a few weeks when you're back on your feet."

I gasp, my eyes widening in surprise. "What? I couldn't possibly put you out like that," I say. I desperately want to take him up on the offer, but it's too kind. I couldn't take advantage of his hospitality like that, especially since he already saved my ass once. Asking for more would be nothing but greedy.

"You can and you will," he says, leaving no room for argument. "Now, shut up and listen to what's going to happen."

I swallow my refusals and nod as Micky continues. "For the next week, I'll get my daughter to come in and train you on everything you need to know about being behind a bar. Layla is a star, she'll have you owning this place in no time. But I'm assuming serving drinks for the rest of your life isn't particularly your dream?" he asks.

"Well, no. I've always dreamed of owning my own hair salon," I tell him bashfully, never having actually said those words out loud. But what's the point in holding back? This is my fresh start, my opportunity to try and make something of myself.

"Hmm, that's manageable," he says, dragging his hand over his beard, deep in thought. "Have you started studying for that?"

"No," I say with a shake of my head. "I've never had the chance to study. I was pulled out of school at fifteen to work for my stepmom's cleaning business so she could stay home and drink."

Micky lets out a sympathetic sigh then reaches out a hand and gently squeezes my shoulder. "That's going to change real soon, Charli," he tells me, and looking into his eyes, I want to trust him. "We'll get you enrolled in classes in the morning."

My jaw hangs open before reality douses my hopes and dreams in gasoline, lighting that bitch up like a bonfire. "That sounds great and all, but how the hell am I going to afford beauty school?"

"Don't worry about that, I'll sort it out. You can pay me back through your wages," Micky suggests.

"I can't," I say with a shake of my head. "Thank you for offering, but it's too much. I can't ask that of you. You don't even know me."

Micky is thoughtful for a moment, both hands resting against his bar when his eyes light up like fireworks, almost as if a lightbulb has gone off in his head. "Have you ever heard of a traineeship?" he asks.

I look at him blankly, completely confused. "Um . . . no."

He lets out a small chuckle. "I had a feeling," he says with a smirk. "It's where you would go to work in a hair salon every day, and the senior hairdresser—or whatever the hell they call themselves—will train you. So, you will get paid to learn while the salon gets an extra set of hands."

"Seriously?" I ask in shock. I've never heard of such a thing.

"Yeah. I'm sure it's a little more technical than that, but leave it with me. I'll look into it in the morning. For now, you should get upstairs and get settled. I'm sure you're exhausted."

What the hell? Is this man an angel sent to earth to rescue me? I mean, maybe he is Santa Claus. It's not Christmas, but perhaps good old St. Nick has a side hustle of saving damsels in distress. "Why are you doing all this for me? You barely know me."

"One day, when you have kids, you'll understand," he explains, a fondness in his deep eyes. "And I hope to God, if my daughter was ever in this situation, there would be someone out there who would look out for her."

Tears begin welling in my eyes again, and I fight them back, having already cried enough for one night. It's time to start living. "Thank you, Micky," I say, letting him see just how appreciative I am of his help.

"Alright," he says. "Enough of that. I'll show you upstairs. I think Layla has some clothes up there you could borrow until you can get some of your own. I think she's roughly the same size as you," he adds as he walks out from behind the bar and gestures for me to follow him. "I'll show you the way."

I follow him out a side door that leads up a set of old, rickety stairs, and I'm thankful that he flicks on a light, showing me exactly where we're going. We reach a door at the top, and he pulls out a bunch of keys from his pocket before fiddling around with them and releasing one silver key from the keychain.

Micky slides the key into the lock and opens it before handing me the key to my new castle.

He pushes his way through, and I follow behind, watching as

he switches on the light, bringing the room to life. It's a small, one bedroom apartment that looks as though it's recently been remodeled. It's perfect. It's so much more than I could have dreamed of.

He leads me around the apartment, showing me where everything is and explaining that there should be enough food and water in the fridge to last a few days, but then I'll need to go shopping. Tears begin to well in my eyes for the millionth time tonight, and as I desperately try to keep them from falling, Micky takes that as his cue to leave.

"Alright, Charli. I'll leave you to it," he says, backing toward the door. "There are clothes in the bedroom drawers and towels in the linen cupboard. I'll meet you downstairs at eleven to introduce you to Layla and get you started on your training."

"Thank you so much," I tell him, wiping at my face and hoping I'm not snotting everywhere. "I don't know how I'll ever repay you for your generosity."

He gives me a tight smile and a small nod, appreciating just how grateful I am. "You're going to be alright, kid," he tells me, backing out of the room and pulling the door closed behind him. The soft thud of the closing door sounds through the small apartment before I hear his muffled tone on the other side. "Don't forget to lock the door." And with that, he leaves me in the safety of my new home.

Rushing over to the door, I flick the lock before turning around and really taking in the apartment before me. I can't believe how amazing Micky has been. A complete stranger has just given me a job, a place to live, and is going to help me achieve my goal of becoming a hairdresser. Within a matter of minutes, the worst day of my life has just become one of the best.

Needing to get myself cleaned up, I search out the linen cupboard and grab a towel before heading off to the bathroom. Reaching into the shower, I turn on the taps, and as I wait for the water to warm, I strip off my wet clothes. Once the temperature is just right, I climb straight in, welcoming the hot water that flows over my chilled body and damp hair, thawing me from the inside out.

The bathroom is fully stocked with everything I could need, and with my feet still aching, I quickly wash off, being conscious of how much water I'm using.

Exhaustion takes over, but I force myself to stay up to dry my hair in fear of becoming sick after being in wet clothes for the past four or five hours. After heading into the bedroom, I scramble through the drawers and find a pair of cute pajamas that I can only assume belong to Layla. There's also an underwear drawer, but I can't bring myself to borrow another woman's panties.

After quickly changing the sheets on the bed, I clamber out into the kitchen and search through every cupboard looking for a glass when I come across a small washing machine and dryer hidden behind a door. A wide grin rips across my face. I've never lived in a home with a washer and dryer. I would always have to lug my stepmother's clothes to the laundromat and wait for hours while they washed. But this . . . well shit, this is like Christmas morning.

Wanting to have something to wear tomorrow, I grab my wet clothes from the bathroom and throw them in the wash before finally finding that cup and getting myself a glass of water.

I lay down in bed moments later and find myself drifting into a deep, well-needed sleep, and for the first time in years, I actually feel safe.

CHAPTER 3

XANDER

Game night is here, and I stand in the locker room listening as Coach Harris hits us with the type of pep talk that only a seasoned professional could possibly muster up. Not gonna lie, I always thought that once you'd heard one, they'd all sound the same. But not with Coach Harris. He really knows how to get his skaters pumped while also instilling the fear of God into them if they were to fuck up.

Within moments the team gets out on the ice, and I look over to Jaxon, who's been in a foul mood all week. I follow his gaze up into the grandstand, noticing he's scowling at some random girl who's fully decked out in a Dragon's jersey. I can't help but wonder what the fuck is going on there. I haven't known the guy for long, but I'm yet to see him be affected by any girl. There's no denying it, she's smoking hot, just like the chick beside her. Although I'm pretty sure that's Bobby's twin sister, Brianna.

Bobby eyes Jaxon through a narrowed stare, and as I skate between them, gaining Bobby's attention, my curiosity gets the best of me. "What's up with Jax?" I ask.

Bobby lets out a small laugh. "Fucker's got his balls tangled, that's what," he grunts with a knowing smirk, shaking his head to himself.

"Right," I murmur, letting it go. After all, who Jax decides to sink his cock into each night really isn't my business.

With our warm-up time almost over, I go to skate away, but Bobby continues. "Just be ready," he warns me, nodding up at the chick in the grandstand. "With Cass here, I have a feeling Jax is going to be on fire tonight."

"Got it, man," I say with a nod as I push on down the ice, wanting to shoot a few practice shots before our time is up. It sounds like it's going to be an interesting game tonight, maybe even a fast one. Hell, I've grown up around guys like Jax, and with the eyes of some chick on them and the possibility of getting their dick wet, there's nothing they won't do to impress the girl.

After taking a few shots and getting in my zone, I skate over to the side and squirt some water into my mouth, which is when I notice *them* sitting up in the grandstand. My fucking parents. Just fucking wonderful.

Noticing my stare, my mom puts on the supportive parent show, waving her hands and showing off her jersey with my number on the back. It's fucking embarrassing. To the crowd around them, it looks like Mom is the best parent in the world, but I know better. It's nothing more than a performance . . . and a fucking terrible one at that.

Knowing Mom won't stop until she gets some sort of reaction from me, I nod my head to acknowledge them both and get a beaming smile out of her. My father simply nods back with his ever-present scowl, though that will soon change. The second the game starts he'll be on his feet, probably down in Coach's ear, hollering at every call the referee makes in his desperate need to feel relevant. It's going to be fan-fucking-tastic.

I ignore them as I get into position and wait for the rest of the boys to fall in line. The whistle blows and everyone springs into action, starting the game strong. Just as Bobby predicted, Jax is on fire. He steals the puck from the opposition, and we follow him down the ice, ready to defend him if need be. The game must only be thirty seconds in when he scores the first goal.

A wide grin rips across my face as I celebrate with the boys. I can't say I don't love the game. It's fast and exciting, and the thrill of getting the biscuit in the fucking net is amazing. Not the same sort of rush that I get from being in the ring, but it's still up there as one of the best adrenaline rushes I've ever experienced.

I'm in my zone tonight, and I must admit, it probably has something to do with Cole's training. The dude is a fucking legend and knows exactly what he's doing, inside and outside of the ring. I feel faster and stronger, and I've only been training with him for two weeks. I've given him my requirements for the team and he's managed to slip that shit into my training so I'm not wearing myself out.

The co-owners of Rebels Advocate are pretty cool too. I've met Caden, Luke and Jace a few times, and so far they all seem pretty pumped about me getting into the Underground. They even think that with Cole's training I could take it out, which also means a shitload of money could potentially be coming my way. Hell, the very thought has my gaze shifting up to my parents. I can't fucking wait to get out from under their hold.

I'm not gonna lie, the idea of entering the Underground isn't one that I'm ready to take lightly. All of the guys from Rebels Advocate have come to speak with me privately, really making sure that I fully understand the dangers of what I'm getting myself into. Which I certainly do. It's simple. If I fuck up, I'm screwed. And if I really fuck up, I'm dead.

Keeping my head in the game, I push myself to my limits, watching the other team with a sharp eye and having my boys' backs at every fucking turn. Just as always, the game flies by, and as expected, my boys step off the ice with yet another win under their belts. There's no denying it. Since I started skating with the Dragons, I've found myself much more exhilarated with the game than I used to be, and despite my current situation, I'm looking forward to the rest of the season. It will be hard and exhausting, but I have no doubt this team will take out the championship. The only question is, will I be here to do it with them?

After getting back to the locker room, I strip off my hockey gear and head straight for the showers, my aching muscles desperate to soak under the hot water. Within five minutes, I'm dressed and ready for whatever the boys decide our night is going to involve.

Half of them are standing around, barely covering their junk as they discuss where we're going, and the second Micky's is suggested, the approval is unanimous. Apparently, heading to Micky's after a home game win is some kind of tradition. One the boys aren't willing to break anytime soon.

After grabbing my shit out of my locker, I head out to the designated athletes' parking lot with Shorty and Aaron when my phone comes to life in my pocket. I dig it out and quickly glance over the text.

Mom - Great game, love. Your father and I are heading home.

Thank fuck. That's one awkward conversation I get to avoid tonight.

I slip my phone back into my pocket and we throw our shit into the back of my truck. Shorty climbs in the front passenger seat and raves about my truck as he directs me to Micky's. To be honest, I'm not really listening. This truck isn't exactly something I take pride in. It's just one of the million things my parents gave me to buy my compliance with hockey.

It only takes a few minutes before I'm pulling to a stop outside the bar, and the second the boys bail out of my truck, it's fucking on. They holler with excitement as we meet up with the others and step through the door of Micky's, the crowd of eager fans treating us as though we're local celebrities.

Shorty looks over at me with a knowing grin as he leads us to a table in the back. "What did I tell you, man?" he shouts over the noise. "We're the fucking Kings of Denver."

His excitement is infectious, and it has a grin spreading across my face as drinks and girls are thrust in our direction. For a change, most of the guys are more interested in discussing how good the game was. They don't need to cater to these girls. All they need to do is pick one as they leave and she will follow without question. Sounds bad, but that's just the way it is.

Some guys from last year, Miller and Tank, have shown up with their girlfriends, Dani and Sophie. Miller and Tank were the Dream Team last season and made it into the NHL with flying colors. Their names are known right across the league, and it's great to finally meet the guys who led this team to victory.

Jaxon shows up with Bobby ten minutes later, accompanied by the two chicks from the grandstand. There's no denying it, Jaxon looks pissed. Bobby, on the other hand, looks like he's ready to get fucked up.

I've only been here a few weeks, and it's already clear that these guys are more than just a team. They're family. They have each other's backs and are constantly pushing each other to be better. As the newbie to the group, I feel like I haven't really broken through that wall yet. Don't get me wrong, the guys are awesome, and they've been extremely welcoming. I feel like they're waiting for me to push through and join them, but there's a disconnect. Almost as though they can tell something is holding me back.

They know something is up with me, that something is keeping me from truly being part of their family, but they have no proof to pull me up on it. I've attended every training session and am always giving my all. Hell, most of the time, I'm the first one there.

All I know is that I'm feeling more at home at Rebels Advocate than I ever have in an ice rink. Maybe the guys can sense that I don't share the same love for the game that they do.

Putting it to the back of my mind, I try to enjoy myself and join in with the celebrations when Sophie asks the bar staff for a bottle of tequila and a bunch of shot glasses. An hour later, after an extremely revealing game of *Never Have I Ever,* the whole table is wasted, and the girls are all but stripping on the dance floor.

I try to signal to the waiter for another drink, but the place is packed. I get up and head to the bar before realizing Shorty and Aaron are right there beside me. The bar is packed with bodies, and we cram our way between them until we get to the front.

"Ooh, fresh meat," Aaron mutters as he looks at some chick behind the bar, appreciation in his eyes as she bends over to grab a schooner glass from under the bench.

I can't help but watch her as she does her thing, and fucking hell, Aaron's never been so right in his life. She's fucking gorgeous. Her straight, dark hair is pulled back into a messy ponytail, and bits of hair are flying around her face. She wears a tight black tank that stretches over her full tits and black jeans that curve around her ass, and I find myself mesmerized.

My eyes travel back up her body only to find her soft blue eyes staring right back at me, her brow arched as though irritated to find some asshole jock gawking over her body. Yet I can't seem to find it in me to care. She's fucking stunning . . . but those eyes. Goddamn, they're drawing me in like a fucking siren.

A forced smile graces her lips as she tears her gaze away from mine and focuses on Shorty. "What can I get you boys?" she asks with a velvety voice, the loss of her stare making me feel as though I've just been shot straight through the chest.

"How about your name, sweetheart?" Shorty asks with a flirty wink.

I scoff. As if that bullshit is going to work on a girl like this. She's probably been hit on a million times tonight already.

The girl gives a playful smile, and I realize it's all for show. The more she plays along with her customer's bullshit, the more likely she'll be tipped. "I'm Charli," she says, her gaze briefly shifting back to me before a slight blush creeps across her cheeks. "What can I get you?"

Shorty orders us all a round of beer, and I watch as she makes herself busy, grabbing three glasses from below the bar. "So, you guys are hockey players, huh?" she asks as she pours our drinks.

Aaron slaps on a panty-dropping grin. "Sure are, babe. Did you catch the game? We were on fire."

"No," she laughs, then indicates around her to prove her point. "I've sort of been busy tonight."

I see the embarrassment in Aaron's eyes as he realizes his mistake, and I can't help but smirk at his idiocy. "What time do you get off?" Shorty asks, cutting off whatever Aaron was going to say to try and salvage his awful pickup.

"You boys are trouble," Charli grins as she puts the glasses up on the bar for us to take, and once again those baby blues come back to me. I hold her stare captive as I reach into my pocket and pull out a twenty before handing it over. She takes it from me, her fingers brushing against mine and making the blush deepen in her cheeks as she holds my stare, unable to look away.

"Keep the change," I tell her, dropping my gaze and releasing the hold between us. Grabbing my drink off the bar, I make my way back to the table through the rowdy customers.

"That chick was into you," Shorty comments as we take our seats, looking slightly disappointed. "She was fucking ace. You should hit that."

Glancing back at the bar, I watch as she busily fills her orders, unaware of just how fucked up that one brush of her fingers has got me. Shorty is right about one thing. Charli is ace. Actually, she's more than fucking ace. She's drop-dead gorgeous with the ability to bring a man to his knees. She looks as though she doesn't have a care in the world, like a bird that's just broken free of its cage, and there's something extremely intriguing about that. A girl so free doesn't need an asshole like me coming around and dumping my shit on her.

Shorty continues when I don't respond. "Fuck, man. If you're not going to hit it, I will," he promises. "Can't let a sweet fuck like that go to waste."

My head whips in his direction as I adopt a strange protectiveness over her, something I don't quite understand. "Leave her alone," I demand with a sharp glare. "She's trying to work. Fuck one of these other thirsty bitches."

Shorty's eyes widen as if he's seeing the real me for the first time, seeing past the black sheep and into the deep void of nothingness. He holds up both hands in surrender. "Chill man, I was just playing. She's all yours."

The way he talks about her as some kind of object grates on my nerves, and I ball my hands into fists below the table. A woman like Charli shouldn't be talked about like that. She should be fucking worshipped. The shy blush in her cheeks and those big blue eyes scream of innocence, and I'll be damned if I let any of these fuckers take that away.

What the hell is wrong with me? I only just met the chick. Hell, I didn't even give her my name, and yet here I am defending her honor. Fucking hell, I must have taken one too many hits from Cole this morning. The asshole worked me hard.

Which reminds me, I have an early session with him in the morning.

Glancing down at my watch, I realize it's almost midnight, which means I should really get out of here. I stand with my glass in hand and throw back what's left before glancing at the few guys left at the table. "I'm out," I tell them.

They all give quick nods as Jaxon speaks up. "Alright man, see you later," he says, his gaze slightly narrowed, a million questions behind his eyes.

I don't dwell on it as I turn and make my way to the door.

My gaze flashes back to Charli as I pass the bar, finding her eyes already on me. When she smiles, I can't help but return it, knowing damn well that I will see her again. I nod my head in her direction and am graced with that sexy as fuck blush again, which only makes my smile turn into a wicked grin. Seeming embarrassed, she tears her gaze away and focuses back on the customer before her, pressing her lips into a hard line as if to smother the smile threatening to tear across her face.

Knowing I have some sort of effect on her is fucking me up, and the need to go back to that bar and claim her as my own is strong, but I need to stay away. My life is a mess and will be for a while. The last thing I want is to burden this girl with it.

Besides, something tells me Charli isn't the hit-it-and-quit-it type of girl, no matter how badly I want to get between those sweet legs. I saw it in her eyes, she's intrigued. She can probably sense the danger in me, just like the rest of them, always wanting to take a ride on the wild side. But when it comes down to it, she's probably after a good boy with morals and values who will drop to his knees and worship at her feet, and one thing is for sure—that ain't me.

CHAPTER 4

CHARLI

It's been three weeks since I arrived at Micky's, and to say I'm on cloud nine is an understatement. For the first time in forever, I feel like I have control over my own life, a future that's mine and mine alone. A life I get to dictate.

I feel free, and it's amazing, exquisite . . . intoxicating.

Micky helped me secure a traineeship at a local hairdressing salon. It starts next week, and I couldn't be more excited about it. The owner is an old friend of his and owes him a favor, so she reluctantly took me on. I don't even care that I didn't get it myself, I'm just thrilled it's happening at all. But I will earn my place there if it's the last thing I do.

It will be a huge change though, and I'll probably be exhausted for a while before I get used to the added hours. I'll be working in the salon five days a week from nine to five and then coming home to start my shift at the bar at six. Micky insists that I shouldn't be working that much, but I don't care. I owe him everything, and I'll work until my fingers bleed.

The only downfall is that I haven't made any friends here, but I'm sure that will come. To be honest, I'm content with how things are. I'm not really sure I need friends right now, but if someone comes along who wants to add positivity and friendship to this new world of mine, I'm not going to say no.

Layla, Micky's daughter, came in for the first week to show me the ropes. I thought at first we would hit it off, but she's older, and a bit too classy for me. She's studying to be a criminal lawyer and is super proper. Don't get me wrong, she's incredibly nice and all, even brought me a bag of her old clothes that I could borrow, but I need friends who are super chilled and drama free. A girl like Layla screams drama. Besides, with everything going on in her life, she probably doesn't have the time to entertain her father's latest charity case.

Layla occasionally works at the bar, usually on busy nights when there's been a hockey game. I thought this place was busy my first few nights. There was always a constant flow of customers, and I had finally gotten the hang of everything. Then the hockey season began, and Micky's became standing-room only. Turns out I didn't know what busy was until it was staring me in the face, quite literally, with hundreds of college assholes screaming orders at me. It was ridiculous. I'd never been so busy in my life, but to tell the truth, I loved it. Not to mention, the eye candy in the room was outstanding, and the tips came rolling in.

The Denver Dragons had won, so the drinks were flowing. The fans were in an amazing mood, and at that point, I thought that was as busy as it was going to get. Then the actual hockey team showed up. I couldn't believe it. I'd heard that they like to come in, but I hadn't expected the whole damn team.

But more importantly, I didn't expect *him*.

The place simply adored the Dragons, while I was busy adoring the ruthless bad boy who looked at me like he was going to bend me over the bar and fuck me right there in front of the world.

When the team first walked in, girls went bat shit crazy, throwing themselves at the boys while every man in the place lined up to congratulate them, shake their hands, and kiss their asses. It's ridiculous how adored they are. I mean, it's just hockey . . . right?

I don't really get it to tell the truth. I've never been much of a sports fan, but I suppose that happens when your stepmother puts a shoe through the TV screen and your ability to watch anything is gone in a flash. But I think I get it now. Those hockey players are simply beautiful. Maybe beautiful isn't the right word. Sexy as fuck? Scorching hot? What wet dreams are made of? Yeah, that's more like it. They're fuckboys. They probably get off on collecting hearts and seeing how quickly they can break them. I swear, each and every one of them had a body carved right out of stone. The type of body men would kill for and women dream of being under. It was like muscle porn.

A freaking wet dream waiting to happen.

Then *he* showed up.

I noticed him the moment he walked through the door. It was like he had some magnetic field around him, and my eyes instantly swiveled in his direction. Knowing my luck, he's probably the biggest player of them all. Dark hair and smoldering eyes, hitting me with that Flynn Ryder shit. He wore a black leather jacket that hugged his sculpted body just right, while his demeanor screamed *bad boy* and made my mouth water.

He made his way across the bar and found a seat, and though he was talking with his friends, he seemed somewhat separated from the group, like he was a bit of an outcast. He could have just been having an off day. Maybe he was tired and not in the mood to party like the rest of them. I don't know, but something about him reminded me of myself.

And then he had to go and raise that magnificent body of his out of his chair and make his way over to the bar. The guy hardly said a word apart from telling me to keep the change, but I was a bumbling mess of nerves as his friends tried to hit on me. I must have been blushing like an idiot, but all that mattered was the way he held my stare. It was captivating and intense. I found myself desperate to look away while also wishing he'd never leave.

From the second he returned to his table, he never took his eyes off me. It was insane. He made me feel some kind of way I don't understand, something I've never felt before, and shit, I think I liked it. But who am I kidding? He's definitely a heartbreaker. Someone I should stay far, far away from.

A man like that could only be bad news.

A man like that could crush me.

A man like that . . . Well shit. He could set my whole body on fire.

Since that night, I've seen him one other time. He came into Micky's one day during lunch with some friends. I was hanging out with some of the waitresses and helping where I could, even though Micky continuously demanded that I go and have a life rather than stay holed up in his bar. I can't help it though, I love it here.

His eyes clocked me the second I came out of the kitchen with a tray full of meals. I almost fell flat on my face and spilled the food all over the place when I saw him. My nerves only got worse when I realized I was taking the food to his table. Hell, I didn't even realize there were other people at the table until I was standing right in front of them.

I unloaded the tray as quickly as possible while his dark, smoldering stare fixated on me, then I ran like a little bitch. I disappeared up to my apartment and clambered into my bedroom, slamming the door closed behind me as though he would come all the way up here and steal my heart right out of my chest. I've barely spoken a handful of words to him, but he's already deep under my skin.

Hell, the guy is running circles in my mind, and I don't even know his name.

"Earth to Charli," I hear Lex, one of the waitresses, say as she starts snapping in my face, demanding my attention.

Shit. There I go again, daydreaming about the sexy stranger.

"Oh, sorry," I say with a cringe, glancing across at her. "What do you need?"

"I was trying to ask if you wanted to come out with me tonight?" she asks as we busily finish up our shift on Thursday night, wiping down the tables and checking everything is in order before we can close up.

"I was completely lost in my own head. Where are you going?" I ask, not really sure I want to be going anywhere with Lex. She's been nice enough, but she's got a wild streak, and the way she openly flirts with the customers is just too much.

"Not sure," she shrugs. "My boyfriend was taking me somewhere and asked if I wanted to bring some friends along."

"I don't know, Lex," I say, glancing at the time and realizing it's after eleven. "It's already late. Plus, tomorrow night is game night, and if the hockey team comes in again, I'll be working until at least three in the morning."

"Come on," she insists with a groan. "Don't be such a bore. You've been here for three weeks and haven't gone anywhere apart from this old bar. It's about time you meet some new people and enjoy yourself, don't you think?"

Damn it. Why did she have to word it like that?

I start mentally mapping out the very limited supply of clothes in my closet, not feeling great about this but knowing I should still take her up on her offer. "I don't really have anything to wear."

"I have my whole closet in my car," she tells me. "I'll grab us a few things and we can head up to your apartment to get ready. It'll be fun. We can have a few drinks and shake our asses, then I'll get Eddie to meet us here."

Shit. Why do I feel as though I'm going to regret this?

"Fine," I grumble, finally relenting.

Lex gives me a beaming smile, showing off those pearly whites. Despite my reservations, I know she's right. I've been here for weeks and still haven't managed to meet any friends or even leave my apartment for a night out. Maybe this is just what I need to break out of my shell.

Just as Lex had promised, she hurries out to her car and returns with a few different options. All of them are much more revealing than I would have liked, but beggars can't be choosers. Once Micky's is closed up, we head up to my apartment and rifle through all the options, mixing and matching with some of the stuff I already have until the look is perfect.

I take myself in and am pleasantly surprised. I've never owned decent clothing before or anything that actually makes me feel like a woman, but this has got me feeling like sex on legs. A pair of baggy suede boots come up to mid-thigh while an oversized sweater drops down below my ass, showing off just the right amount of skin and a black leather mini-skirt peeking out below.

Lex insists on doing my hair and makeup and starts pulling at me before I have a chance to tell her no. She takes my hair out and fluffs it up a bit, saying it needs some volume, then proceeds to put black eyeliner around my eyes and adds just a touch of mascara.

Once she's done, I take a look in the mirror and gape at myself, completely blown away. I've never worn makeup before. I would have loved to, but I've never been able to afford it. Come tomorrow, I'm heading to the store and loading up on this shit.

The kohl-black color around my light blue eyes makes them pop in a way I have never seen before, and I absolutely love it. I take the whole look in, my dark hair, the makeup, and the outfit with the high boots. I look like a whole new person.

I'm busy admiring the way the heels make my ass look when Lex gets a text saying her boyfriend is downstairs. As she drags me out the door, I make sure to lock up before rushing downstairs and checking that the bar is locked up too.

We get into Eddie's beat-up car, and Lex immediately climbs into his lap before shoving her tongue down his throat. I look away while I roll down the window, trying to dull the overwhelming stench of stale cigarettes—a smell I'm all too familiar with after living in it for the last twenty-one years.

Wanting to get going, Lex climbs over to the passenger's seat, and Eddie drives like a fucking maniac through the city, no care for the others on the road or anyone in his car. Soon enough, he pulls to a stop outside an abandoned building in the worst part of town.

My hands start to shake, not liking the look of this, but an encouraging smile from Lex has me pushing the door wide and stepping out into the street. There's a slight chill in the air, but at least it's not raining, so that's gotta be a positive, right? Lex loops her arm through mine as if we're best friends, and she pulls me along toward the abandoned building.

I swallow hard, certain I'm about to be raped and murdered, but I put one foot in front of the other until we're walking through the back entrance of the building. It looks like some kind of old paper mill, dusty and dirty with not a soul in sight, but I hear the familiar sound of heavy bass rattling beneath my feet.

"What the hell is this place?" I ask, slightly freaked out.

"Chill out," Lex sings with a big grin, excitement brimming in her eyes. "You're going to love it."

My brows furrow as Lex and Eddie lead me through the building to a door, and as they open it, loud music flows through. My eyes widen hearing the sound of a raging party below, men chanting, booing, and screaming.

Eddie barges out in front of me and Lex before skipping down a small staircase and into some kind of pit below, and as my heart starts to race, I follow him in.

The room is swarming with people, and my jaw drops as I take it all in. There's a bar set up with tables and chairs, but that isn't what has my attention. It's the big boxing ring in the center with two guys going at it and blood dripping from a nasty cut above one of their eyes.

"Holy shit," I whisper to myself.

"Tell me about it," Lex grins. "Isn't it awesome?"

Sure, it's awesome, but it's also fucked up. I could get in so much trouble if I get caught here. Well, actually, I don't really have anyone to get me in trouble anymore, except for maybe Micky. But he would just say he's disappointed in me and give me the *look*.

I hold onto Lex's arm a little tighter as I realize this place is filled with the kind of people who wouldn't hesitate to try and get me alone. "Oh, look," Lex squeals in my ear, pulling my attention away from the people around us. "He's here."

"Who's here?" I yell back, trying to be heard over the music.

Lex glances back at me, a wide grin across her face. "Your date."

"My what?" I ask, horrified, more than ready to cut and run.

Lex lets go of my arm and races toward a guy who looks eerily similar to the guy who tried to get a little too friendly on that storefront. He looks me up and down, and I see the interest in his eyes as Lex drags him back toward me and Eddie. "You can thank me later," Lex says as though this loser is some kind of big prize.

"Hey," the guy says with hooded eyes. "I'm Chris."

"Um, hi," I say, reluctantly, trying not to let my disgust show. After all, this guy hasn't done anything to deserve my hostility. At least, not yet, but the night is still young. "I'm Charli."

Chris steps up beside me and throws his heavy arm over my shoulder while dipping his head toward me, the stench of rum wafting off him. "Let's find a seat, babe," he says in my ear right before running his nose up the length of my neck and sniffing me.

Ugh. I slide out from under his arm and cringe at the feel of his damp nose on my skin. What a fucking creep.

I turn to leave, but the next fight is announced and the crowd pushes toward the ring, giving me no chance to escape. With no choice but to follow the crowd, I move closer and find a space near the front with a perfect view. Lex shuffles in beside me with Eddie hugging her from behind, a drink in his hand despite the fact he's supposed to be driving me home.

Chris attempts to move in behind me just as Eddie is doing with

Lex, but I push him off and fix him with a scathing glare. "Touch me one more time and I'll beat you harder than these assholes in the ring," I warn him. He holds his hands up in surrender, but I see the challenge in his eyes. He isn't finished for the night. Not even close.

A voice booms over the speakers, announcing the fighters as the crowd roars in anticipation. The first guy comes out in nothing but a pair of shorts, and he looks angry. The look is only emphasized by the scar that leads from his right eye straight down to his lip. The crowd cheers for him, but when the announcer brings out his opponent, the crowd goes nuts. Money exchanges hands, and I watch in fascination as terms are settled and bets are made. People yell obscenities at the fighters as they stare each other down, and all I can do is watch.

The fight starts, the brutality of it all rendering me speechless. This isn't like the fights that are highly publicized in the professional circuit. This shit is dirty. The fighters are quite literally beating the shit out of each other. Blood spills all over the ring as the guy with the scar lays into his opponent, easily getting the upper hand.

"Aren't there rules or something?" I ask, leaning toward Lex as the guy with the scar gets his opponent on the ground and sits on top of his chest, keeping him pinned as he pummels his fists into his face, easily breaking his jaw.

"No," she scoffs. "Not in the Underground."

Holy fuck.

This is terrifying, but I can't look away. Within seconds, Scar knocks his opponent out cold, and a dude wearing black comes into the ring and holds his hand up to the sky, declaring him the winner of this round.

Fight after fight goes down, and I'm amazed at how much blood coats the floor. The last guy who went down tried to move his arms and legs as he attempted to get up and unconsciously made a snow angel. Or . . . a blood angel? I don't know, but it was gross.

The smell of alcohol surrounds me and people continue to make bets on each fight, but my eyes remain solely on the ring. The announcer calls the final fight and introduces a new guy, explaining that this is his first time in the Underground.

A strange hush flows through the room as everyone seems to lean in just a little, intrigued by the idea of having fresh meat in the pit. The announcer introduces him as *The Widow Maker* and as he strides out into the blood-soaked ring, the crowd goes wild.

The Widow Maker is wearing a black robe with his hood pulled up right over his head, and as he pulls it off, my gaze becomes glued to his body. He's like a work of art, so perfectly sculpted with a wide, strong chest and perfectly defined abs. My gaze locks onto that deep V with hunger when he lifts his head to the cheering crowd and everything comes to a standstill. The noise of the crowd fades around me, my gaze so intimately focused on him that everything else blurs.

I stifle a gasp, not believing what my eyes are clearly showing me.

It couldn't be *him*. He's supposed to be a hockey player, not a fighter.

Unease rocks through me. I'm intrigued to see him fighting it out in the ring, but I'm also terrified of what could happen to him. The idea of this guy getting hurt makes my stomach clench, but why the hell do I care?

Damn it. I wish I knew his name.

I find myself creeping even closer to the ring, almost gripping the bars as my stare remains locked on him. As if sensing my eyes on him, his head snaps up. He looks straight up at me, that dark, dangerous stare locking right onto mine.

Surprise flickers in his eyes, but there's something else there that I can't quite figure out. It's almost as if he's happy to see me, pleased to find me lingering in the rowdy crowd, as though I've given him something to fight for. It's clear I was the last person on earth he expected to see hovering around the ring, but none of that should matter right now. He should be focused on this fight, not me. Although, the fact that he can't seem to tear his gaze away from mine is getting me all kinds of hot and bothered.

My thighs clench, and I watch as he catches the slight movement, hunger coursing through his stare.

My tongue rolls over my bottom lip, the tension growing between us, and goddamn, if this man doesn't look away soon, I'm going to burst into flames right here for the world to see.

CHAPTER 5

XANDER

The Underground is fucking insane. It's my first fight, and I have to admit, my nerves are starting to get the best of me. I know I'm prepared, but I've never seen my opponent fight before. How do I know what to expect? Is he good? Is he a clean fighter or a dirty one?

Who am I kidding? If he's in the Underground, it's a fucking guarantee that the motherfucker is dirty. There's a reason these assholes aren't working the professional circuit.

"You've got this," Cole says as he takes both my shoulders and gives them a tight squeeze.

Luke and Jace stand next to Cole, both giving me encouraging smiles, but I can see the nervousness in their heavy stares. "Don't let him get you off your feet," Jace reminds me. "Get in and get it done."

I nod, taking any last-minute advice they've got and holding onto it with both hands. After all, I don't want to screw up my first fight of the season and tarnish my reputation before I've even got one. Besides, there's five grand on the line for tonight. Compared to my trust fund, that's just spare change, but it's going to make a difference when I need to get my own place and live on my own two feet.

The announcer echoes over the speaker, and I shudder when I hear myself referred to as *The Widow Maker*. Who the fuck comes up with this shit? That's gotta be the lamest name I've ever heard for a fighter, but I don't have a chance to dwell on it as Cole pushes me out into the ring with my robe and all.

The crowd's going nuts as they try to get a good look at the fresh blood, trying to gauge what kind of competition I'm going to be. Little do they know, this competition is mine. I'm just that good, and it's not my ego talking. It's straight-up facts.

Slowly pulling off my robe and doing a turn, I give the chicks a good show before tossing it to Cole, who snatches it out of the air with a smirk, knowing damn well what I'm doing. The chicks scream obscenities at me, giving detailed descriptions of exactly what they want me to do with my cock. Hell, I get shit like this right before a hockey game, but nothing on this level. This is insane.

I'm barely getting started on the Xander Show when I feel a familiar piercing stare that has my heart kicking into gear. There's no fucking way. She couldn't be here.

My gaze snaps up to the crowd, right to where I feel her stare. I find her instantly, those baby blues boring into me.

My heavy stare locks onto her, and I watch as her eyes widen, realizing exactly who stands before her in the ring. She gawks at me. Clearly I was the last person she'd expected to see here tonight, and I have to admit, I'm fucking shocked too. What the hell is Charli doing here? Sweet, innocent Charli at a place like this.

A strange need pulses through me to get out of the ring and rush up to her just so I can drag her ass out of this shithole and take her home. She doesn't belong here. But what do I know? Apart from a two-second conversation weeks ago, I've never actually spoken to the girl. How would I know if she is an innocent, sweet girl? Hell, she works in a bar for fuck's sake, and now she's at an underground fight. Maybe she isn't the kind of girl I thought she was. Maybe she's the kind of girl I could bend over and . . . No. I need to concentrate.

Either way, she's here now, and there's no way I'm leaving this ring without my first win under my belt. The tension builds between us, so fucking thick it's amazing no one else can sense it. The seconds seem to tick by, but I keep my eyes trained on hers. I'm more than ready to scale the side of the ring to get to her when some asshole drops his arm over her, leaning his whole body weight against her small frame and making her stumble forward. Anger fires through me, but I must admit, it's satisfying as hell to watch the way she cringes in disgust and shoves the prick off.

The loser wobbles behind her, but she clearly doesn't give a shit about the guy. A smirk comes ripping across my face, and I watch in amusement as the corners of her lips begin to rise.

Fuck, this chick is a little spitfire. How the hell could I have missed that?

One thing is for sure, I'll be finding her after the fight.

The announcer starts to introduce my opponent, and I know it's time to stop staring at Charli and get my head in the game. Hating the idea of looking away, I send a wink in her direction and grin as her face flames the same way it did that first night at Micky's.

Turning away, I face the opposite side of the ring and watch as someone moves through the crowd, making his way toward the ring with his team at his side, just as mine had been.

My opponent is introduced as *Hellraiser* and I scoff at the pathetic excuse of a fight this is going to be. The guy is scrawny with barely any muscle mass. He looks like a fucking child, barely out of school. I have to be smart about this, though. He wouldn't be here if he couldn't fight, which means the guy must be fast. Jokes on him. I've never met an opponent faster than me.

My gaze settles on him, not looking away as I watch him peel out of his robe. He makes his way into the center of the ring, looking up at the crowd with both hands raised as if he's already the undefeated champion. To me, he just looks like some asshole kid who needs to be put in his place.

After taking a slow walk around the blood-soaked ring, he focuses his attention on me and comes to a stop, sizing me up as though I'm nothing but an obstacle on his way to the top.

Without warning, Hellraiser lashes out, not bothering to wait for some kind of official signal to start the fight, but I suppose there's none of that shit here in the Underground. His fist flies close to my face and I spring back, narrowly missing my jaw being shattered. I have to give it to him, this bastard really is quick.

He smirks at me as if his deadly secret has been revealed and I should suddenly be shaking in my boots, but I've got a few secrets of my own.

Hellraiser pushes forward, but I won't let him make a fool of me. Especially not with Charli in the crowd. I match his advance and let him have it, my fists striking out like fucking lightning. He springs back but seems put off, so I use that to my advantage and nail the kid in the gut, following it up with a quick combination. Jab, cross, knee, repeat.

It's almost like a game. The adrenaline pulsing through my veins has me ready to face down anything. Add that to the fact Charli hasn't been able to tear her eyes off me, and I'm feeling good. A-fucking-mazing.

We get well into the fight and I've barely broken a sweat, dancing around him like it's nothing more than a warm-up. Hell, I'm almost fucking pissed he hasn't given me a good fight. The second I saw Charli, my game plan shifted with my new number one goal being to impress her, and damn it, I'm hardly able to do that with this guy.

Hellraiser attempts to fight back, but he's worn down way too quickly, using all his energy in a bid to intimidate me. Rookie error.

"Quit playing with him," Cole scolds from the side, his voice roaring over the sound of the enthusiastic crowd.

I smirk at the kid, taking note of the sweat dripping through the center of his brows, his busted lip, and that ferocious scowl as he realizes he severely underestimated me. I almost feel bad finishing him so quickly. The kid hardly got a chance to impress anyone, which will not benefit the rest of his competitions, but I came here to do a job and build a reputation. From this point on, no one will doubt my skill, and no one will enter my fucking ring as cocky as this idiot had.

Knowing I need to get this done, I swallow my morals and finish him. My fist comes up and springs out like a fucking freight train, clocking the bastard at his temple.

Hellraiser goes down like a sack of shit.

A guy comes rushing into the center of the ring and grabs my wrist, holding it high above my head and speaking into a microphone. "Winner by KO—*The Widow Maker*."

Ahh, fuck. There's that ridiculous name again.

The crowd cheers as I look up into the stands, focusing on that piercing stare I felt every second throughout the fight. Charli watches me with a ferocious hunger in her eyes, and it almost brings me to my knees, much faster than Hellraiser ever could. Those soft blue eyes flame as she takes me in, her bottom lip disappearing between her teeth, and I know without a doubt those delectable thighs are clenching together, desperately trying to relieve the throbbing ache between them.

Her need has me wanting to do all sorts of wicked things to her, especially when the blush creeps over her cheeks, realizing she's been caught.

God, she's so fucking gorgeous.

Unable to help myself, a smirk pulls across my lips, but I don't get to watch her for long before Cole, Luke, and Jace are tackling me to the blood-soaked ground. "I knew you could fucking do it," Luke roars, grabbing me by the shoulders and shaking me with excitement.

Cole claps me on the back, a wide grin taking over his whole fucking face. He doesn't say a word, but he doesn't need to. The words *fuck yeah* are practically stamped across his forehead.

The boys drag me out of the ring while Jace reminds me of the five grand I've just won. But none of it matters to me right now.

She does.

Not wanting her to slip away before I get a chance to talk to her, I look back over my shoulder just as that asshole from earlier throws his arm over her petite shoulder again, wrapping the rest of his arm around the front of her neck, keeping her pinned against him. He starts dragging her toward the exit and panic flashes in her blue eyes as she tries to pry him off, her gaze flicking around as if searching me out, desperate for help.

"Hey," I call to Cole, trying to get his attention back from his friends. He turns with a raised brow, and I don't hesitate. "I got to go. Can you grab the money?" I ask as my eyes flick back toward Charli, tracking their every step.

Cole looks confused, probably wondering why I'm suddenly desperate to get out of here and not ready to party the night away. "Um, yeah. Sure, whatever, man. I'll see you at Rebels tomorrow. Don't be late."

"Yeah, thanks," I mutter before taking off like a bat out of hell, barely able to spare him a backward glance. I'm all too aware of the fact I'm wearing nothing but a pair of gym shorts.

I head toward the exit, one foot slamming down in front of the other, adrenaline spurring me on. I dash up the stairs and into the abandoned building, but can't find her through the mass of people all trying to get out of here before it turns into a fucking raid.

After racing out front, I look up and down the car-lined street before hearing a feminine growl tearing through the night. "Let me go, asshole."

I run, my feet pounding against the pavement.

"Chill, babe. We're having fun," some guy responds. "Don't start acting like a bitch now. You've been teasing my cock all night and now suddenly you're not into it?"

"This is your idea of fun?" the girl scoffs. "Get your dirty as fuck arm off me."

I pick up my pace and follow the sound of her voice before turning down an alleyway and finally finding her. Charli is standing next to the asshole, his arm still locked around her, and there are two other people already sitting in an old beat-up car, just waiting for Charli to play along with their fucked-up games.

A girl hangs her head out the window, and there's something familiar about her. Maybe a waitress at Micky's? I don't know. All that matters is the way she's staring at Charli. "Come on. Hurry up already. We'll head back to Eddie's and Chris can show you a good time," the girl slurs as she tries to light up a joint. "God knows you fucking need it."

The guy beside Charli, who I'm assuming is Chris, grins down at her and takes her by the wrist. He gives a sharp tug, yanking her toward the car and making her stumble under his force. "Don't," Charli shouts out, trying to yank her arm free, the desperation in her tone almost killing me.

"Hey," I call as I finally catch up to them, my tone having all four of their stares whipping in my direction. I focus on Charli and relief surges through her blue stare. "You okay?"

The guy reluctantly lets go of her wrist and steps around Charli as if blocking her from me. The two in the car watch me with suspicion while Chris watches me as though I'm some kind of competition. Charli though, she looks at me as if she's about ready to fall into my arms and let me whisk her away.

"Um, yeah," Charli says, hesitantly taking a step away from Chris. "I'm okay." Her silent *now* is deafening.

I nod, my gaze shifting over her company once again before coming back to her as I continue to make my way toward her, Chris getting antsy with every new step. "Cool. Do you want to get out of here?"

Charli narrows her eyes on me, and I know she's hesitant about me, but not nearly as much as this other asshole. The relief in her eyes is evident, and I know without a doubt that she'd rather risk it with me than this guy. "Uh . . ." she cringes, almost looking for some kind of way to politely excuse herself from her current company. As if they deserve that much.

"Dude, back off," Chris says, inching toward me. "She's with me." Quickly realizing he's not about to intimidate me, he turns back to

Charli, reaching for her wrist again. "Let's go. Get in the car already."

"Dude," I say, mimicking him as Charli flinches back from his touch. "Are you fucking blind? She doesn't want to go with you."

"Come on," the chick in the passenger seat whines as she blows a cloud of smoke out into Charli's face. "Let's go already."

"Um," Charli says, finally speaking up. "I'm going to go with this guy," she announces, hooking her thumb in my direction.

Chris gapes at her as if her response is truly baffling to him, and as Charli steps further away, he rolls his eyes. "Whatever," he grunts before getting into the car. "She's fucking frigid anyway." He slams the door behind him, and Charli has to jump back out of the way as the car takes off up the alley.

She stumbles back, and I have to quickly catch her before she falls. "Thanks," Charli murmurs, looking up at me as I hastily drop my hands away, not wanting her to freak out at my touch. "That guy was a bit . . . much."

"No shit," I scoff, before looking her over, really making sure she's alright. "You're really okay?"

"Yeah, thanks," she says with a shy smile as her blue eyes meet mine, knocking me the fuck away. The move has that same blush creeping over her cheeks, and I have to admit, this chick has somehow got me by the balls.

"Come on," I say, indicating with a flick of my head for her to follow me. "Let me take you home."

CHAPTER 6

CHARLI

If someone had asked me this morning how I envisioned the rest of my day going, this sure as hell wouldn't have come to mind.

Tonight has been seriously fucked up. All I wanted was to finish my shift at Micky's, go upstairs and crash. Yet here I am, two thirty in the fucking morning, in a dark alley with the hot-as-fuck guy from the hockey team, who just happened to save me from being gang-banged in a dirty alley by Chris and Eddie, and probably whoever else they decided to invite.

How do I keep getting myself into these fucked-up situations?

One thing is for sure, I'll never trust Lex again. What a stupid move that was. I should have trusted my gut when it told me she was no good. Of course, the only girl I meet just happens to be a crazy skank whore who has no understanding of what being a good person really is.

Go me, I'm fucking winning at life today.

I don't know what I would have done if Mr. Widow Maker wasn't here. He came in like my knight in shining gym shorts. Though, who knows what kind of situation I've gotten myself into now. I've met this guy once. He could be a serial killer for all I know. Maybe a rapist, like apparently every other guy in this goddamn city.

I stand motionless, staring at his defined back as he starts to make his way back up the alley. Should I go with him? Maybe I should wait until I can order an Uber, but then I would have to spend what little money I've managed to save over the last few weeks.

Shit.

Sexy guy turns around when he realizes I'm not following. "Are you coming?" he asks over his shoulder, before flashing a panty-dropping smile that has me right back in that abandoned building, remembering exactly what this man is made of. Not to mention, the wink he gave me before his fight. Goddamn, I swear, my panties disintegrated. I probably would have jumped him right then and there if there wasn't a barrier keeping me from him.

Crap. Now is not the time to be thinking about screwing this guy. I just need to get myself home where I'll be safe and sound, then I can go right ahead and forget that tonight ever happened.

Realizing he's still waiting for my response, I reluctantly swallow my fears and nod. I mean, how else am I going to get home? It's not like I have a phone to actually order an Uber. I'd have to ask this guy to save my ass, again. "Yeah," I murmur, swallowing hard. "I'm coming."

Something settles in his dark stare, almost as if he was scared I would say no, and not wanting to keep him waiting, I hurry to catch up with him before walking out of the alley side by side. He leads me back past the door where I entered the building and right around the back to a small parking lot. He seems to be leading me toward a black truck, and if I have to be honest, I'm impressed. I don't know much about cars, but as far as this one goes, it's sexy as fuck. Just like its owner.

A few other people are lingering around, and I jump when I hear someone calling out. "Hey, kid."

My head snaps in the direction of the voice and Mr. Widow Maker takes off at a quick jog. I recognize one of the guys who was at his side after the fight. I stand motionless, unsure if I should follow, but it turns out there's no point. The guy hands him some kind of envelope before shoving a bunch of clothes into his hands. They do that bro clap-on-the-back thing, talk for a second, and then go their separate ways.

He starts making his way back to me as he pulls his jacket on. "Sorry," he says, stepping in beside me and motioning to the big black truck, unlocking it as he goes.

"It's fine," I say, climbing up into the passenger side and waiting as he walks around to the driver's side and climbs in beside me. The tension between us burns the moment he closes his door.

He tosses his stuff into the back before glancing at me, the intensity in his eyes making me struggle to catch my breath. "Where to, Charli?"

The way he says my name sounds like a caress, and it has shivers spreading all over my body. I'm impressed about the fact that he actually remembered my name from all those weeks ago. "Oh, you can just drop me back at Micky's," I tell him.

His brows furrow, and something tightens behind his eyes. "Uhh, no offense, but no," he says with a scoff. Unease blasts through me as my heart starts to race, and seeing the alarm on my face, he throws his hands up as a show of innocence. "Woah. No, girl. I just mean, it's nearly three in the morning. The bar is not somewhere you should be going at this time of night. Besides, it's probably closed."

I let out a small breath, which turns into a soft laugh, unsure why I like his response so much. "I didn't mean that I wanted to go party," I clarify, unable to quit grinning like an idiot. "I live in the apartment above Micky's."

"Oh," he breathes, understanding flashing in those dark eyes. "Well, I guess I can drop you there."

"Shit," I laugh, shaking my head as he hits the gas. "What kind of a girl do you think I am?"

"Honestly, I've got no fucking idea," he tells me, a smirk playing on his lips. But I guess I deserve that. Showing up at an illegal underground fighting ring really doesn't really make me out as a good girl. "I kind of got the impression that wasn't really your scene."

"Not even a little bit," I scoff, before realizing that I might have just offended him. After all, that clearly *was* his scene. "Shit, I, ahh, don't mean any offense by that. It's just, I'm more of a *hang out at places that won't get me thrown in jail* kind of girl, and by that, I mean I don't ever get out."

He laughs as he peels out of the parking lot and into the deserted street, the crowd now long gone. "Don't stress. I get it," he tells me. "But it leaves me wondering how the fuck you ended up there."

I let out a sigh. "That girl I was with, Lex," I start. "She's sort of the only girl I've met since I've been here, and she insisted I get out and have a good time. You know, meet new people and all that," I say with a shrug, rolling my eyes at just how stupid I was. "I kind of figured that meant we were going to a club or a party. I don't know, something like that. I mean, how the hell was I supposed to know she was taking me to some bullshit illegal fight club to set me up with a possible rapist who has no understanding of boundaries?"

"Shit," he laughs. "It's really not your night."

"You can say that again," I murmur before looking up at him and studying his face. "I guess it was a good night for you, though, Mr. Widow Marker," I say with a grin, watching the way he rolls his eyes at that ridiculous name. "Tell me you didn't come up with that name yourself?"

He laughs and shakes his head. "Shit, it really is that bad, huh?" he laughs. "If I had a say in it, it wouldn't be something so lame."

I lift my brows, finding it so easy to tease him. "Right. Whatever you say."

He rolls his eyes, and I can't help but notice the way those eyes are so perfectly lit up. It's like Christmas morning. Not that I've ever really experienced a good one before. "For what it's worth," he says with a cocky grin before pulling an envelope out of his jacket pocket and holding it up between two fingers. "Won myself five grand."

My jaw drops, never having seen that much cash in all my life. "WHAT? Five grand? Holy shit. No wonder you can afford a truck like this," I exclaim, forgetting to filter the words that come flying out of my mouth. My eyes widen in horror, realizing just how rude that was. "Shit, sorry. That's really none of my business."

He laughs, his lips still pulled wide into a cocky grin that's doing wicked things to me. "Don't worry about it. That was actually my first fight, which makes this my first payday," he declares proudly as he stuffs the envelope back in his pocket. His tone changes as he continues. "The truck, however, was a gift from my parents. Just another way to buy me off."

"Oh," I murmur, suddenly seeing the truck through new eyes and realizing this guy has some ghosts of his own. I desperately want to pry and find out as much information about him as I can, but who am I to ask?

"So, you're a student at Denver?" he asks, moving right along.

"No, not exactly," I say, really not knowing how to explain it, but also not wanting to go into my life story right now. "But as of next week, I'll be a sort of student."

He glances at me as he flies down the street, curiosity flashing in his eyes. "A sort of student? The hell is that supposed to mean?"

A wide, cheesy smile stretches across my face just at the thought of my new traineeship, and I find myself more than eager to tell this perfect stranger all about it. "So, I've always dreamed of having my own hair salon, but I haven't had the chance to study or learn anything about it until now. I got a traineeship with a local salon, and the senior stylist is going to be my mentor and teach me everything I need to know."

"No shit," he says with delight, glancing at me again. "That's fucking awesome. It's like you're getting paid to learn."

"Yeah, pretty much," I grin.

"I guess congratulations are in order," he says, his tone lowering to something a little more intimate. It has a shiver sailing over my body and making me clench my thighs.

"Don't get carried away," I scoff, trying to think of anything but how desperately I want to jump him. "I need to wait and see if I'm actually any good first. I might end up fired before I make it past my first day."

"Don't be so hard on yourself," he tells me, the way he so casually holds the steering wheel with just one hand making my mouth water. "No one could possibly be that bad."

I can't help but laugh. "Oh, I don't know. Apart from doing my own hair, I haven't really had any practice," I tell him. "Well, actually. That's not entirely true. I did cut all my dolls' hair when I was a kid, but that was before I realized it wouldn't grow back. That was a really hard day for me."

He lets out a laugh that wraps around me, the sound holding me captive. It makes me wish I could hear it every day for the rest of my life. My heart starts to race, my hands growing clammy as I shake my head, realizing just how stupid I'm being over this guy. I've got to get a grip. I mean, he's hot, but he's just a guy. Why am I letting him have this kind of effect on me?

He makes a stop at a red light and turns to look at me. "I think you'll do great," he tells me with sincerity, those words making me crumble from within. I'm more than ready to throw myself at him.

I force myself to look away as I feel a blush take over my cheeks, making me so damn happy we're sitting in the dark. "Thanks," I murmur as I try to get myself under control, the tension in the truck making it almost impossible. Hell, I wonder if he can feel it, too.

Needing something else to focus on, I turn my attention back to him. "What about you? I mean, you're a great fighter, but I thought you were a hockey player?"

He lets out a heavy sigh, and I hope I haven't struck a nerve. "Yeah, I'm a hockey player," he confirms, "but I love fighting. There's just something about it I can't explain."

"Like?" I ask, hanging on every detail he can give me.

"I don't know," he says, thoughtful, turning his intense stare back to the road and allowing me a moment to simply gaze at him. "Maybe it's the power I have over my opponent or the rush of adrenaline before the fight. I'm not sure. I guess it's a mix of things."

"Right, I get it," I say, realizing it's probably the exact feeling my stepmom got each time she smacked me across the face. "So, were any of the guys from the team there tonight?"

"No," he scoffs before turning to me with a cringe. "Look, about the whole fighting thing," he starts. "You won't tell anyone you saw me there, right? I mean, if anyone found out, I'd be off the team."

My eyes widen in shock at his admission, but at the same time, it makes sense. Being found participating in any illegal activities would jeopardize his position on the team, no matter how good he is. "How can I tell anyone when I don't even know your name?" I say with a cheeky grin.

He matches my smile with one of his own. "I'm Xander," he tells me, a sparkle lighting his eyes and making my inner goddess pant for him. Hmmm, Xander. I could get used to that. Perhaps I could even get used to screaming it every time I come. "You won't say a word?"

"No, Xander," I say, his name feeling like silk on my tongue. "I won't say a word."

He stops dead in the middle of the road and turns to face me with an intense stare before his hand lifts off the gear stick, his pinkie finger rising with pride. "Pinkie promise," he insists, not daring to look away.

A wide grin stretches across my face. "What the hell? Are you twelve?" I laugh.

"You gotta do it," he insists, waving his finger around, making sure I know just how serious he is.

I can't help but roll my eyes as I lift my hand to his. "Fine," I groan, curling my pinkie around his. "I pinkie promise that I will not tell a soul that you spend your nights sloshing around in piles of other men's sweat and blood while beating up poor, defenseless kids in an underground ring."

He gives me a blank stare. "First off, he was no kid. He might have looked twelve, but that asshole had to be at least nineteen. And second," he says as he twists his hand around mine to press our thumbs together as if to lock in the promise. "Despite your attempt to make it sound like I actually enjoyed playing in that bloodbath, thank you.

That was single-handedly the most disgusting thing I've ever done, but I appreciate you keeping this to yourself."

A smile pulls at the corners of my lips, and I nod my head. "Of course. I wouldn't dream of breaking the sanctity of a pinkie promise," I tell him as our hands fall apart, my fingers suddenly so cold and empty. "Are you satisfied?" I ask as he gets back to driving.

His gaze darkens and an intense hunger pulses through his eyes. "Not even close," he tells me, that thick tone sending hot jolts of electricity pulsing right through my body.

I suck in a gasp but he hits the gas again, shifting his gaze back to the road and turning the corner. I realize we're nearly at Micky's, and I wonder how the time has possibly gone so fast. "So," I say, swallowing as the heat in the truck suddenly puts me in a choke hold, "if you want to be a fighter, why don't you stop hockey and fight professionally? I mean, I can't pretend to know what it takes to go pro, but from what I saw, you're pretty good."

"Just *pretty good?*" he questions, glancing at me as he pulls up onto the curb outside Micky's. I roll my eyes and give him a blank stare before he finally takes pity on me and answers the question. "The plan is to go pro eventually, but it's complicated."

Something hardens in Xander's gaze, and I cringe, hoping I haven't brought up something that's a sore spot for him. "Sorry," I murmur. "I didn't mean to pry."

He lets out another one of those intoxicating laughs. "I get the feeling you can't help it."

"No, I guess I can't," I tell him honestly, admitting to my nosey habits. "But for the record, I know complicated. Not the same brand of complicated as you, but complicated all the same."

Xander nods as he considers my response, but then his eyes soften and something tells me his complicated life has been long forgotten. "When do I get to see you again, Charli?" he murmurs.

He holds my stare and my jaw drops just a little, trying to work out what to say, but not a damn word comes out. This is a dangerous game. This man has the ability to destroy me. I need to duck and run before I get sucked into the chasm with no way out.

I open the door and climb out onto the walkway before thinking better of it and turning around. How could I possibly leave without another word spoken between us? A wide smile cuts across my face as I lean back in through the open door and meet his intense stare. "I don't know, Mr. Widow Maker. After what I saw tonight, you seem like more trouble than I can handle."

He smirks back at me. "Says the girl who found herself in the Underground with a guy who wanted to fuck her in the back of his friend's car?" he asks with a questioning, raised brow.

I shrug my shoulders as if not having a clue what he's talking about. "Who, me? No. You must have me confused with one of the other damsels you've saved tonight," I tell him. "Just how many were there?"

"Only one that counts," he says with a wink.

Goddamn. This man.

Backing away before I do something I'm not ready for, I close the door and turn my back, a stupid grin stretched wide across my face. I dash up to the door of Micky's and fumble with the keys like an idiot before finally getting myself inside.

How stupid could I be? Getting involved with a guy like that could only be bad news. Hell, he looks like he breaks hearts for sport. But shit, he's such a smooth talker, knowing exactly what to say to make my heart race. I'm in real trouble with this one, and what's worse, he doesn't strike me as the type to back away slowly. No, he's going to come in with the full force of a freight train.

After setting the alarm and double-checking the main doors are locked, I hurry up the stairs to my apartment. But the curiosity is too much and I can't resist rushing over to my window and peering out. I gasp, finding the familiar black truck right there, still up on the curb, only now there's a grinning Xander staring up at me from the walkway.

No. I'm not just in trouble. I'm completely and utterly fucked.

Xander grins up at me, clearly knowing just how much he's affecting me. "I'll see you around, Charli," he calls up to me before walking back around to his driver's door. He glances up at me one more time, his eyes sparkling with wicked desire. Before he's even gotten in his truck and driven away, I'm melting into a puddle on my bedroom floor.

This is not what I need right now. I need to concentrate on getting my life back on track. I have a new job starting in a few days, and I don't need any distractions. Especially distractions that come in the shape of an extremely ripped hockey player/fighter in a leather jacket with a panty-dropping smile.

Oh God. Just the thought of that smile has something burning up inside me.

Heading into the bathroom, I strip out of Lex's skanky-ass clothes before splashing cold water on my face and scrubbing off my makeup. Deciding I need to completely wash off the night, I jump straight into a cool shower and scrub the stench of Lex's joint out of my hair before washing the sticky, spilled drinks off my body.

After my shower, I grab a cold glass of water and head into my bedroom before dropping my towel and finding a pair of pajamas. I climb into bed and am instantly hit with the images of Xander in the ring, dominating his opponent in nothing but a pair of gym shorts. His ripped body glistening with sweat as he smirks up at me.

My eyes close as the burning need within me intensifies, and I know there's only one way I'll be falling asleep tonight.

My hand travels beneath the covers, and I suck in a breath, Xander's face and body keeping me hostage. My fingers trail over my clit and I groan, rolling over it again. My eyes roll to the back of my head, and not being able to resist, I push them lower before sliding my fingers deep inside of me.

More images fill my mind. His body. His eyes. His cocky smirk. His everything.

My other hand comes up, skimming across my waist and up to my nipple, gently pinching as my back arches up off my mattress. My thumb works my clit as my fingers curl inside of me, imagining just how good it would be with Xander.

He'd know exactly how to touch me. How fast and hard, how raw and wild. Fuck, I'll never be able to resist him.

I push my body right to the edge until I detonate around my

fingers, my pussy convulsing around them. I cry out his name, my eyes rolling in my head as my orgasm pulses through my body. And as I come down from my high and stare up at my ceiling, desperately trying to catch my breath, I know that I will never be the same.

CHAPTER 7

XANDER

I don't know what it is about this girl, but something had me waiting outside Micky's like a fucking stalker, watching and waiting until I could see that she was inside her apartment, safe and sound.

I just stood there like a fucking loser. Who the hell does that?

All I know is one minute she was slipping through the doors, and the next, she was beaming down at me from her apartment window. I told her I would see her around, and I have never uttered truer words in my life. There's something about her. Something that pulls me in and refuses to let go. She has her claws in deep, and talking to her in my truck made me realize just how genuine and ambitious she is, not to mention gorgeous as fuck. She has goals, dreams, and a damn backbone to make it happen. It's fucking admirable.

Unlike me, who's biding my time, waiting for the shit to hit the fan rather than making the change for myself. She's a force to be reckoned with, an inspiration, and a damn sexy one at that. One I can't seem to get out of my head.

Charli told me about wanting to own her own hair salon, and I couldn't believe how similar her dream was to mine of owning a gym. She would chat and get carried away with the conversation as if she was too excited about her future to stop, but then it was almost as if she remembered she was shy and would suddenly cut herself off and start blushing. It was the most adorable thing, and made me desperate for more.

One thing's for sure, when she's on a roll, she has absolutely no filter. I found myself excited to see what other shit would come flying from her lips. Whatever she's thinking comes out like word vomit, and I have to admit, it was damn hilarious listening to her trying to backtrack each time she thought she had crossed some invisible line.

Sleep came easy that night with thoughts of Charli roaming around my head, coupled with the added exhilaration of winning my first fight and getting that first bit of money to put toward my future. Not to mention, I've been thoroughly exhausted from all my extra training, but I'm hoping my body will adapt to the change soon.

I wake on Monday morning and groan as my alarm screeches into the early morning. "Damn," I grumble before pulling the sheets back and dragging my ass out of bed. After pulling on a pair of sweatpants, I head into the bathroom and take care of business before trekking downstairs to get ready. I take a seat on my couch and tie up my shoes before heading out into the early morning breeze.

Most of the hockey guys are already at our meeting spot, so I join in on a few stretches as we wait for the rest of the guys to show up. After another few minutes, we're ready to go, and we head out for our usual run and workout in the park. Before I know it, I'm back home, showering and preparing for my business lecture.

My lecture drags on, and I pass the time by rerunning my conversation with Charli in my head before switching it up and imagining just how good she would taste. Once the lecture wraps, I head out to my truck, desperate for an afternoon nap before I have to go to training at Rebels Advocate.

As I reach for the back door handle of my truck to shove my shit in the back, I notice a bank branch across the street. It's probably a smart idea to open a separate bank account for my winnings, keeping them separate and hidden from my parents. After all, making deposits into my normal account is too risky, considering my parents like to believe they have a right to check up on my finances.

Skipping out on an afternoon nap, I hurry across the road, and an hour later, I return back to my truck, one step closer to my goal. Glancing at the time on my phone, I realize I have just enough time to grab something to eat before getting my ass down to Rebels Advocate.

Monday's fucking suck. They're always so busy. After my morning workout and lecture, I have training with Cole in the afternoon and then a late hockey session before I finally get to call it a day.

Twenty minutes later, I'm barging through the doors of Rebels Advocate and Cole clocks me the second I step through to the foyer, putting me straight to work. "Alright, kid. Drop your shit and get started. We're doing circuit training today."

Fuck. Circuit training. My damn favorite.

There's nothing more exhausting than circuit training. It's fast and hard. Designed to use as many muscle groups as possible, and when it's run by Cole, it's nothing short of excruciating. However, he's the best trainer I've ever had. He gets me and knows how to push me to my limits without getting on my nerves. I always had a healthy respect for my old trainer, Rex, but we were too comfortable. Stuck in a routine that I needed to break free from.

Heading over to the treadmills, I jump on, making sure to warm up properly before Cole comes and kicks my ass. I watch as he makes his way around the gym, giving his other fighters encouragement as he collects everything he needs for my session, and from the looks of it, he's planning a good one.

"Get your ass over here, Xander," Cole hollers a few minutes later and I spring into action, stopping the treadmill and sipping at my water on my way across the gym. It doesn't pay to be tardy with Cole.

Within ten minutes of working my circuit, I'm dripping with sweat and regretting the day I walked in here. I don't know how Cole does it. I can skate for hours without breaking a sweat, and yet here with Cole, I'm a dripping mess in minutes. There's no denying that Cole is fucking good at what he does.

"That was a good fight on Friday night," Cole mentions, giving resistance to the back of my punching bag as I pound into it.

"Hmm," I grunt in agreement, not able to manage a proper

response.

"You could do better," he tells me. "You were just playing with the kid. I didn't get you there to fuck around. But someone seems to think your little show was worth something. The bets have been raised for your next fight."

"Really?" I grunt, my gaze snapping up to meet his as my tired arms fall to my sides.

"Did I say you could stop?" Cole scolds.

Fuck.

I pick my pace back up, pushing myself to my limits.

"As I said, you seem to have impressed some big players, and they're putting more money on you. We already know you have a shot at taking this thing out, but now, they know it too. They see you as a real contender," he explains before indicating for me to move over to the free weights for some rapid movement. "You went in there with no reputation and came out with a fucking great one, but they know that kid, Hellraiser, was no contender for you. They're gonna step up their game. They'll make you work for it."

I hold back a childish grin, his words like music to my ears. "So, when's my next payday?"

"Next fight is scheduled for Wednesday. Eight grand is up for grabs," he tells me, double-checking that no one can overhear. "I'll find out the location the night before."

"Eight grand?" I breathe with raised brows. If I keep going like this, keep winning, it won't be long before I can afford to get out from under my parents thumb. It's dirty money, but it's mine, and I'm earning every fucking cent of it.

"Yep," Cole confirms as he hands me the jump rope with a wicked grin, knowing damn well I can't stand the fucking jump rope. All it takes is one foot out of place and this motherfucker is leaving a welt on the back of my legs.

An hour later, I collapse to the ground. How the hell am I going to get through hockey training tonight? I lay on the mats with my eyes closed, concentrating on my breathing as I wait for the feeling to come back to my arms. This must be what it feels like to be on the brink of death.

"Get out of here, kid," Cole says as he walks by, making sure to bump into me as he passes. "You'll need to get something to eat before you go to hockey. Replenish your energy."

Yeah, I should probably take his advice. "Fine," I groan, needing a second before I get up off the floor and head into the bathroom, desperately trying not to hurl.

After taking a quick shower, I drag my feet out to my truck, wondering how the fuck I'm supposed to skate tonight. I'm exhausted, but Cole is right. Something to replenish my energy will go a long way.

I down a full bottle of water and sit in my truck for a few minutes before finding the energy to drive back toward campus. Pulling over across the street from a café, I hop out of my truck and jog across the road. Pushing through the doors, the heavenly aroma of food assaults my senses in the best way. Not having been here before, I take a second to study the menu before settling on a chicken salad and hoping it gives me just enough energy to get through training. I'll definitely need a big dinner afterward, though. If I could, I'd be hitting up a steak or burger right now, but I can't risk it coming back up on the ice. It wouldn't be pretty.

Getting everything I need, I make my way out front when movement across the street catches my eye. A grin stretches across my lips as I notice the pole dancing studio, and recall Jax and Bobby bitching in the locker room about Cassie and Bri taking a class. Though, to be honest, I would have loved to have seen that. Those girls are wicked fine.

Only having a few minutes until I have to get going, I head back across the street and lean up against my truck. My eyes continue scanning the street, as I inhale my food, and then stop when I come across a familiar dark-haired beauty standing inside a hair salon, and my grin only widens. I'd parked right outside her salon and didn't even notice.

I'm unable to resist watching Charli work. By the way she's watching and listening to the hairdresser beside her, today must be her first day working at the salon, and the lively spark in her eyes tells me everything I need to know. She fucking loves it.

She seems to be in deep concentration as she stands with an older lady working on a client. From what I can tell, the senior stylist is teaching her everything she knows, and Charli is soaking up every last bit of wisdom like a fucking sponge.

Pride surges through me seeing how seriously she's taking her new role, and just as I finish wolfing down my meal and go to get back in my truck, that stunning face of hers turns in my direction with absolute joy in her eyes. Noticing me out on the street, a dazzling smile graces her face, and like clockwork, a sweet blush spreads over her cheeks.

My grin widens, and I have to stop myself from going in there and claiming her, caveman style, right there for the world to see. Instead, I send her a wink and laugh as her eyes widen. Then before I get her in trouble on her first day of work, I step up into my truck and haul ass to training, suddenly with a shitload of newfound energy.

CHAPTER 8

XANDER

The crowd roars as the final buzzer sounds, declaring us the undefeated Kings of Denver once again. Coach Harris has a red face from the constant string of demands he's roared throughout the game, and he claps each and every one of us on the back as we step off the ice.

"Fuck, yeah," Shorty roars as we make our way into the privacy of our locker room. "That's one way to guarantee some easy pussy tonight."

We crack into laughter, each of us high on the adrenaline of yet another win. I know my dream is to be a fighter, but it still feels damn good to take out the competition.

I sit down on the bench to take off my skates when the boys strike up their usual after-game chatter. "Where are we heading tonight, boys?" Bobby asks as he pulls his jersey up over his head and carelessly throws it into his bag.

"I vote for Micky's," Shorty declares as he pulls a towel out of his locker, wiping over his face.

"Nah," Jaxon grunts with a firm shake of his head. "Not Micky's."

I try to hold in a groan. I should have seen that coming. Some dickhead grabbed at his girl a few weeks ago, so it only makes sense that he wants to avoid the place. Honestly, I feel for the chick, but us avoiding Micky's really fucking sucks for me.

"I know of a frat party not far from here," Bobby suggests as he loses his pants, his dick hanging out with no shame at all. Not that he's got nothing to be ashamed of, anyway. But fuck, I didn't realize the big bastard had his cock pierced. Good for him. I bet the girls love that.

"Yeah, I'm keen," Aaron shrugs while Shorty murmurs a soft "Damn."

The rest of the guys agree to the frat party, and just like that, it's settled.

Coach Harris comes in and tells us just how great we were as we finish getting cleaned up, before reminding us of next week's schedule and making sure we've all got our heads in the game. Once he's done, I head into the showers and return a moment later, fresh as a fucking daisy and ready to party.

We try our best to make it through the crowds of fans who wait by the door, some asking for autographs while others beg for pictures. Some just want to say congratulations, but there are those diehard fans who are waiting to hear where we're celebrating tonight.

Finally making it through the crowds and out to my truck with Shorty and Aaron on my heels, we throw our shit in the back and climb in. Aaron gives out directions and soon enough, we're pulling up at the frat party.

The place is packed, and the moment we walk in, I lose the guys as they scatter to find a drink, or in Shorty's case, probably the chick he will be screwing later tonight.

One by one, the rest of the team shows up, and it turns from a house party into a massive rager. Within half an hour, the place is so packed that the majority of the party has spilled out into the street, and I don't doubt the cops will be showing up at some point to shut this shit down.

It's been a massive week, and after the fifth time of having some drunk sorority bitch spill her drink all over me, I've had more than enough. Hell, I lasted an hour though, so I get credit for that, right? I slip out front and dig my keys out of my pocket with every intention of going home to crash, yet only a few minutes after hitting the gas, I'm parking my truck outside of Micky's.

It's almost closing time, and there's no doubt in my mind that Charli's working tonight. She's always working. Making my way through the door, I'm pleased to find the place is starting to clear out and is much calmer than the bullshit frat party down the road.

Taking a seat at the bar, I clock her straight away. Her back's to me, but I really don't mind as I take in the view of that perfect round ass wrapped up in those tight jeans. As if sensing my stare, she turns around and gasps as that bright blue gaze locks onto mine. She tries to act as though my very presence hasn't startled her as she reaches under the bar for a new glass to fill with beer, giving me a good view down her top.

Charli silently places the beer down in front of me before moving on to fill her next customer's order, and I find myself watching her with an intrigued grin as she goes about her duties. I don't know what it is about this chick, but every fucking step she takes is mesmerizing. Without even trying, she's got me hooked like a fucking junkie desperate for his next fix.

I sit here for half an hour before I'm startled out of my reverie when a steak lands in front of me. I know it has everything to do with Charli, even though she doesn't look up at me to acknowledge it. The blush spreading across her cheeks is a dead giveaway. Either way, I won't be wasting a perfectly good steak, I'm fucking starving. Hell, I don't know why I didn't consider ordering one in the first place.

Not wasting another second, I dig in and watch as Charli smiles to herself before walking away from the bar, clearly very proud.

My steak is cooked perfectly, and I lose myself in the flavor. Before I know it, the bar is practically empty. I glance around, wondering how the fuck I managed to lose track of time like that. Charli is busy wiping down the tables, humming along to the music, and lost in her own world as she prepares to close for the night. She heads into the back and turns down the music, giving the remaining customers the hint to get the hell out of here.

She returns to the bar a moment later, and I lift my chin, gaining her attention. "You need a hand with anything?"

She gives me a grateful smile but declines the offer. "No, it's okay. I'm nearly done, but thanks though."

Rolling my eyes, I get up off the stool, not surprised by her response in the least. I make my way around the bar and stride right up to her, smirking as she freezes. Then without a word, I take the spray and towel from her hands and make myself useful, wiping down the rest of the tables and bar countertop for her.

By the time I'm finished, every last customer is gone, and it's just me and Charli left in the bar. That familiar tension is back, steadily growing between us. Taking my seat again, I watch as she grabs my plate off the bar and ducks into the back. She's gone for only a moment when the lights go out, sending a wave of darkness throughout the bar. She leaves on the lights directly above the bar and completely shuts the music off. After such a long few days, the dead silence in the bar is the most blissful thing I've heard all week.

Charli comes back out and pours me another beer before pouring a chick drink for herself. She comes around to my side and takes the stool beside me, making me grin at her initiative. I didn't expect her to be so forward, but I like this side of her. Apparently, I haven't got a shy Charli tonight . . . at least, not anymore.

"Thanks for helping," she murmurs, sipping on her drink. "You didn't need to do that."

I shrug off her thanks. "I wanted to," I tell her as I swivel on my stool to face her more directly, my knee brushing up against her thigh.

"You had a game tonight?" she asks, her brows furrowed in

question as if she can't quite recall if that's true or not.

"Sure did," I say as a smirk takes over, unable to look away. "You keeping tabs?"

Her whole face flames, but she recovers quickly. "The audacity of this man," she laughs. "After parking your big-ass truck outside the salon on Monday, you have the nerve to ask if I'm keeping tabs? You expect me to think that was a coincidence, Mr. Widow Maker?"

I groan at her casual use of that ridiculous name, knowing she's only using it to tease me. "Would you believe me if I said it really was a coincidence?" Charli presses her lips into a tight smile before slowly shaking her head, refusing to believe me. I roll my eyes but continue anyway. "How was your first week?"

A beaming smile takes over her face, lighting up her features like Christmas morning. "It was incredible," she tells me, making me wonder how it'd feel to have her talk about me in that way. "I feel like I've already learned so much."

"That's great. What about your mentor? Has she realized you're too good for her yet?"

Charli's face flames again before really considering my question. "Oh God, I wish I could be that good, but Gina is great. She tends to get a little grouchy if she misses her afternoon coffee, but she really knows what she's talking about and is cool with me learning from the other girls as well."

"Sounds like you've hit the jackpot."

She nods and sips her drink. "Uh-huh," she says. "Most of the girls are really nice. Maybe even nice enough to make some proper friends."

I give her a pointed look. "Are you sure you're really the best judge of character? After that last chick you hung out with, I'm wondering if maybe I should be finding you some friends instead. I could set you up with a few girls. Some of the guys' girlfriends are pretty cool."

Charli rolls her eyes. "I think I can manage to make my own friends," she tells me. "But what about you? Win any illegal fights lately?"

I can't help but laugh. "Yes, actually, last night. I killed it. I was against this big Scottish guy and people were still wondering if I just got lucky last week, but then I smashed him. So bets will rise again for the next one."

Her brows crease in concern, and she begins to worry her bottom lip. "That's great," she says, sounding distant and unsure.

I hold her stare, not liking the way she's starting to shut down on me. "What's wrong?" I ask, itching to reach over and take her hand.

Charli cringes before finally speaking up. "When you say you *smashed him,* what does that mean exactly? You didn't really hurt him, did you?"

I let out a breath, relief pounding through my veins. "No," I tell her honestly, watching the visible relief in her eyes and the way she seems to breathe just a little easier. "The guy is fine, just a little knocked around. The Underground is a dirty competition, but I fight clean. Besides, if I'm gonna go pro one day, I can't have any of this shit coming back to bite me in the ass."

"Apart from the whole illegal underground fighting thing," she grins, her eyes sparkling with a wicked playfulness.

All I can do is grin right back at her. She's so fucking sassy. I love uncovering these little traits of hers. First, it was the innocence, then the shyness, then the blushing—which drives me wild—and then her inability to filter her mouth. But now I'm finding out that she's a sarcastic smart-ass, and that's just the cherry on top.

I haven't figured out why yet, but this woman pulls me in for some reason, and it's not just because of her killer body or stunning good looks. This woman has something more, something that I've never found in anyone else.

Charli watches me a moment as I do the same to her, both of us clearly trying to figure each other out. "What's your story, Charli?" I ask softly, so she doesn't think I'm prying and understands that I truly want to know her.

She considers me for a moment before her eyes drop to her glass and she begins drawing patterns in the condensation on the side. She lets out a heavy breath. "My dad died when I was twelve, leaving me with a stepmom and a massive debt," she says, not holding back as she goes in with the hard stuff. "She wasn't very nice, but she tolerated me. Well, she did until a few years later when she started drinking and I suddenly became a burden."

The need to creep my hand along the bar and take hold of hers fires through me, but I hold it back, not sure if she's ready for that. Instead, I wait for her to continue. "She became abusive, always telling me that I was nothing and complaining about how she was stuck with me. So, the moment I turned fourteen, she pulled me out of school. She decided that because the debt was my father's, it made it my responsibility."

Fuck it. My hand has a life of its own. It makes its way across the bar, and I place it right over hers, gently giving it a squeeze. An electric current shoots through my hand, right up my arm and into my chest, making me feel like my whole body has finally come alive. Who knew just touching her could have such an effect?

Charli's hand flips over on the bar, and I lace my fingers through hers. Something feels so fucking right about this moment. She looks down at our joined hands, and I see something settle within her. Something that gives her the strength to keep going, and goddamn, it feels good.

"I was made to work her cleaning business while she stayed home each day drinking. It had gotten pretty bad by that stage, and because drinking is an expensive habit, she forced me into a second job, which is ridiculous for a fourteen-year-old girl. At first, I refused, and that was the first time she hit me." Charli scoffs and glances away, as if ashamed of sharing this part of her life. "I guess she must have liked it because it became her new favorite thing after that."

She takes a second to have another drink, this time taking a longer sip. "I hate that I never fought back. I was always so scared that I had no place to go, so I put up with it for years until her new boyfriend introduced her to drugs."

"Babe," I say, cutting her off, fearing what direction this could go in.

"Don't stress," she says, reading the fear in my tone. "It doesn't get much worse."

I press my lips into a hard line, not sure I believe that, but I listen as she goes on. "She was always on drugs, hitting, and yelling at me. The boyfriend hardly came around, so that wasn't much of a problem, but it made her more aggressive. I stuck to my routine and would stay out 'cleaning' as long as I could, came home, cooked dinner, and then hid out in my room. She would pass out by nine most nights and not wake until ten or eleven the next day, so I could generally avoid her in the mornings," she says, then takes a breath.

"Anyway, a few weeks ago she found a stash of money I'd been hiding to get myself out, and she blew it all on pills. When she passed out for the night, they were just sitting there on the counter, and I don't know what possessed me to do it, but I flushed them," she says with a cringe. "She had misplaced drugs before and lost her shit on me, but because of how much was there, I knew this time would be worse. So I packed my things and ran. I walked for four hours during the worst storm we've seen all year. Had no money and no phone, so I couldn't get help or even order an Uber. I just had to keep walking. I was getting tired, and I couldn't find anywhere to crash, so I stopped at a storefront where there was a bit of shelter from the storm. I thought I was about to spend my first night on the streets when this asshole tried to grab me."

My whole body tenses and she stops, looking up at me in alarm, and suddenly she's the one soothing me. "It's okay. Nothing happened," she practically coos. "He tried, but I nailed him in the balls and ran until I got here. I almost broke the door down trying to get inside. I had no idea if the guy had followed me or not, I just knew I had to find somewhere safe. And I guess the rest is history."

"Fuck, Charli," I mutter, unable to calm down. Who the fuck would treat this beautiful woman so poorly? Every person in her life has let her down until she came here.

Getting up off my stool, I put myself right in front of her, taking her chin and lifting her face so her soft eyes meet mine. "You are the strongest woman I have ever met," I tell her honestly.

Her eyes grow watery, and I realize being strong is something she's never considered of herself before. But she needs to know. I'm in awe of her. With all the shit she's been through, she's still managed to pull her life together. She has taken control of a shitty situation and turned it around. She has set herself on a path to freedom, which is something I desperately wish I could do for myself—take control and make the changes. I always hold back, only taking small steps at a time. But Charli, she fucking leaped, making her the most inspirational woman I know.

I capture her stare with my own, holding her captive as the tension grows between us. I slowly lean in, and she sucks in a breath, seeing my intention crystal clear. She closes her eyes just as my lips press down against hers, and it feels so damn right. Her lips are so soft against mine.

I kiss her gently at first, giving her a chance to pull away if this is too much, too soon, but she lets out a soft moan as her hand lifts from the bar and presses against my chest. She pushes it up over my shoulder and around the back of my neck before pulling me in closer, claiming control, and fucking hell, I give it to her.

Charli's lips begin moving against mine, and I welcome every fucking second of it. She keeps it soft and controlled, never once losing herself, despite the intense hunger between us. My hands fall to her waist, and I grip her tight before lifting her from the stool and sitting her ass on the bar so that I can step in closer between her thighs.

Charli gasps and locks her legs around me, holding me as close as our bodies will allow. Her fingers knot into the back of my hair, and just as I feel her control begin to slip, she pulls back, dropping her forehead to mine as she catches her breath. "Holy shit," she whispers, a smile playing on her lips.

I can't resist dropping my lips to her neck and kissing her there, unable to explain what this pull is between us. All I know is that if I don't get more, I will die a starved man. "There's something about you, Charli," I say, my lips moving across her skin.

Charli groans as her fingers tighten in my hair, pulling me back to meet my eyes, and I find her bottom lip pulled between her teeth, desire pulsing in her stare. She wants to invite me upstairs, but I know she isn't ready, and I'll be damned if I push her too quickly and mess this up.

"If you don't go . . ." she mutters, her chest heaving with heavy breaths.

"I know," I whisper, my feet rooted to the spot, desperately needing to stay right here with her while knowing I should leave. I reluctantly take a step back, putting just enough space between us, her hands falling away as I try to find just a fraction of control. "You're gonna destroy me."

Her eyes blaze and she shakes her head. "Not if you destroy me first."

Fucking hell. This woman. It's almost as though she's daring me to try.

I take another step away before I end up throwing myself at her and bending her over the bar. "You and me, Charli. Don't fight it."

A grin pulls at her lips, her eyes sparkling with silent laughter. "Get your ass out of my bar before I drag you out."

Stepping back toward the door, I can't help but grin back at her. "Why don't you come over here and say that?"

Charli laughs and shakes her head, knowing damn well just how that would end. "Goodnight, Xander," she purrs.

Not wanting to push my luck any further, I send her a wink and watch how her eyes darken with hunger once again. Leaving her high and dry, I say goodnight and slip out the door before this goes somewhere she's not ready for.

CHAPTER 9

CHARLI

I've been working at the hair salon for a few weeks now, and I'm loving it. The girls are amazing, and Gina is incredible. From the moment I walked in on my first day, Gina took me under her wing and has been teaching me everything I need to know. She's starting off slowly, so I have a chance to really master each thing without getting overwhelmed. It's been amazing. So far, I've been working on basic cuts, and though I'm dying to move on to the advanced stuff like coloring, I'll have to be patient. Despite how badly I want it, both Gina and I know I need to take my time.

The very first time she handed over the scissors and let me take the reins, I almost shit myself. I was a nervous wreck. My hands were shaking, and I did what I could to plaster a confident smile across my face and not freak out my client, but I can't lie. I've never been so nervous in my life. Thankfully I aced it, even though I took my time, and the poor lady had to sit there for much longer than necessary. I've managed to speed that shit right up, though.

The only downfall is that with the title of being the newbie, I also get stuck with the shit jobs like mopping and sweeping the floor after each client to keep the place presentable. But I get it, it's how the food chain works. You have to start at the bottom and work your way up. Not to mention, these are the kind of jobs that kind of come with the territory of owning my own salon.

After my first paycheck, I was able to go and buy my first brush kit. By no means was it an amazing one, but it's more than enough to get me started. Next up, I'll be going for the scissors, but I don't want to be stingy with them and end up with a poor quality set, so I'll have to save for a few more weeks. You know, in between slowly building up a new closet and paying rent.

I'm finishing up the trim on my five o'clock client, and I am more than impressed with my work, when I glance up at the clock. Holy crap, it's nearly closing time already. Every single day I've been here has flown by. It's awesome, but it also has me wishing for a few more hours in the day. Though, working for a few extra hours would probably kill me.

With my weekday shift working for Gina, my night shifts at Micky's, and my constant daydreaming about Xander and that kiss on the bar, I'm utterly exhausted. A good exhausted, though. For once in my life, the feeling of spending a day working has me feeling on top of the world, and it has everything to do with the fact my work is contributing directly to my future rather than someone else's substance addiction.

It's amazing. Having control of my own life and money has given me my happiness back and allowed me to feel free for the first time in nearly ten years. I will never trade it for anything.

After checking over my client one more time, I decide she's done and remove her cape before watching as a smile spreads over her face. She does a few hair flicks, trying to get all the angles, before thanking me and grabbing her purse off the table.

Gina approaches as I'm sorting out the payment and chats with the client as she makes another booking with me in four more weeks, managing to boost my ego in the process. "You're really getting the hang of this," Gina tells me as the door closes behind my client.

"Thanks," I smile, really feeling like I'm getting somewhere. I'm more than appreciative that Gina has also taken the time to notice. "Today felt really good."

"Excellent. That's what we want," she replies as she opens the till to start closing up for the day. "Why don't you head off? I can take care of the rest."

"No, no," I say with a shake of my head. "You've been here since seven. I can take care of it and close up."

"Are you sure? I don't want you overworking yourself," she scolds like an overprotective mother. She knows about my night shifts in the bar, and while she doesn't approve of me working so many hours, she also understands my drive to build a life for myself.

"Really, it's fine," I tell her. "I managed to have a clean-up between my afternoon clients, so there isn't too much to do. I'll be out of here in fifteen minutes."

"Fine," she groans, realizing that fighting me on this is a lost cause. "Suit yourself."

With that, I dash off into the back and grab the broom before getting straight to work. If I make this quick, I'll have just enough time to finish closing up, power walk back to Micky's, and grab a fresh change of clothes before downing something to eat and being ready for my shift in the bar at six.

Gina says a quick goodnight, and as she leaves, I allow my mind to wander. As usual, it takes me straight to Xander. I haven't seen him this week, but I know I'll probably see him again in the next few days. He seems to somehow always find his way back to Micky's, no matter what he's doing. To be honest, I love the random surprises.

Especially that night he came in and watched me finish my shift. I felt his piercing stare the whole time, though I don't know what could have been that interesting. I was mostly wiping down tables, but then he went and helped me close. I don't know why, but something inside me found it incredibly romantic. So, of course I spent the rest of the night swooning like an idiot.

I don't know what possessed me to open up to him the way I did. I've never told anyone about the shit I've dealt with from my stepmom over the years. I had opened up to Micky that first night, but not on this level. I'd just given Micky the need to know stuff, but with Xander, I wanted him to understand me. To really know why I am the way I am.

I felt ashamed telling him how I allowed myself to be mistreated for so long, but then I saw the way he looked at me and that feeling washed away. He thought I was strong, like a survivor, and at that moment, I started to see myself in the same way. It was exhilarating—like I'd claimed back a part of myself.

After finishing up my jobs, I do a quick once over, straightening up all the chairs and equipment before turning off the lights and locking up. I check the clock one last time and grin, realizing I've spared myself a few minutes to dawdle rather than having to haul ass back to Micky's.

After keying in the pin for the alarm, I pull the door closed behind me, making sure I hear the familiar click before shoving the key into the lock and quickly twisting.

Putting one foot in front of the other, I head off down the road, feeling on cloud nine. Things couldn't be going better. You know, apart from the whole being too fucking shy to really go for this thing between me and Xander. I hate that I have so many reservations and not enough balls to just take what I want, but I'm so scared he's going to hurt me. I'm already in too deep, and if it turns out I'm just a game to him . . . he really will destroy me.

Xander gives me the impression that he's more than experienced in the bedroom, and I'm not going to lie, that makes me nervous. I mean, I've fooled around with guys before, but when it comes to sex . . . this bitch is still rocking her V plates. Xander has probably seen and done everything there is to offer. Threesomes, foursomes, maybe even a little bit of kinky fuckery. Which makes me wonder what the hell he sees in me. Why does he keep coming back? Am I a game to him? Does he just want to corrupt the sweet girl from the wrong side of the tracks?

One thing's for sure. I want him in a way I have never wanted a man before, and the thought terrifies me. Wanting him like this is handing him the power to hurt me.

I'm so caught up in my inner battle that I don't notice them until it's too late. *Far too late.*

Thoughts of Xander are lost the second a set of hands shove hard into my chest, and I'm jerked back against a brick wall along the main road. My eyes barely have a second to bug out of my head before I'm dragged into a side alley, hidden away from the rest of the world. I try to scream as panic tears at my chest, desperately trying to figure out what the fuck is going on.

With another shove, my head rebounds against the side of a building, and my heart rate spikes, focusing on my bitch of a stepmom before me. I swallow hard, fear pulsing through my veins. How did she find me so soon?

The bitch gets so close in my face that I hardly notice her drugged-up boyfriend has come along for the ride. "You have a lot of explaining to do," she spits as she grips me by my arms, pulling me back enough so that she can slam me against the wall again, my head bouncing off the brick wall with a sickening thud.

Pain rockets through me as my head spins, feeling like that terrified little girl she turned me into. "I . . . I . . ."

"How cute," she mutters, her lip pulling up in an irritated sneer. "Stuttering like a piece of shit."

Anger pulses through me, but I zip my lips, terrified of what's going to come next. I just hope she says her piece and leaves me alone rather than dragging me back to that house.

Clearly not getting what she's asked for, she slams me against the wall again, getting a sick enjoyment out of my pain. "Where the hell are they?" she demands, finally releasing me and ripping my handbag off my shoulder. She shoves it into her boyfriend's chest, and he immediately dumps its contents out onto the ground, searching through all of my things . . . things I've worked hard to purchase over the past few weeks.

"I don't have them," I yell, devastation crippling me, watching as her boyfriend destroys all of my things in his desperate bid to find the flushed pills. I plead with her, hoping it's enough to make her go away, but I know better than that. She won't be going anywhere until she knows exactly what I did to her damn drugs. And when she realizes . . . well, fuck.

She slaps me hard across my face and I cry in agony, gripping the side of my cheek. "You're a liar, Charli. You always have been, just like your deadbeat father. Now tell me where they are," she demands, raising her voice too loud for the side street we're on.

The mention of my father has the blood boiling under my skin, and I can't hold it back any longer. I shove against her chest, forcing her back a step as my head continues to spin. "Don't you dare speak about him, you fucking dirty junkie," I spit. "I told you, I don't have your damn drugs."

"Oh, getting smart, are we?" the boyfriend says, taking a step closer. He pushes my stepmother out of the way, and she falls to the ground in her drunken stupor. He grabs me by the neck of my shirt and slams me hard against the brick wall. My eyes lose focus, but I don't have a chance to dwell on it before he's in my face. "Tell me where they are before I have to teach you a fucking lesson."

The rage is like nothing I've ever known, and instead of shrinking away from the asshole, I find a twisted smirk stretching across my face. I look up at the bastard, letting him see the vile disgust in my stare. "They're long gone, asshole. Probably in the middle of the fucking ocean by now."

"Fuck," he roars, his grip too tight on my body. "You fucking whore. You're going to pay for that."

"Funny," I scoff. "I did pay for them, with the money *her* broke ass stole from me."

I see the anger in his eyes, and I know I'm moments away from being slammed into the wall again. I shrink back against the wall, trying desperately to find a way to lessen the blow, only it never comes. Instead, my body is torn away from the wall with the force of the boyfriend being ripped off me.

My eyes fly open as I scramble, trying to catch myself before I fall, but the sound of flesh being beaten has my stare readjusting.

Xander stands at the opening of the alley, my stepmother's boyfriend pinned beneath him as he pummels his fists into the asshole's ribs, filling the alley with the sweet sound of crunching bone. My jaw drops in shock, but I don't get a moment to watch the show before my stepmom is back in my face, trying to grab at me.

Only this time, Xander's very presence provokes a change in me.

After all, he was the one that helped me see that I'm not worthless, and I want to prove to him that he was right. But first, I need to prove it to myself.

The bitch comes for me, but I don't let her get close enough. Instead, I face her with a newfound determination. Swallowing my nerves, I shove against her, the same way she had done to me earlier. Only I step with it, putting in the force she couldn't possibly muster up in her drunken stupor.

Her eyes widen, unsure of this new me. I've never fought back before. I've always succumbed to her evil. "Get the fuck out of here," I growl, letting her hear the venom in my tone. "I'm not some kid you can push around anymore, and I'm sure as hell not your little bitch you get to use and abuse. You're a coward, a fucking junkie, and a drunken whore. Look at yourself. You're fucking pathetic, coming into the city just to start shit over a bag of pills that you bought with money you stole from me. Here's an idea. You want a fix? Fucking pay for it yourself. I'm done letting you drag me down. So take your little junkie boyfriend and fuck off. You're not welcome here."

She attempts to recover, but I don't give her a chance as I push her back once again. "What the hell are you waiting for? Go."

I give one final push, sending her right out of my way. She stumbles back with shock on her face, and I realize that after so many long, agonizing years of torture, she has finally given in. She's done with me. She won't bother with someone who fights back.

My head spins from the hits I took to the wall, but it's not over yet. I need to get away from them, and I need to get Xander out of here before he kills the guy. I've seen him in the ring, and I swear, with the right motivation, he'd be lethal.

I rush up to him, ignoring the way his muscles ripple with each move. Blood coats his knuckles and runs down the guy's face as I reach out and grab hold of the first thing my hand comes into contact with. I tug hard on Xander's arm, hoping I'm not too close to get hit in the face. "Xander, stop," I yell, frantically. "That's enough."

His head whips around to me, his fist frozen in the air. His eyes are wild and definitely not the kind ones I've come to know. "We have to go," I say, pulling on his arm with urgency, noticing the people who've gathered around to watch the show.

Xander blinks a few times before finally coming back to himself. He scrambles to his feet, pressing both hands softly against my face to check me over. "Are you okay?" he murmurs as his sharp gaze sails over my body, taking in every little mark they left on me.

I shake my head, a heavy pounding making my vision blur. "Not sure," I tell him honestly. "He got my head pretty good."

Xander's hand moves over the back of my head, and I feel a sharp sting as he passes over a big bump. I wince with the pain, and he immediately pulls his hand back, his palm now coated with blood. "Shit, you're bleeding," he tells me. "You've probably got a concussion."

I look down at his bloody palm. "You sure that's mine?" I ask.

"Yeah," he sighs as he pulls me into his side and away from my past, walking by the boyfriend so he can kick him in the ribs one last time. "Come on," he says, as he scoops my things up off the sidewalk and shoves them into my handbag. "I'm guessing you're not going to allow me to take you to the hospital?"

I shake my head. "I just wanna go home."

Xander nods as he leads me to his truck that's parked halfway over the curb with the rest hanging out into the middle of the road, blocking traffic. He must have been driving past and saw what was going on. Either I'm just lucky he has impeccable timing, or he was keeping tabs on me again.

Without another word, Xander helps me up into his truck, and I prepare myself to face Micky, knowing damn well how this is going to go down.

CHAPTER 10

CHARLI

Xander brings his truck to a stop outside Micky's, and I glance toward the bar with a heavy sigh before turning back to him. "Thanks for the ride," I say with a forced smile as I reach for the door handle, the movement making my head spin even more.

"No problem," he says, killing the ignition and getting out of the truck before making his way toward the entrance. My feet hit the pavement as I stare after him, my brows furrowed. What the hell does he think he's doing? After the smackdown I just gave, I think I can handle walking to the door by myself.

Realizing I'm not following him, Xander stops and turns back around just as he had in the alley with Lex, only now he doesn't look as though he'll be as forgiving of my shit. "Are you coming or what?" he asks with a raised brow, his tone suggesting I better hurry the fuck up.

Ugh, I guess I'm going to have to deal with a handler for the time being. Closing the big truck door, I hurry to catch up with him and step into his side. "You don't need to come in," I tell him as we walk the rest of the way to the door. "I'm a big girl. I can handle myself."

"Bullshit," he grumbles under his breath, reaching for the handle. "If I don't follow your ass inside that door, you're going to go up to your apartment, get ready for your shift, and work all night."

"Um, yeah," I reply, a little confused.

"You've got to be fucking kidding me," he mutters to himself before eyeing me. "After what you've just been through, there's no way I'm letting you work tonight. I would have taken you to the hospital if I thought there was even a slight chance you'd let me."

"Not letting me work tonight?" I repeat with probably a little too much attitude, but seriously? "Who the hell do you think you are? I have a job to do, and I intend to do it. And for the record, I don't require your permission to do so."

As I attempt to rip him a new one, he smirks at me, which only infuriates me more. "Fuck, you're a little firecracker, aren't you?"

All I can do is stare. I mean, honestly, who is this guy? I know he's sexy and all, but would he hold it against me if I clocked him in the jaw?

"Come on," he says, cutting off whatever I was about to say. He holds the door open for me, and I huff as I give in and walk through.

Micky stands behind the bar and looks up at our entrance. "Hey,

Charli, how was work?" he asks as he busily goes about his bar, preparing for the night ahead.

"Great," I tell him as I take a seat at the bar. "Got a few new clients."

"Good work, kid," he commends, both hands filled with tequila bottles. "I knew all your hard work would pay off." Once he has replaced the bottles, he turns to face me but notices Xander by my side. He eyes him warily, trying to work out what kind of people I've been hanging out with. "Who are you?" Micky grunts through a narrowed gaze, clearly not approving of me hanging out with random guys who just happen to be covered in dried blood.

"I'm Xander. Her boyfriend," he replies, more than earning himself a good castration.

"You're my what?" I sputter, looking at him as though he's gone nuts. I mean, I know I got a knock to the head earlier, but I'm sure I would remember the conversation where an illegal underground fighter became my man.

Xander raises his chin to me, daring me to challenge him, and I realize that would only make his day. A small grin plays on those stupid lips that I haven't been able to stop thinking about all week. "You heard me."

I narrow my eyes at him, ready to blow when Micky cuts me off. "Can you two sort this shit out later?" he groans as he continues straightening up his bar. "I do not care for your little couples squabble. Now, what's going on? Why are you down here instead of preparing for your shift?"

Xander cuts in before I have a chance to come up with some kind of excuse as to why he is here. "Figured I'd tell you about her afternoon seeing as though she won't."

Micky's brows crease as he turns to me, his sharp stare filled with suspicion. "What's he talking about?" he mutters in a tone that suggests I better hurry up and spill every last detail.

"Nothing," I groan as I hop up off the stool, ready to make my way to my apartment. "I'm fine. Now, if you will excuse me, I have to get ready for work."

"Sit your ass back down, Charli," Micky scolds, and I see the pleasure flashing in Xander's eyes, realizing that Micky isn't about to let me off the hook. Since I got here a few weeks ago, Micky has easily slipped into the father figure role that's been so absent in my life. And as much as I love that, it only infuriates me that Xander likes it too. "You have three seconds to tell me what's going on, girl, and why the hell do you have a red handprint across your face?"

After sending Xander a sharp glare, I focus my gaze back on Micky and let out a heavy sigh. "I had a visit from my stepmom and her boyfriend," I tell him, watching the way his stare tightens. "They thought I had their pills and got pissed when I told them I'd flushed them. So naturally, they had a few things to say about that."

"Fuck, Charli," Micky scolds, his jaw clenching. "You're not telling me everything."

I cringe, not wanting to give him further details. I know it's only going to make him worry, but apparently, Xander doesn't quite give a shit. "They roughed her up. She's got cuts and bruises on the back of her shoulders and arms. Also has a cut on the back of her head where he slammed her against a brick wall. Pretty sure she's got a concussion. Had I not gotten there in time, I'm sure she'd be passed out in the trunk of his car right about now."

"Fuck," Micky roars, slamming his hands down on the bar before muttering to himself and marching up and down the length of the bar.

"With all due respect, sir, I don't think Charli should be working tonight," Xander suggests. Though I think we all know it's not a suggestion and more of a demand.

Micky turns to me, and I notice his eyes quickly roaming over every inch of me, checking for any other wounds that Xander might have missed, but there's no way. Xander checked over every inch of my body. "Get upstairs and get cleaned up. I'll call Layla. She can cover your shift."

"What?" I demand. "I'm fine to work."

"You are not," Micky challenges. "If anything, you're lucky you're not passed out in a fucking ditch somewhere. Now, get your ass upstairs."

I let out a huff as I move away from the bar. How did I go from having nothing to having two overprotective, intimidating men in such a short time? This is ridiculous.

"Shit, kid. Thanks for bringing her home," I hear Micky murmur to Xander as I practically bust down the side door that leads to my apartment. "You better go after her or she's going to fume all night. Then we'll both be in trouble."

"BOTH YOU ASSHOLES ARE ALREADY IN TROUBLE,"

I yell over my shoulder, stalking up the stairs as the internal door between my apartment and the bar swings closed behind me.

I don't hear Xander's reply, but the familiar sound of a stool moving out from under the bar tells me he's making his move.

Nerves shoot through my body, as I unlock my apartment, hearing Xander on the stairs behind me. Hell, knowing we're about to be closed in together suddenly has me forgetting why I'm so pissed at him.

Xander stands at my back as I finish unlocking the door, and as the nerves overwhelm me, he places his hands on my hips and the electricity flies. My breath picks up as I eventually get the door open, and he trails in behind me, his hands falling away.

The door closes with a soft thud, and I feel suddenly all too aware of how alone we are. I mean, I've been alone with him a few times now, but nothing quite like this. In an apartment . . . with a bed.

My head pounds from the bump, but I hardly register it. All that exists is Xander, and needing to put some space between us, I head for the kitchen, but he stops me with a hand at my elbow. Xander gently pulls me back to him until my hand lands on his strong chest, and I'm looking right up at his devilishly handsome face. His eyes search mine, and I'm drowning in a sea of darkness, completely mesmerized by everything that he is.

"Are you okay?" he murmurs, his soft tone wrapping around me.

"My head kind of hurts, but I'm fine," I tell him.

He nods in understanding but continues. "I meant *are you okay?* After seeing them?"

"Oh, umm. I guess. Maybe. I don't know," I say with a shrug, not really having the chance yet to process everything that just went down. All I know is that the second Xander showed up, I felt like I could do anything. "You know, if you hadn't been there, I never would have stood up to her."

He pushes a stray lock of hair behind my ear, his fingers lingering on my face. "Yes, you would have," he tells me. "That was all you, Charli. You just realized that you're not the same frightened girl she made you believe yourself to be. You're strong, and you'll never allow another person to treat you like that."

"You really think so?" I question.

"I know so," he says, leaning in and giving me a gentle kiss on my lips, making butterflies soar through my stomach. Before I know what's happening, he releases me and makes his way into the kitchen, searching through the cupboards.

He finds a glass and fills it with water before searching out painkillers and indicating for me to get a move on. I step up to the counter and gratefully take them from his hand, my fingers brushing across his and making electricity spark between us. After swallowing the painkillers, I place the glass down on the counter, and the second I do, he takes my hand and leads me into the bathroom.

Xander pulls a first aid kit out of the vanity and instantly gets to work cleaning up the wounds on my back. I can't help but wince as he applies a cream, even though he's being as gentle as a big guy like him possibly could. He takes a look at the cut on my head, but there really isn't much we can do for that apart from cleaning it up and putting an icepack on it.

He finishes up and goes to make his way out of the bathroom. "Wait," I say quietly, still a little nervous around him, even though he hasn't given me a reason to be. Xander turns and looks back at me with a curious stare, but I order him to sit on the edge of the bathtub before he gets a chance to tell me no.

He does as he's told and I grab a washcloth out from under the sink, soak it under the tap, and make my way over to him. I take his hand in mine and gently wipe the dried blood off his knuckles, terrified that I'm going to hurt him.

Once I'm finished with his other hand, he stands before me, and my gaze lifts to meet his, the silence so heavy between us. His body brushes mine, and he gently takes the washcloth from my hand before tossing it toward the sink, neither one of us looking to see where it lands.

Xander raises his hand and twines it around the back of my neck as nerves pulse through my body. My eyes close briefly with his touch, but I don't want to miss a moment. His other hand wraps around my waist and he slowly pulls me into him, as those lips come down on mine in the softest kiss.

I moan into his mouth, melting into him as his lips move against mine, overwhelming my senses with the sweetest pleasure. Needing more, I bring my hands up. One snakes around the back of his neck while the other takes possession of his strong chest, my fingers splayed wide, claiming as much of him as I can.

His fingers slip beneath my tank, sliding across my skin and making me crave more. He sets my body alight with every touch, and a moan slips from between my lips, so desperate to feel him all over me.

Our kiss grows heated, hungry, and intense as the nerves continue bubbling up within me. Am I ready for this? What's he going to expect of me? Is he going to fuck me and then I'll never see him again? He declared he was my boyfriend barely ten minutes ago, so maybe this is as serious for him as it is for me.

"You're thinking too much," he murmurs against my lips, his fingers tightening around my waist.

"I can't help it," I tell him. "Boyfriend, huh?"

"Yeah, babe," he confirms. "Boyfriend." Xander pulls back slightly and looks me in the eye. "Do you need to stop?" he asks as his hands both come to rest on my hips.

Stop? Hell no.

If Xander is confirming he wants to be a part of my life as my boyfriend, then why the hell would I hold back? Hell, I'd be stupid to pass up an opportunity like this. I just wish I could guarantee that he's never going to hurt me.

Oh, hell, I'm going for it. I'm ready for this. I'm a grown-ass woman, and it's about time I took complete control. I don't know why all of a sudden, but I know it has something to do with Xander. It's his very presence, the way he draws me in and makes me feel things no other man has ever done before.

I shake my head and his eyes flame with need. His hands lower around my ass and he picks me up with ease, his lips fusing to mine. My legs lock around his waist and he walks us out of the bathroom and into the bedroom.

Xander lays me down on the bed, coming down with me and being careful to avoid the bump on my head. His lips pull from mine, trailing down the sensitive skin below my ear, making my back arch up off the mattress. I groan as the pleasure rocks through me, my body already coming alive for him.

I've never felt anything like it, and I can only assume it's going to get better.

His hand roams down my waist, slipping under my tank before pushing it up and over my head, leaving me in nothing but jeans and a bra. His arm slips beneath me, unclasping my bra as his lips come back to mine. He frees me of my bra as my hunger for him reaches new levels.

Gripping his shirt, I pull it over his head and toss it aside, desperate to feel my skin against his gorgeous muscles. He's so defined and sculpted to perfection. My mouth waters for him, and before I know it, my jeans are flying off the end of the bed, and his warm mouth is closing over my pebbled nipple.

I groan, my fingers knotting into his hair as his hand slips down between my legs, cupping my pussy. He grinds the heel of his palm against my clit and my body jolts with electricity, the need for him all too much. "Xander," I pant, my desperation too much to handle.

God, I need to feel him. I need him inside of me.

I feel his smile against my skin just moments before his tongue flicks over my nipple, making my back arch off the mattress again. I groan, my head tipping back with undeniable pleasure. He's barely touched me and already I'm on the edge, more than ready to explode.

His hand dives a little lower, and I feel him at my entrance before his hungry, animalistic gaze lifts to mine, silently asking if this is okay. I nod and he doesn't hesitate, roaming his fingers through my arousal before slowly pushing them deep inside.

"Oh, God," I groan, my fingers digging into the strong muscles of his back.

He curves them, and I see stars, but it's nothing compared to the way he massages my walls. His thumb stretches to my clit, and I vow to spend the rest of my days worshipping at his feet. Pleasure like this should be a crime.

Needing to touch him, I reach down between us and work his belt before pushing his pants down just far enough for his thick, heavy cock to spring free against my hip. I bite down on my lip and curl my fingers around his length before moving up and down.

He's so thick and big, and for a moment I panic, wondering how the hell he's going to fit. I guess I just need to trust him, to know that he'll take care of me.

My thumb roams over his tip, and he groans, pushing his fingers deeper as his thumb continues working my clit. "Fuck, Xander," I gasp. "I need—" he adjusts his fingers, curling them just right, and my whole body jolts, my pussy clenching around his finger. "Oh, God. Yes."

A wicked grin pulls at his lips, more than enjoying himself. Just to show my appreciation, I tighten my grip around his cock and get the best kind of pleasure, watching the way his eyes flutter with satisfaction. "Fuck, Charli," he mutters, clenching his jaw. "I've gotta have you."

"I'm all yours," I whisper, more than ready to feel the way he'll stretch me.

Xander groans, and without hesitation, he pulls his fingers free from my pussy. I almost cry from his absence, but then he's right there, settling between my legs with his heavy cock pressing at my entrance.

As if sensing my nerves, he drops his lips to my neck, kissing just below my ear, and my body starts to relax as he begins pushing inside me. Just as I knew he would, he stretches me wide, slowly pushing deeper and claiming my virginity.

I gasp, my pussy burning around his size, and if he weren't taking it slow . . . fuck, I can imagine how much it would hurt. He inches inside me, little by little until he's fully seated inside of me. As his lips continue moving over my skin, I start to get used to his delicious intrusion.

I let out a shaky breath and Xander stills, his lips freezing against my neck. He rises up just enough to meet my eyes, and I see the question there, putting all the pieces together. My nervousness, my hesitation, the way I've been needing to take things slow. "Are you . . .?"

My body tenses, which makes the pain that much worse, and I suck in a breath through my teeth, desperately needing to relax again. I can't help but wonder if not telling him wasn't okay. If I've crossed a line I didn't know existed.

That nervousness returns, and all I can manage is a small nod. But when a brilliant smile spreads across his face, all my worries fade away. He drops his lips to mine, kissing me deeply, and just like that, I start to relax around him, the pain quickly turning into the sweetest pleasure once again.

"Are you okay?" Xander murmurs against my lips. "Can I move?"

I nod again, swallowing hard and preparing for the worst, but as he slowly pulls back, I find it's not so bad. Actually, it's kinda nice.

He pulls nearly all the way back out before slowly pushing back in, filling me to the brim. My eyes flutter, and I suck in a breath as it quickly turns into undeniable pleasure. "Oh my God," I breathe, my fingers knotting into his hair and holding him tight, getting used to this alien feeling.

Xander reaches down between us, and as his lips move back to my neck, he slowly rubs tight circles over my clit, causing stars to burst behind my eyes. Reading my body, he knows exactly when I'm ready for more. He picks up his pace and a loud groan pulls from deep inside of me, desperate with need.

Xander pushes me right to the edge, working my body just right, and I feel that familiar build starting deep inside of me. My eyes roll to the back of my head, and as if sensing just how close I am, Xander pushes himself deeper.

I explode, reaching my high as my orgasm rocks through me. I cry out his name, my nails digging into his back. I've never felt anything so intense.

My pussy shatters, convulsing around his thick cock, and I tip my head back, the pleasure almost too much to bear. Xander doesn't stop. He keeps thrusting into me and rolling his fingers over my clit as my orgasm continues pulsing through me. I feel it when he comes, shooting hot spurts of cum deep inside of me, and just knowing that my body was enough for him makes me feel like a goddess.

After coming down from my high, Xander locks his arms around me and gently rolls us, being careful not to jostle or touch any of my injuries. He doesn't stop until his strong back is flat against my mattress and I'm straddled over him, his cock still buried deep in my pussy.

His fingers trail over my body, taking me in as though he can't believe what he's seeing. He reaches up, gently brushing his thumb around the curve of my breast, watching as my nipple becomes pebbled under his touch. "You should have told me," he murmurs, his dark gaze lifting to mine.

I drop my hands to his wide chest, slightly leaning forward and feeling his cock moving within me. "I'm sorry," I murmur in my blissful state. "Between Micky's lecture and my sulking, there wasn't really a good chance to tell you."

"I could have hurt you," he insists.

"But you didn't," I smile, loving this caring side of him and shifting my hips again, exploring how it feels.

His hands drop to my hips as his eyes roll with my movement. "That's bullshit. It hurt. It was written all over your face."

"Really?" I question, rocking my hips just a little more and feeling him hardening within me. "If it hurt me so much, then why the hell am I so desperate to do it all over again? Don't ruin this, Mr. Widow Maker. I trusted you to take care of me, and you more than rose to the occasion. It was perfect. Hell, more than that. It was amazing."

"Amazing, huh?" he rumbles, his eyes becoming hooded as I circle my hips, gasping at the deliciousness of it all.

"Uh-huh," I say, my tongue rolling over my bottom lip and

excitement brimming in my eyes, more than ready to take him again. "Mind blowing."

Hunger sparks in his eyes, and he goes to take my hips, wanting to throw me down and do it all over again, but I shake my head, shoving harder against his chest to keep him pinned. "Don't even think about it," I tell him. "It's my turn."

Xander raises a brow and relaxes back on my bed, his hands on my body, as I discover just how good it can really be.

CHAPTER 11

XANDER

Charli and I have officially been together for three weeks, and to say they've been amazing would be an understatement. I've never had a serious girlfriend before, but this one has me wanting to throw myself at her feet, worshipping every fucking step she takes. I'm not afraid to admit that this chick has me by the balls. I'm pussy whipped to the max, and I don't give a shit. She's my woman, and I'm damn proud of it.

Since our first glorious night together, I have spent every waking hour with her that I can. Between training and her work schedule it's hard, but we somehow make it work.

Apart from the nights when I have fights, I generally go over to her apartment, despite her arguing that she'd rather come to mine.

She flat-out refuses to allow me to come pick her up, some bullshit about not being a burden, but she doesn't understand just how quickly I'll drop anything in the world to be there for her. She's a new and improved version of herself, someone who now doesn't need to rely on anyone. Just as I told her, she's a strong and beautiful woman. I just didn't realize how fucking stubborn she was too.

However, she did agree to let me get her a phone. That argument didn't go down so well, but I used her own safety against her, and her argument died abruptly. The very next morning, I showed up at her place with a new iPhone in hand. She's never had a phone before, and she grabbed it out of my hand like it was Christmas morning, then played with it until she had completely worked it out. Although, despite being one of the smartest girls I know, she somehow couldn't wrap her head around the app store.

It's Friday night, and I've just gotten off the ice after winning another game, one my parents just happened to show up to. They left without so much as a hello, so I guess it's sort of a win in my book.

We're well into the season and are still the reigning champions, and man does it feel good. The game was great, and I have a feeling it has something to do with the fact that Jaxon has sorted out his shit with his girl. The two of them are tied at the hip, basically living in each other's pockets, but he seems happier, and that's rubbed off on the guys. Which makes game nights all that much better.

The only thing that would make it better would be if Charli didn't have to work so much and actually got to come watch a game, but I know she will eventually. After all, she can't shut up about it. Micky has been insisting she work more lately as he finally sacked Lex, leaving him down on staff. And it doesn't help that he has a guilty conscience about needing to call his daughter in all the time. Not to mention, Charli doesn't know how to say no to the big guy. She sees him as her saving grace, which honestly, is exactly what he is. I will forever be grateful that he was there that night because she is quickly becoming the love of my life.

I get showered and dressed in the locker room and wait patiently for the guys to decide where we're partying tonight. Apparently, they're still avoiding Micky's out of respect for Jaxon's girlfriend, which honestly, I get it. But after meeting Micky and spending some time with the guy, it doesn't sit right with me anymore. Micky deserves the kind of money our presence brings to his bar, but I'm just one man in a team full of guys who want to party, so tonight it looks like we're heading off to some bullshit house party.

Sounds fucking awful to me. But I guess it really doesn't matter. I'll show my face for an hour, then head off to see Charli before leaving for my fight.

It's a big one tonight, so I'm fucking pumped for it. The last few weeks I've won all of my fights, and I can't describe the feeling when the referee comes in and raises my fist to the ceiling, declaring me the winner. It gives me a rush and leaves me wanting more, like a fucking junkie desperate for his next hit.

I've made a reputation for myself within the fighting circle, a bit like I have with hockey. I'm the black sheep. The dangerous, unpredictable one. For hockey, a reputation like that works against me, but with fighting, it couldn't be better. My opponent never knows what I'm going to do. They can't read me, so they enter my ring unprepared, and that's the way I like it.

A few hours later after spending way too long at that stupid house party and then chilling with Charli, I lean across the bar and press a kiss to her lip. She wishes me luck, though we both know I don't need it. I'm just that good.

After hopping in my truck, I double-check the message from Cole with tonight's location and type it into my GPS before hitting the road. I drive just outside the city and come to an old building that looks like it used to be some kind of club.

There's a huge parking lot and cars fill nearly every space. It hasn't gone unnoticed that the further we get in the competition, the more spectators come to watch. That's why the location has had to get bigger. I love the energy of a large crowd. No matter if they're cheering for me or not, their energy is my motivation. Not to mention, the more people that come through the doors, the more money that rolls in with them.

Putting my truck in park and cutting the engine, I head around back just as Cole instructed, and I find him with Luke by the back entrance, talking with a few other guys. They spot me and do the introductions. Apparently, the guys are also trainers who are here with some of the other fighters. They look at me with appreciation, but I honestly don't care. I'm here to do a job and get paid.

I nod in acknowledgment, and Cole gets the hint that I'm ready to get the show on the road. He walks through the entrance with me and instantly pulls me up on my bullshit. "Would it kill you to be nice?" he questions. "I've known those guys for over ten years. They couldn't stop talking about your takedown last week."

My mind flicks back to my epic win last Thursday, and I have to grin. I had taken the guy down in under a minute. It was the quickest and easiest twelve grand I've ever made. Cole loved my performance, but he did request that I at least put on a decent show if it's going to be an easy takedown. The bigwigs here like their entertainment. After all, a good show brings in a good audience.

"I'm not here to make friends," I tell him as he leads me through the back rooms of the old club. The place is lit up with big industrial lights and power cords running all over the place. I step over an overfilled power strip that screams *fire hazard* and continue on my way.

"Clearly," Cole grunts as we enter a large room filled with punching bags. All the other fighters and trainers fill the room, some warming up, while others have their trainers wrapping their knuckles.

I find the schedule pinned to the back of the door, and I search for my name. I pull out my phone and quickly check the time. "Looks like I'm up against some kid called *Crusher*," I tell Cole, wondering if this asshole got to choose his name or was lumbered with it in the same way I was.

He nods his head as he looks over my shoulder at the schedule. "There are three ahead of you, so I'd say you've got about forty minutes until go time." I nod, and we go find someplace to get ready.

Jace shows up halfway through my warm-up and gives me a string of advice, but really all he wanted to do was tell us about some chick he is meeting up with after the fight.

It's been at least half an hour when Cole instructs me to sit my ass down and begins preparing me for my fight. I search the room as he wraps my hands, trying to figure out which one of these guys is my opponent, but I come up blank. So instead, I ask Jace what he knows, and as if on cue, he rattles off every detail he can possibly remember about *Crusher*. Within minutes, I've got my whole game plan figured out.

Twenty minutes later, I stride out of the ring, fifteen thousand dollars richer and without a single scratch or bruise on my body. Turns out, the guy wasn't much of a *crusher* after all.

With a few more fights left in the night, I grab a beer with Cole and Jace and check out the rest of the competition. I try to relax, but I'm so fucking exhausted, I bail after ten minutes.

Climbing back in my truck, I have to crank the music to keep from falling asleep. Mixing fight night with game night is hard work, especially after a day filled with a morning run, an on-ice training session, and my session at Rebels Advocate. My body yearns for a break, and the fact that it's creeping into the weekend has me on cloud nine. Though I don't know how much sleep I'll get, not with Charli around. She's a fucking she-devil, always ready for more.

I'm a few blocks away from Micky's when I pass an ATM under a street light and decide to stop. There's nothing I hate more than having a shitload of cash on me. It makes me feel like a walking target. I pull over and leave the ignition running as I quickly deposit the cash into my bank account.

The moment I'm done, a feeling of relief settles over me, knowing I'm one step closer to my future. I'm heading back to my truck when a beat-up car screeches to a halt, blocking me from my truck. There's something familiar about it, but I don't get a chance to figure it out before four guys are coming at me.

Letting out a sigh, I prepare to kick their asses, wishing they could have tried this shit when I wasn't feeling so fucking tired. But hell, if they insist on coming after an MMA fighter, then that's their problem. They'll be the ones suffering the consequences.

Taking note of the assholes as they come at me, I recognize one of them, and understanding dawns on me. It's the prick who had my girl pinned to a brick wall, Charli's stepmother's piece of shit boyfriend. I suppose this is his attempt at payback after I beat him to a pulp a few weeks ago, and I have to give him credit for being able to track me down like this.

The boyfriend and one other guy look fucking stoned, one is fat, and the fourth guy looks as though he's just busted out of prison. I'm not sure if I can handle four against one. It's not exactly something I've had to do before. It'll be messy, but I'll give it a go. Hell, maybe Cole could add something like this to my training. I'm sure Jace, Luke, and Caden would be down for it.

The four assholes are on me in seconds and start one by one, which is their first mistake. The boyfriend gets an uppercut to the stomach, the other high one gets a kick while the fat one and shady one both get swift punches to the jaw, each of them gaping at me as though not understanding where they went wrong.

They try it again, coming at me one at a time, and I have to admit, I even start to enjoy myself a little. Only it doesn't take them long to work out that they're going to have to use teamwork, which is when things get a little harder. My eyes frantically jump between the four as they all come at me at the same time.

The exhaustion from the day quickly catches up with me, and they start gaining some ground. The boyfriend disappears, and I have no idea what happened to him because I know I haven't taken the fucker out yet. Hell, I've been holding back where he's concerned. I want to leave him for last.

Grunts and curses echo throughout the street, and it's my bad luck that it's so late at night and the streets are deserted. The fucker rejoins the fray, and my eyes glance in his direction, only it's a second too late. I have just enough time to notice the baseball bat in his hands that's already swinging toward my face. And there's not a damn thing I can do about it.

The bat clocks me at what feels like a hundred miles per hour, instantly knocking me to the ground, my world fading to darkness.

A nasty ache pounds through my skull as I come to, remembering what the fuck just went down. My eyes spring open as I frantically search the area for another threat, but it doesn't take me long to realize they're gone. And so is my fucking truck.

I get to my feet and my ribs protest in agony. I've had more than my fair share of broken ribs to know just how fucked up they are. Stepping back toward the ATM to get some light, I lift my shirt to check the damage. Cuts and bruises cover my skin, but the worst of all is the massive, almost black bruise across my ribs.

I'm certain they're broken and that those fuckers continued their beating once I was down because before that bat came out, I was holding my own pretty well. But what kind of odds are four against one anyway?

Letting my shirt fall back into place, I search my pocket for my phone and let out a frustrated groan. Not only is my truck gone, but my phone and wallet are too. I've got no way to get home apart from a long walk with broken ribs.

I find myself heading in the direction of Micky's, and forty-five minutes later, I turn the final corner to see the lights still on inside. A breath of relief falls from my lips as I struggle to keep myself up.

Thank fuck for late nights.

Knowing I don't have much time before passing out, I pick up my pace and bang against the locked door with what little energy I have left. I hear groaning and grunting coming from within, but it doesn't take long before Micky is staring back at me, annoyed by having been disturbed.

His eyes widen and barely catch me just in time. "What the fuck happened?" he grunts, holding my weight as he ushers me through the door and into the bar, kicking the door closed behind him.

He leads me back into his office and sits me down on his couch, being careful not to jostle me around. "The stepmom's boyfriend came looking for round two," I say with a grunt, wincing as I try to lean back against the couch. "He brought three friends and a baseball bat."

"Shit," he grunts.

"Yeah," I agree. "Took my fucking truck as well."

"Motherfucker," he roars before walking to the kitchen and returning moments later with a bag of frozen peas. "Here, put this on your face," he instructs. I take the peas from his hand and hold them against my face, wincing with pain. Micky heads out to the bar, and just when I think I'm going to pass out, he returns with a first aid kit and a bottle of water. "I'll get you cleaned up, but then you are Charli's problem."

"No, don't wake her," I tell him as he starts cleaning up my wounds.

"Don't fucking argue with me, kid," he scolds. "I'm not playing nurse all night, and believe me, from the look of you, you're going to need one."

Damn, he has a point. "Fine," I grunt.

Gripping my shirt, I peel it off so we can see the extent of the damage, and every little movement leaves me in agony. Micky cringes, spying my ribs, but he's determined to get this over and done with.

It doesn't take him long to clean me up, but despite his best efforts, I'm still going to need a shower to wash off the dried blood. Micky gets up and makes his way out of his office, and assuming he's done, I get up and try to figure out where I'm supposed to go from here.

As I painstakingly make my way back out into the bar, I hear Micky's gruff voice coming from upstairs and groan before hearing

Charli on the stairs, knowing what she's about to see. Hell, if I could have gotten upstairs and showered first, then it wouldn't look nearly so bad.

Charli barrels through the door and skids to a stop, finding me barely holding myself up against the bar. "Fuck," she cries as she takes me in and rushes toward me, her eyes already filled with tears. She stops herself before she actually touches me, but I see the need to reach out in her eyes. "Are you okay?" she asks, her gaze sailing over my body, cataloging my injuries and trying to figure out just how badly I'm hurt.

I take her hand in mine. "I'm fine. It looks worse than it is."

"Bullshit," Micky grunts to himself. I give him a hard stare and he pulls his phone out of his pocket before pressing it into my hand. "I'm going to give you two some privacy," he states. "You'll need to call your bank and cancel your credit cards before the fucker can do anymore damage. Then be sure to call the cops and report your truck stolen."

I nod, glad to have a guy like Micky looking out for me. After everything that's happened tonight, canceling my credit cards was the last thing on my mind. The door clicks gently behind Micky as he leaves us in a heavy silence.

Charli carefully wraps her arm around my waist and helps me up the stairs to her apartment, taking it slow while making me feel like a fucking loser. I hate being cared for; it makes me feel weak. I should be the one taking care of her. "You take my bed tonight," Charli tells me. "I don't want to roll into you while I sleep."

I give her the same hard stare I gave Micky not five minutes ago.

"The last thing I want is for you to be out on the couch."

She looks at me like she's preparing to put up more of a fight, but I stare her down. She knows a losing battle when she sees one and reluctantly gives in, though I see the irritation in her eyes. Getting into her apartment, I take a seat on the couch while Charli heads into the kitchen to find some painkillers.

Pulling out Micky's phone, I let out a sigh as I dial my father's number.

"Hello," the prick answers, clearly pissed off at being disturbed in the middle of the night. I can't blame him, though. I would be, too.

"Dad, it's me," I say as I hear my mother in the background questing who it is.

"Xander? Why are you calling so late?" he questions before he sighs. "What kind of trouble are you in now?"

I roll my eyes at his attitude and let out a sigh of my own. "No trouble, Dad. The boys and I went out to celebrate after the game. I was mugged by four guys on my way home. Took my truck, wallet, and phone."

"Shit," he grunts. I can just imagine him, sitting up on the edge of his bed, elbows braced against his knees while he rubs his eyes in annoyance.

"My bank card for my trust was in my wallet," I explain.

"Right," he says, instantly getting where I'm going with this. "I'll call the bank now," he says, taking on his usual businesslike tone. You can always rely on my father to look out for his money. "What about the truck?"

"I'm calling the cops after this to make a statement," I explain. "I'll report the truck stolen. I'll probably have to call the insurance company too."

"No, the truck's in my name. I'll have to do that," he mutters, the irritation loud and clear in his tone. "I'll get the bank to send you out some new cards. You'll need new identification as well," he reminds me.

"I'm on it, Dad," I tell him.

"Right. Well, I'll speak with you soon," he says before promptly hanging up and not bothering to check in on my wellbeing, even after I just told him I'd been mugged. I mean, shit. Is it really that hard to ask how the fuck I'm doing? Hell, considering this could potentially fuck up hockey for me, one would think he'd be all over it.

Putting the phone down beside me, I take the painkillers that Charli has set out on the coffee table and quickly swallow them, not bothering with water. "That sounded like fun," she comments, pointing toward the phone on the couch.

"Oh, yeah. It was the time of my life," I scoff, watching as she yawns. "Why don't you go to bed," I suggest as I reach out and give her hand a gentle squeeze. "I'll be a while on the phone with the cops and then I need to take a shower."

"No," she says, shaking her head. "I'm right where I need to be."

"Okay," I murmur. She's not the only one who can see a losing battle. I lean back on the couch and draw Charli into me, internalizing the pain so she won't worry about me.

Half an hour later, I already called the cops and spoke to Officer

Samuels, who took my statement and reported my truck stolen. Unlike my dad, I told her exactly what happened and why. She mentioned that as it was near an ATM, there may be CCTV footage to help nail a charge. Wanting to give her as much information as possible, Charli took the phone and was able to help with their identities from my descriptions. Despite that, Officer Samuels said she would need to compare it to the footage to make a positive ID.

Following that, I call my own bank and make sure they cancel my bank card that holds my whole future. I'm so fucking grateful that I deposited that cash before they jumped me.

Not having the energy for more calls, I place Micky's phone down on the couch. Seeing that I'm finished, Charli helps me to my feet. She maneuvers me into the bathroom and strips me of my bloodied clothes before stepping out of her sleep shorts and peeling her cropped tank over her head.

Seeing her so confident in front of me has me reaching out to touch her, unable to help myself. "Don't even think about it," she scolds, pushing my hand away. "Not until you're better."

"You've got to be kidding," I groan as I watch her lean into the shower and turn the taps, putting that perfect ass of hers on display. My cock twitches to life, but it also fights with the exhaustion from the day.

"Not kidding, Xander," she says. "Now get your ass in the shower so I can take you to bed."

Goddamn. I'm more than just falling for this woman.

CHAPTER 12

CHARLI

There's nothing more satisfying than playing nurse to Xander Phillips.

When Micky came pounding at my door last night, I'd been all snuggled up in my bed, fast asleep. He had gotten only halfway through his explanation before I bolted down the stairs, desperate to check on Xander.

His shirt was off, and I noticed the cuts and bruising to his chest first, then of course, the devastating bruising across his ribs. I don't doubt there's a broken bone in there somewhere, but Xander is a stubborn asshat and refuses to get checked out, saying he's had more than enough broken ribs to know how to care for them.

My eyes traveled up to his face and took in the lump on the side of his temple, and it was clear someone had done a number on him.

Seeing him like that took me by surprise. After seeing him fight all those weeks ago, I've seen Xander as invincible. Untouchable. No one could take him down. Until I learned he was up against four of them and a baseball bat. I mean, he's incredible, but he's still human.

Anger tore through me. Without even hearing the explanation, I knew what had happened. I was so stupid to assume it was over. I can't help but feel this is all my fault. If I hadn't flushed the pills, they wouldn't have come after me. I could have just left and that would have been it. I never would have seen them again. Or maybe if I'd just stayed there and never met Xander in the first place, he'd be safe and sound in his own bed, pain free. But instead, I brought this down on him.

I hate myself for the harm my actions have caused, and I will spend every day of forever trying to make it up to him.

Xander puts on a brave face all night, but underneath the stubborn facade, I know he's in a lot of pain. Not that the big idiot would ever admit to it.

I wake early on Saturday morning after feeling like shit all night. Each time Xander moved in his sleep he would cringe and grunt in pain. I tried to give him space, but he would just keep pulling me back to him. It was like sleeping on eggshells. I was terrified of making a single move.

I dash around my room pulling on my jeans and boots before searching high and low for my favorite bra. Finding it hanging from the ceiling fan, I reach up, barely being able to grip the fabric, and yank it down. I'm unable to help the wicked grin stretching across my face as I'm putting it on, remembering exactly how it got up there in the first place.

After pulling on a shirt, I head to the bathroom and brush my teeth before ducking back into the bedroom and leaning down to press my lips to Xander's.

He wakes with my touch, and his arms fly up and around my neck, holding me to him so he can take advantage of my kiss. "Stop," I chuckle against his lips. "You're gonna hurt yourself. I'll be back soon."

Xander frees me before taking a second to notice I'm dressed and ready for the day. "Where the hell are you going?" he pouts.

"Out," I say, grabbing my purse and phone off the bedside table. "I won't be long."

"Oh," he says, throwing the blanket back. "Give me two minutes. I'll come with you."

"The hell you will," I scold, pulling the blanket right back into position. "You're staying right there until you're feeling better."

Xander gapes at me, looking as though I just pulled his heart right out of his chest and stomped on it. "Bullshit."

I shake my head before going around my room, making sure I have everything I need. "I don't want to hear it."

A slow grin spreads across his lips as his eyes darken with hunger. "That's the kind of attitude that earns a lady a good spanking."

"I'll make you a deal," I say as I spritz a little of the perfume Xander had gotten me last week onto my wrist. I watch him out of the corner of my eye as he raises his brow in curiosity. "If you're a good boy over the next few days and let me look after you, then I'll be a bad girl for you." I creep in closer, kneeling on the end of the bed and slowly crawling toward him, my gaze locked heavily on his. I watch how his hunger turns into intense desire, and it makes me feel like I can do anything. "Whatever you want, Xander. On the bar, in the ring, spread out on the ice as you feast between my legs . . ."

Xander groans, reaching for me, but I spring back out of the way before he can catch me. "Gotta be faster than that, *Widow Maker*."

His gaze darkens, knowing damn well I'm taking a stab at his claim of being one of the fastest guys in the game. But hell, egos were made to be shot down, and besides, teasing this incredible man is the best fun I've ever had.

Xander shakes his head and, taking pity on him, I stride around the side of the bed again and press my lips to his in a feather-soft kiss. "Why don't you go back to sleep?" I suggest. "I won't be long."

His hand shoots up, knotting into my hair to hold me still, and kissing me deeper. "How am I supposed to sleep now that I'm thinking about spreading those pretty thighs and tasting that sweet pussy?"

Oh, God. I clench my thighs, a fierce yearning rocking through me. I should have known better than to play games with Xander Phillips. I need to bail before this big idiot is out of bed and bending me over.

Pulling away from him, I try to find my bearings and remind myself of the bruises across his ribs. The last thing he needs right now is to be getting worked up. "Remember," I say, backing toward the door. "You need to be a good boy before you can be a bad one."

"Fuck, babe," he whines as I slip through the door and try to make a hasty exit. "Come back."

I keep walking when I pull up short, cursing myself at how desperate I am for this man. Fighting a smile, I double back and shove my head into my bedroom, getting the perfect view of his body, the bedsheets riding low across his hips. "Need something?" I purr.

The corner of his lips pull up into a wicked smirk, his eyes drawing me in. "Yeah, you need to deal with this," he says, throwing the blanket back and showing off that delicious, rock-hard cock. My mouth waters, even more so when he grips the base of it and slowly begins stroking himself.

My pussy throbs.

The need is too much, and I go to take a step back into my room, mesmerized by the way his fingers move up and down his cock, when reality comes slamming back to me. I remember the way he looked hunched over the bar last night, blood smeared across his body. I can't. He needs to heal, and I'll be damned if I'm the reason for it taking any longer than it should.

I shake my head, a manic grin stretching across my face. "Nice try," I tell him. "Tempt me all you want, but it won't change the fact that you'll be fucking nothing but your hand this morning."

"Babe," he groans.

"I'll see you soon." I wink as I exit the room and dash out the front door before he has a chance to try and change my mind again.

"You owe me," he calls.

I laugh as I make my way downstairs and out the front door of Micky's, knowing damn well that I owe him, and I plan on making it up to him in a big way. But he'll be fine with blue balls for now. Besides, his blue balls will match his bruises, and I can't resist a coordinated man.

Heading down the street, I enjoy the early morning breeze as it brushes past my face and blows my hair back behind me. I turn into the mall and search the stores until I come across the pharmacy. Quickly making my way inside, I get busy stocking up on everything Xander could possibly need over the next few weeks—painkillers, antiseptic cream, bandages, and more.

Next, I hit up the grocery store.

Figuring a guy like Xander is going to rid my home of all its edible contents within the first half hour, I stock up on everything that I know he likes, being careful that I don't get anything that goes against his strict diet. But it's not easy. I've never had to think so hard about nutrition in my life, and I hope I'm picking up all the right things.

As I'm heading back out toward the street, I walk past a lingerie store. Glancing through the window as I pass, something inside has me stopping and backtracking to the door. A wide grin stretches across my face, knowing I don't really have the funds to spend the extra money, but I can't possibly resist. I push through the door, my gaze fixed on the costume before glancing at the store attendant. "I'll take that one."

By the time I get home, my arms ache from the shopping bags, and I realize it probably would have been a good idea to let Xander tag along. You know, if he weren't in bed recovering from being jumped by four assholes with a baseball bat. Besides, if he had come, his surprise would be spoiled.

"That was quick," Xander calls out from the bedroom as I dump all the bags on the counter and start putting groceries away. I roll my eyes. That wasn't even close to being quick. He must have dozed off without even realizing.

I grin to myself before the comment flies out of my mouth. "Not as quick as you were the other night."

"Fucking smart-ass," I hear him mutter.

Walking into the kitchen, I start putting the groceries away. "Are you hungry?"

"Depends."

I shake my head as a smile rips across my face. "On?" I ask, already knowing what he's going to say.

"Are you on the menu?"

"Ha, ha. You're so very original, Xander Phillips," I tease.

"Please," he scoffs. "I'm fucking hilarious."

I roll my eyes as I ignore his comments and get started on breakfast. A few minutes later, I call out for him, letting him know the food is ready and place it down on the coffee table. Moving into the bedroom to help him, I find him already out of bed and striding toward me, doing a good job of ignoring the pain that must be tormenting his whole body.

We eat on the couch then put on a movie, which the big guy promptly falls asleep during. Wanting him to rest, I quietly get up and take our dishes back to the kitchen before cleaning up and putting on another movie, keeping the volume down low.

As I'm singing along to *"(I've Had) The Time of My Life"* at the end of *Dirty Dancing*, Micky's phone rings on the coffee table. Not wanting the call to wake Xander, I quickly jump up and answer it, assuming it's most likely a vendor. Accepting the call, I shove the phone against my ear and start making my way to the door, ready to find Micky if the call is important.

"Hi, this is Officer Samuels from the Denver Police Department," a feminine voice says through the phone, bringing me to a stop in the doorway. "Is Xander Phillips available?"

"Oh, hi. This is Charli. I spoke with you last night," I say, realizing this is about Xander's attack. "He's asleep. Can I pass along a message for him to call you back?"

"Sure thing, Charli. How is Xander doing today? He had quite the night," she says.

"To be honest, he's being a stubborn ass," I scoff.

"Yeah, well. He is a man after all. You shouldn't have expected anything less," she chuckles to herself. "Anyway, the reason for my call is, I wanted to let Xander know that CCTV did indeed catch the footage of the attack. We shouldn't have any issues positively identifying his attackers, and that has a lot to do with the names you supplied last night."

"Oh, wow. That's great news."

"Indeed, it is. They'll be charged, and we'll send out a recovery team to locate Xander's truck," she explains.

"Thank you," I say, "Xander could use some good news today."

"That he could," Officer Samuels agrees.

Sounding as though she's trying to wrap up the conversation, I suck in a breath through my teeth, hoping this doesn't come back to bite me on the ass. "Um," I cringe, not really sure I should be saying it, but after those dickheads hurt Xander, I'm going to make sure they pay. "When you pick them up, you should probably search their place for drugs."

"Understood. Thanks for the tip."

"No problem," I mutter, feeling sick to my stomach. She quickly wraps up the call and promises to let us know how things go with Xander's truck, hoping to have more good news for us later today.

I end the call, and as I make myself comfortable on the couch, Xander stirs beside me. He cringes in pain before realizing what he's done and schools his features, remembering his ridiculous need to be viewed as the toughest guy in the room.

Getting up, I pad into the kitchen to find the painkillers, and after making my way back to him, I practically force them down his throat. Once he's comfortable, I fill him in on the phone call from Officer Samuels, and that little bit of good news is enough to help him relax.

By the afternoon, we're both bored out of our minds. There are only so many movies one can watch in a day, so I decide it's time to finally blow his mind.

Xander is chilling on the couch, begging to leave the apartment, when I excuse myself for the bathroom. I rush through the process so he doesn't become suspicious. I fluff up my hair, apply a little red lipstick, and put on my new sexy nurse outfit before stepping into the high heels I'd stashed in here earlier.

Taking one last look in the mirror, I decide it doesn't get much better than this.

Nerves pound through my body as I step out of the bathroom and lean against the doorframe. I bite down on my lower lip, doing everything I can to show him just how hungry I am for him.

He clocks me the second I step out of the bathroom, and I watch in amusement as his eyes widen in shock, before quickly morphing into an intense appreciation. "Fuck me," he murmurs as he adjusts himself on the couch, his morning activities doing nothing to stop the raging erection growing in his pants.

"Did someone call for a nurse?" I purr, managing to say it without breaking into embarrassed laughter. I push off the doorframe and slowly make my way over toward him with hooded eyes, loving the way he watches me right back.

He tracks every move I make as his sharp gaze roams up and down my body, his intensity knocking the breath right out of my lungs. Xander adjusts himself on the couch, sitting up as I step between his knees.

He places his hands on the back of my thighs and runs them over my thigh-high, fishnet stockings, a low groan rumbling through his chest. Leaning forward, I place my hands on his knees and gently push them further apart, giving myself plenty of room to drop down between his legs.

Reaching out, I slip my fingers into the waistband of his sweatpants, and he leans back against the couch, raising his hips to allow me to slide them down. His cock springs free, and my mouth waters, seeing just how ready he is.

Xander watches me, his eyes flaming with red-hot need, and I wrap my fingers around the base of his cock, slowly moving up and down his impressive length. I keep my eyes locked on his and watch as those flames turn to molten lava. My thumb rolls over his tip, and he groans low, the sound like music to my ears.

Wanting to give him exactly what he deserves, I lean forward and take him into my mouth deep enough that I can feel him at the back of my throat. His hand knots into my hair, gripping it tightly as my pussy aches for sweet relief. Working him up and down, I run my tongue over his tip as I tighten my grip around his base. "Fuck, babe," he hisses, his hips jolting beneath my touch, already close to the edge.

His words spur me on and the louder he groans, the more I need to feel him empty into my mouth. I don't dare stop, giving him all I've got, working him up and down, my tongue continuing over his tip as his fingers tighten in my hair. Finally he comes hard, shooting hot spurts of cum down my throat as he hisses my name.

Pulling back, I release his cock and look up at him as he tries to catch his breath, watching me with wonder in his dark eyes.

"Fucking hell," he mutters, reaching for me. "Get up here so I can fuck you 'til you scream."

My tongue rolls over my bottom lip, and I shake my head. "Nope. Not until you're better."

"Don't give me that shit," he says, ignoring his ribs and leaning forward. He grips my arms and pulls me toward him until he can get a better hold then hauls me up onto his lap. I straddle his hips and his cock grinds against my clit, making my eyes roll to the back of my head. "I fight for a living," he says, taking hold of my hips and gently rocking me back and forth as if knowing just how badly I need him. "I can handle a little pain."

I'm desperate to slide down onto his thick cock, but the thought of hurting him kills me inside. He can clearly see the desire in my eyes, but he can also see the hesitation. "Either you're going to sink that sweet pussy down over my cock, or I'm going to throw you down and fuck you over the coffee table. Your choice."

Fuck. This guy is such a stubborn ass.

Not leaving me a chance to respond, he slips his hands up my skirt, taking hold of my black thong and tearing it off my body.

The desperation is too much, and I rise up higher on my knees as Xander positions himself beneath me. Then putting us both out of our misery, I drop down on top of him, sinking low over his cock and taking him deep. He stretches me wide, and I groan, the instant satisfaction sending hot pulses of pleasure rocking through my body.

Gripping onto his strong shoulders, I pick up my pace, needing so much more. Needing to feel my body beneath his fingers, he tears the nurse outfit up over my head, leaving me in nothing but a red, lace bra.

His eyes flame with desire, and he pulls the cup down, freeing a nipple before closing his mouth over it, his tongue flicking over the pebbled peak.

"Oh, fuck. Xander. I'm gonna come," I warn him as I continue to ride him with everything I've got.

"Hold on to it, babe," he grunts as he raises his hips off the couch, plunging himself impossibly deeper.

"Shit," I cry. "I can't."

"You can," he insists through clenched teeth. He begins pounding up into me, joining my rhythm. Once, twice, three times. "Now," he demands.

His words are my undoing, and I explode around him, my pussy convulsing as the high rocks through me. He stills beneath me but allows me to keep moving as I ride out my orgasm. I tip my head back, the raw intensity almost too much for me to take.

"Holy shit," I pant, bracing myself against the couch over his shoulder to keep from collapsing against him.

His arms slide around my waist as he pulls me closer, not giving a single fuck about his pain. "You can say that again," he murmurs, his lips finding their favorite place below my ear. "You're not that innocent girl you were a few weeks ago."

I can't help but laugh. "You've corrupted me."

"Damn straight, babe."

"Maybe you'd prefer if I went back to that girl," I tease.

"Don't get me wrong, I loved that innocent, shy girl who would worry if she was doing it right, but this," he says, his eyes raking over my body, taking in the red bra with one nipple still protruding out the top before dropping his gaze lower to where his cock remains buried deep inside me. "This is downright sexy. It's fucking amazing."

I grin at his comments until I go over them in my head. Did he just say he loved that innocent, shy girl? As in he loved those traits or he loved me?

He notices my head has gone somewhere and concern flashes in his dark eyes. "What's wrong?" he asks, running his fingers down the side of my face and pushing a stray lock of hair behind my ear.

"Nothing." I smile with a slight shake of my head, intent on enjoying this moment.

"What is it?" he insists, not capable of letting it go.

I look him deep in his eyes, hoping it's the right time, but now that it's on my mind, I have to let it out. "I love you," I whisper.

His eyes search mine, and he goes quiet for a moment before the softest smile graces his lips. He wraps one hand around the back of my neck and pulls me to him, pressing his lips to mine before kissing me with every ounce of passion he possesses.

Once he's thoroughly done rocking my world, he pulls back just an inch, his forehead resting against mine. "I fucking love you, too."

CHAPTER 13

XANDER

My alarm sounds on Monday morning, screeching through the quiet room like a damn banshee. Rolling over with a groan, I reach for my new phone and grunt in pain, the move putting me directly over my ribs. Quickly adjusting myself, I try again before finally silencing my phone and hoping I haven't disturbed Charli too much.

I hate the idea of going back to reality today. The weekend with her has been nothing short of amazing, apart from the whole attack thing. That shit kind of sucked. Like, really fucking sucked. But not having to train all weekend and being looked after by nurse Charli definitely had its perks. That nurse's outfit blew me the fuck away, with the matching bra, red lipstick, and thigh-high stockings. Fuck, I wasn't expecting that from my innocent Charli, so I guess she has a wild side after all. A wild side that drives me fucking crazy.

Then she went ahead and told me she loves me, and those three little words whispered from her lips made me drown in a sea of raw emotion. It was like my heart exploded with undeniable happiness. All I could do at that moment was pull her to me and kiss her like it was the end of the world.

I've had girlfriends tell me they love me before, but nothing ever felt the way it does with Charli. She's real. She's the woman I'll be spending the rest of my life with. I know it's only been a few weeks, but when you know, you know.

The thought of leaving her to go to hockey training almost has me rioting, but what can I do? Despite not being what I really want, hockey is a part of my life, and I honestly do love it. I want to be part of the team, which means showing up for my boys. I can only imagine how the shit is going to hit the fan when they discover my secret life, but the longer I can keep it quiet, the better.

Leaning over, I press a kiss on Charli's lips before climbing out of bed. She caved last night and agreed to stay at my place so it would be easier for me this morning, as all my shit for training is already here.

My ribs still ache, but the rest of my body seems to have calmed down enough to at least pretend I'm good. Don't get me wrong, without clothes on, it's damn obvious that something went down. I just consider myself lucky that I wear long clothing for hockey and I'll be able to hide most of it. After all, we all know where questions lead.

Shuffling around my room, I gather my shit for my morning run as my ribs scream in protest, but there's nothing I can do at this point apart from keeping them bandaged and taking some painkillers. The bruising has completely come out, and to be honest, it looks fucking bad. Worse than it had that first night.

I head out to the landing and sit down on the top step to tie my shoes, hating the awful feeling that each movement makes. It's still early in the day, and I need to allow my body a chance to wake up. I'm sure once I get started on my run, all the aches and pains will begin to settle.

Ducking back into my room, I can't resist giving Charli another kiss to let her know I'm leaving. I'm a whipped motherfucker like that. "Don't be stupid," she mumbles through her sleepy haze, still trying to take care of me.

"I know. I'll be careful," I promise her. But let's face it, whatever is required of me during our training session, I'm always going to give one hundred percent, no matter what. Even if it fucking kills me.

Then heading downstairs, I make my way into the kitchen before ripping out a piece of paper from a notebook. I begin writing with a stupid as fuck grin plastered across my face.

Babe,
Just in case I'm not home when you leave.
In fact, you better keep it.
I love you.

Taking the spare key from my keychain, I place it down on the piece of paper before grabbing a drink out of the fridge and hitting the road.

I meet the boys at the park, just like every other morning, and we get straight into it. Just as I predicted, my body begins to relax, and after a decent warm-up, the pain is tolerable. This is only a run though. Getting on the ice is going to be a whole new issue.

I have a fight in a few days and I'm not stupid enough to assume it will be better by then, but if I take care of myself, I might still have a chance of winning. It takes months for a broken rib to heal, and getting in the ring with a broken rib is fucking stupid. It will be obvious to my opponent that I have a weakness, and that area will be targeted. Not to mention, if I get hit and a piece of my rib dislodges and punctures my lung or heart, it's game over for me.

A few hours later, I step off the ice completely exhausted. Who would have known that training with an injury would be so hard? But I gave it my all, and I don't think anyone noticed that I was lacking or favoring my left side.

As I make my way toward the locker room, I pass Coach Harris and can't help but notice the way he narrows his gaze on me, a strange mix of curiosity, concern, and suspicion flashing in his eyes. I look away almost immediately. Perhaps I didn't go as unnoticed as I'd hoped.

I've never given him a reason to doubt me, so maybe he'll put it down to me just having a bad day. After all, I'm only human. We all have bad days.

After making my way into the locker room, I take my sweet time removing my skates and hockey gear. I'm usually the quickest to get out of here, so it's damn frustrating. I feel like I'm going at a snail's pace, but I can't risk the guys seeing my ribs in the showers and asking questions.

When the majority of the boys have cleared out, I finally head in and get cleaned up. I'm the only person in here, so I make it quick, but when Jaxon walks in as I'm turning off the water, I realize I'm not getting out of here without being seen.

He minds his business, just as he should in the showers, but I make it quick nonetheless. I towel off and pull my jeans on before heading out of the stall, and as I raise my hands above my head to pull my shirt down, a voice stops me in my tracks.

"Dude?"

I whip around finding Jax gawking at my ribs. Fuck.

"It's nothing, man," I say, shrugging it off, but this is just the beginning. I see the questions and curiosity in his eyes. The fucker is already suspicious of me. I see him watching me after game night, noticing how I leave earlier than everyone else, and until now, he's let it slide. But I doubt that's gonna be the case now.

Not giving him the chance to question me further, I quickly pull my shirt the rest of the way down and get the fuck out of there.

My blades cut through the slick ice as I push forward with the puck at the end of my stick. I shoot it across to Bobby to avoid getting body slammed into the barrier. I have a fight tonight, and turning up with another injury is not going to work in my favor. Especially after Cole chewed me out all week when I didn't let on just how badly I was injured.

I stick by Bobby's side, ready and waiting if he needs me. Jaxon comes flying up to Bobby's other side so we each flank him as the rest of our teammates work defense and make a clear line for Bobby to shoot the puck straight into the net. The crowd roars in excitement as their favorite team scores yet again. Bobby claps me on the back right before Jaxon comes out of nowhere, slamming into him in excitement.

Coach calls us to the side to talk through our plan of attack, pointing out weaknesses on the opposing team and firing us back up again before sending us back to the center of the ice.

The game is hard, and I push myself a little too much, but it's a necessary evil. I committed to giving my all to my team, and despite how fucking bad it hurts, that's exactly what I do. No pain, no gain. At least, that's the bullshit my father always used to feed me.

The sweet agony pays off when the final buzzer sounds, declaring victory for the Dragons. An hour later, I'm sitting back with a beer in my hand, staring at my girl as she effortlessly works the crowded bar.

I sit with the boys at our usual table and watch as they go hard on the beers, especially Shorty, who for some unknown reason, absolutely loves Micky's. It probably has something to do with the easy pussy he gets here.

Rather than calling the waitress over, I head up to the bar to order a drink, and Charli practically boots the new girl out of her way to be the one to serve me. She pours me a drink and hands it over with a flirty smile that has me ready to take her up to her apartment and nail her on the kitchen counter.

Despite having my drink in hand, I find myself sitting at the bar, chilling out with my girl as she works. A moment passes before Charli glances up and subtly nods behind me. "Head's up," she mutters. "You've got company."

Glancing over my shoulder, I find Jaxon making his way over here, and it's clear I'm his target. I let out a heavy sigh, knowing this is it. He's been riding my ass all week, and I've managed to avoid his questions, but something tells me my time has run out.

He takes the seat next to me, nursing a beer in his hands. "Hey, man. What are you doing all the way over here? There's a party going on, and we're the guests of honor."

Shit, what the hell am I supposed to tell him? "Just chilling out with Charli here," I say, motioning behind the bar to Charli. She turns at the sound of her name and gives Jaxon a nod before getting back to work, not liking having the attention on her.

I down the rest of my drink and subtly check the time, knowing I'm going to have to leave for my fight soon, but I also know it would be way too shady to just get up and leave without a word.

"Let me guess. You've got somewhere to be?" Jaxon says, letting me off the hook, though the disapproval in his tone has something tightening in my gut.

Shit. That just made me feel like the biggest douchebag around. I wish I could be honest with these guys, but our whole relationship would change. I know they sense I'm hiding something from them, something big, and that makes them question my loyalty to the team.

But I can't tell them, not yet. Besides, the second they realize my heart is somewhere other than on that ice, the game will change. They won't see me as their teammate, their family . . . I would just be some guy who happens to be wearing the same jersey.

With a sigh, I look up at him with regret, hating how deceitful I have to be. "Yeah. Sorry, man."

He's silent for a moment before finally asking the question that's been on his mind all week. "Is there something you need to talk about?" he asks before getting a little more serious. "You're not in any kind of trouble, are you? I can't have shit coming down on the team, especially now we're getting closer to the finals."

If only he knew.

"Nah," I tell him, shaking my head, trying to make light of the situation. "No trouble. Just got stuff going on."

He seems to take my word for it before flicking his gaze back to Charli. I can practically see him trying to work it out. It's like he knows there's some kind of connection between us, but he has no idea what.

I don't know why I haven't told the boys about me and Charli. I guess, at first, I wanted to keep my fighting life and my hockey life separate, and Charli was put firmly on the fighting side, but that's not the case now. She comes under a whole new section. She's my fucking girl, through thick and thin. She's so much more than a fucking side I can put her on.

"Alright, man," Jaxon says, getting up off the stool and wrapping this shit up. "You know where to find me if you need anything."

I give him a nod, taking his comment for what it is—an open

invitation to spill my fucking guts. "Thanks," I say before turning away. I give Charli a quick wink and she blows me a kiss before mouthing "Good luck."

"Hey," I hear Jaxon calling after me. I turn back around and practically have to lip-read over the noise of the bar. "Don't show up to training covered in bruises. I need your head in the game if we're going to take out the championship again."

Yeah, the fucker definitely knows.

I give him a tight grin. My head in the game? My head is always in the fucking game, no matter what. He should know that by now. "Sure thing, man," I say before ducking out the side door, and heading back up the alley to my truck, reminding myself how lucky I am to have it back.

Officer Samuels had called during the week to let me know that my truck had been recovered during a raid on a chop shop, and that I could pick it up anytime. Though it had a few scratches and dents, it's nothing that my insurance won't cover.

I pass some shady-looking asshole in the alley, who looks like he's smelling a pair of lace panties. But hell, everyone has their fucking kinks, right? The fucker scowls at me, but I continue on my way. I've got places to be, people to fuck up. Cole is going to kill me if I miss the fight. Not to mention, I'd miss out on twenty grand and forfeit it to the other guy.

Not fucking happening. Not on my watch.

Getting in my truck, I hit the gas and peel out of my parking space before sailing down the street, my mind already deep in tonight's fight.

I get a minute down the street and am just pulling onto the main road when a text comes through on my phone, and I groan as I read it.

Jaxon - Dude, left your wallet on the bar.

Fuck. I consider telling him to leave it with Charli, but you never know when you're going to need it. I've always made a habit of never going anywhere without it. Besides, it's brand new. I don't want to lose another fucking wallet in less than a week.

Xander - Shit. Be there in a sec.

I whip my truck around and head straight back to Micky's, knowing this shit is bound to make me late. I park in the spot I'd been not a few minutes ago, and throw the door open before flying out. I dash back down the alley to find Jaxon beating the ever-loving shit out of the shady fucker with the panties. I rush forward to break it up, when I realize it's the asshole who'd gotten too handsy with his girl here a few weeks ago. The very reason we all avoided coming to Micky's for so long. Rather than break it up, I let Jaxon have at him.

It doesn't take him long to knock the guy out. I guess he does have anger on his side. I find my wallet laying on the ground and dash forward.

"Dude," I say, trying to pull him back to reality, looking as though he's about to go for round two. "I didn't know you had it in you." Jaxon's head flies toward me, ready for another attack, but quickly realizes it's just me. "Everything good here?"

"Yeah, man," he responds, his gaze shifting back to the asshole, sprawled across the dirty ground. "Just had a little misunderstanding is all."

Little misunderstanding, my ass. "Right," I scoff, remembering the wallet at my feet. I pluck it up off the ground, giving Jaxon a look. "Thanks for this."

He gives me a slight nod and I take off up the alley again, hoping I haven't wasted too much time. I get to the end when I hear noise back at the bar's side exit. I turn back around, hoping the fucker hasn't regained consciousness, when I realize it's just Shorty with some chick.

I roll my eyes, knowing exactly what's going on there.

Fucking Shorty. Such a whore.

CHAPTER 14

XANDER

After pulling up at tonight's venue, I rush out of my truck. The clock on my dash tells me I still have a few minutes to spare, but Cole is going to kick my ass for cutting it this close.

I head around the back of the building to find Caden and Luke waiting for me. The moment they see me, matching looks of relief and anger fall over their faces, and I know they're dying to knock some sense into me. We don't have time for that shit, though.

"Thank fuck," Caden breathes as he practically claws at my arm to get me inside. "That was too fucking close."

"Don't I know it," I grunt, hating the way he pulls my arm, which sends a shooting pain right to my broken rib.

We rush down the hallway while Luke spurts out every last detail I should know about my opponent, but I've seen the guy before. He's the kind who likes to go for the kill, so as annoying as it will be, I'll have to fight with my weaker side so he doesn't get an opening on my ribs.

I enter the fighters' room and find Cole speaking with some official, trying his luck at delaying the fight, but we all know the rules around here. If you're not here at your scheduled time, you forfeit.

Cole clocks me the second I enter and his panicked features morph into a heavy scowl. Yeah, I'm fucked.

He storms over to me, already pulling the tape out of his pocket, and lets me have it. I tune him out while he begins wrapping my hands and adding extra tape to my ribs. Noticing someone else in the room, my stare locks on his, and I recognize him from some of the fights I've stayed to watch.

Pitbull is the favorite to take out the competition, with me coming in close second. To be honest, the guy is bad news. Really fucking bad news. He got his name because that's the way he fights—like a fucking dog. He's brutal in the ring, and I'm not looking forward to facing off against him.

Every single person he's fought has been rushed to the hospital with life-threatening injuries. He's nothing short of dirty, but I'll get my day with him, and I'll put the fucker right in his place. All I know is that it's going to be the hardest fight I'll have to endure. On the other hand, if it's the finals, it's rumored the winner is set to take home something like two hundred grand. So you can bet that I won't stop until that cash is in my hand. One thing has me extremely nervous though. He's just watched Cole tape up my ribs, and without a doubt, he's storing that piece of information away, ready to use it against me.

Snapping back to reality, I find Cole finishing on my ribs, leaving me a few minutes for a warm-up with Caden. He grunts and whines as I pummel my fists into him, but he knows it's what I need right now. He'd rather end up with bruised hands than see me enter that ring unprepared.

Two minutes later, the same official comes in and calls me to the ring. I hate being rushed for a fight, but even with my injury and lack of warm-up, I'm still confident I can win. The guy I'm against is only eighteen and a little too cocky for his own good. He usually wins by knockout, but so do I.

I have to admit, he's a strong contender, but he still has a lot to learn about what his body can do. Maybe in a few years, I might see him in the professional circuit. Hell, I don't know why someone as young as him would even be in the Underground yet.

I step out into the arena with Cole and Luke heavy on my heels. Cole is still pissed at me, but it's game time, so he shelves it for now. "Alright, kid," he says as we wait for the announcer to call me into the ring. "The guy is shorter than you, so remember to keep low. His footwork's good, but not as good as yours. Use that to your advantage. The second he realizes you're injured, he's going to aim for your ribs for an easy kill. Keep your left side forward and don't let him in."

I nod my head as I keep my mind focused on the fight ahead.

The announcer calls me in, and I come out as the music pumps up, the crowd roaring for *The Widow Maker*. I strut around, putting on the show my fans have come so accustomed to. I do my usual strip down for the ladies before throwing my black robe over to Cole, which is when shit gets serious.

The music dies down and I face my opponent, who looks down at the tape across my ribs. A sick smirk comes over the fucker's face, and it's damn obvious what his game plan is. The idiot. Everyone knows you don't give away your secrets, no matter how obvious they are. Always leave them guessing, which is a lesson I'll gladly teach him the hard way. After all, he's only eighteen, and needs a few years to learn the tricks of the trade.

The fight begins, and just as expected, he aims his first punch right at my ribs. I turn away and use his momentum to grab his arm and flip the idiot onto his back. I stand back with a grin and watch as he scurries to his feet, figuring I might as well have a little fun with this one and teach him some of those lessons he truly deserves to learn. I mean, I could have taken him out while he was down, but the crowd enjoys a good show.

The kid scowls at me, pissed for having made a fool of him in front of a crowd this big, and so early on in the fight, too. But he has only himself to blame. His anger radiates off him, but it's no secret that you don't fight with anger. You fight with your mind in the game. Error number three for the kid.

He comes at me with fists flying, but I block each and every one, which only manages to piss him off more. He pushes forward and tries to get me in a headlock so he can single out my ribs, but once again, all attempts fail when he tries to play with one of the big boys.

I land a few combinations, all of which he's too slow for, but credit to the kid, he can take the hits. I see the moment he starts to get his head in the game, and it turns into a decent fight for a little while, but he's wearing out quickly. My blows have him backing up step by step, and as I grow bored of this game of cat and mouse, I decide to put him out of his misery and take him down.

Pushing forward with a kick to the chest, he stumbles back against the ring. Keeping on him, I hit him with a combination punch then a sweep to knock him on his ass. The kid doesn't even see it coming.

I flip him to his stomach and pull his arm behind his back, keeping him pinned as I put him in a headlock. He struggles for a bit, but he knows he can't get out of it. He can continue struggling all he wants, but we all know if he waits too long, he's going to pass out. So instead, he does the one thing I'll never do in front of a crowd—he taps out, giving me some of the easiest money of my life.

I get to my feet and help the kid up just as the ref comes out to hold my hand up and declare me the winner. And hell, maybe in a few years when he's got some more training under his belt, I might even enjoy taking him on again.

I strut out of the ring, pretty damn pleased with myself, and wondering why the hell I didn't get in the ring years ago. Hell, with the money I'm pulling in right now, I'll be buying my own place pretty soon. Though, I might wait to see just how far I make it in this competition before purchasing anything. After all, if I win the final, it will change what kind of place I could buy, and hell, I plan on buying something really nice. Especially considering I have every intention of taking Charli with me.

The second I'm out of the ring, Cole launches himself at me along with Luke and Caden, who beam and boast about how great that was. Though to tell the truth, it seems too easy to boast about. When I get further into the competition and actually earn the win, then I'll be happy to brag. Hell, beating this guy was almost easier than taking Caden down during the warm-up.

The guys lead me back out to the fighters' room, and Cole puts me through a cool down, clearly forgetting about being pissed at me before the fight.

Dropping onto the bench, I peel off the tape around my knuckles. "Alright, see you later, kid," Cole says once we're done.

"Yeah, see ya," I say, shoving my shit into my bag and turning to the door.

"Don't think I've forgiven you for being late," he reminds me. "There'll be hell to pay in training tomorrow."

Fuck.

I give him a curt nod before saying my goodbyes to the boys and a few of the other fighters I've gotten to know over the past few months. Then after collecting my winnings, I make my way out, dying to get home to my girl.

I'm nearly at my truck when a movement through the darkness pulls me up short, and I find someone leaning up against my truck. My stare narrows, slowly creeping closer. I've already been jumped once, I'm not looking to make it twice. As I get closer, a strange familiarity starts to nag at me, until finally, I can make out his face.

Shit. Game over.

Aaron leans against the side of my truck with his foot propped up on the tire, his hands buried deep. His stance is casual, but after being on the team with the guy since the start of the season, I know his stance isn't casual at all. Hell, he's furious.

"Hey, man," I cringe as I throw my gear in the backseat.

He doesn't say a word, just looks at me with anger and betrayal pouring out of his eyes as he continues leaning against the truck. His head tilts slightly, and I know he's ready. "You could have told us. We wouldn't have said anything."

"Seriously? You get why I can't tell anyone about this, right? It's the fucking Underground. It's illegal. If anyone found out that you guys knew, you'd all be going down right along with me," I explain. "Each and every one of you would have to kiss your NHL dreams goodbye."

"Really? That's the bullshit excuse you're going with?" he scoffs. "We're not fucking idiots. No one would have said a word. Hell, we probably would have been here after the games to cheer you on instead of getting fucked up at some ridiculous house party. We've all been wondering what the fuck is going on with you."

"Sorry, man," I grunt, unapologetically. "I'm prepared to risk my future, but I wouldn't risk the whole fucking teams' future."

Aaron lets out a frustrated sigh, clenching his jaw. "Fuck," he spits, pushing off the side of my truck as his hand comes up to scratch the back of his neck. "I don't know whether to be pissed at you or impressed with how fucking good you are."

"Yeah," I grin. "I don't suck."

"A guy in there said you could win this thing?" he questions.

"Do you think I would be risking it all if I didn't think I could win?"

"Who fucking knows," he snaps. "It's not like you've allowed anyone to get to know you."

Yeah, I deserved that. "And now you know why," I say, holding his stare as I narrow my gaze on the big fucker. "How did you know I was here?"

He grins at the question and looks guilty as shit. "Dude, you're the shadiest motherfucker around. I was curious."

The meaning hits me like a fucking fist to the gut. "You followed me from Micky's?"

"Eh," he shrugs, unapologetically. "You keep disappearing, saying you have things to do, but seriously, what kind of normal person has shit to do in the middle of the night? Then you show up to training covered in bruises, pretending like we couldn't fucking see them. You didn't leave me any choice, man. It was like you were daring me to figure it out."

I let out a sigh. I guess he's right, which means it's only a matter of time before the rest of the guys work it out. "You'll keep it to yourself?"

"Yeah, man," he says. "But honestly, the guys know something's up with you. You're like a puzzle they haven't been able to work out, and they're curious. It won't be long before they're following your stupid ass here too."

"I know," I say with a heavy sigh. "I feel like a dick not being honest about it, but if I were, I'd be off the team."

"Yeah, I get it," he says with a forgiving smile. "Come on. While we're here, we may as well enjoy the night."

"Fine," I groan as he convinces me to head back inside. "But then I'm going home to my girl."

"The fuck?" he grunts. "You've got a girl? How did I not know this? Fuck, I bet it's that chick from the bar, isn't it? Man, she's fucking hot," he says, hardly giving himself a chance to breathe. "Shit, I feel like I hardly know you at all."

I can't help but grin. Tonight is going to be interesting.

CHAPTER 15

CHARLI

Dropping my ass into the chair in the salon's break room, I give myself just a minute to annihilate my lunch when I hear the familiar buzz of my phone deep in my bag. I groan, flying back off the chair to grab my bag, and scouring through it until my fingers close around the cool metal.

Seeing Micky's name across the screen, my brows furrow. He rarely calls me, and if he does, it's something important. "Hey," I rush out. "What's up? Everything okay?"

"Have I got you at a good time?" Micky questions, getting straight to business. "I couldn't remember what time you said you went for your break."

"Yeah, all good. I'm having lunch now."

"Good, listen," he says, a strange hesitation in his tone. "The bar's shut down until further notice."

"What?" I screech in outrage as I try to figure out what the hell he's talking about. "Who would do that?"

"The building inspector," he mutters, sounding as though he's about ready to rip out throats. "There's a problem with the drain in the kitchen. The whole place is flooded, which means the bar is closed until it's fixed."

"Shit, Micky," I sigh. "That sucks."

"Sure does, kid," he says. "But unfortunately, that means you no longer have access to your apartment."

"Oh," I breathe, not having expected that, though it makes sense. I should have put that together.

"Can you stay with Xander for a few days?" he asks. "If not, you can crash on my couch. It's nothing special, but it'll do."

"Thanks, but it's fine," I say, not put off by the idea at all. "Xander gave me a key."

"Well, shit," he says before a loud belly laugh rumbles through the phone. "Getting serious, huh?"

I roll my eyes, a stupid, dopey grin spreading across my face. "Shut up."

Micky just keeps laughing. One of his newfound loves in life is teasing me until I want to throttle him. "Alright," he says, and I can just picture the way he would roll his eyes and smirk. "I'll let you know once we've got the all-clear."

"Sure thing."

"Be safe, Charli," he says, easily slipping back into that father role that comes so naturally to him. Then he ends the call.

Dropping back into my seat, I continue with my lunch when one of the other stylists walks in. Zara gives me a smile, but it shifts as she takes me in. "Everything okay?" she asks, concern lacing her tone, making me realize my worry for the bar must be plastered across my face.

"Oh, yeah," I say, trying to school my features. "The bar is going to be closed for a few days, so I'll be staying with Xander for a while."

"Well, that hardly sounds like a problem," she grins.

"Believe me, it's not," I laugh, more than thrilled about the idea of spending the next few nights locked in his strong arms. It's not much different than what we're doing now.

"Haven't you been wanting to go to one of his games?" she asks. "If the bar is closed, it's not like you'll be working. Why don't you go? I think the Dragons are playing tonight."

Hmmm, interesting.

I don't know why I didn't think of it first. A wide smile takes over my face as excitement drums through my veins. "He does have a game tonight," I confirm. "I could surprise him."

"Sounds like a good plan," she laughs, my excitement becoming contagious.

An idea hits me, and I suddenly feel a wave of nervousness. "Do, umm . . . do you want to come with me?" I ask, realizing that Zara could potentially make a really amazing friend. After all, I don't get any weird vibes from her like I did with Lex.

Zara beams up at me. "I thought you'd never ask."

"Really?" I gasp, my eyes widening with surprise. "I think it starts at seven."

"Okay. Did you want to go for some cocktails first?" she asks. "I mean, we finish at five, so we'll have a few hours to kill."

I can't help but grin. I think we're gonna get along just fine.

Zara and I make our way up the grandstand, and I'm already in awe. The place is packed, and I'm surprised to see just how many people I recognize from the bar. We practically stumble up the stairs after having a few too many cocktails, but I don't have the decency to be ashamed of my near drunkenness because I think I've actually made a good friend.

We find our seats, and the moment we get comfortable, I rip into the packaging of the jersey I just bought with Xander's name and number on the back. The moment I pull it over my head, something settles within me, like I'm finally getting the chance to show the world that Xander is mine.

Zara hands me a massive foam finger, and we both break into giggles as we pull them on. I can't wait until Xander comes out and sees me. With the foam finger and jersey, I don't know if he'll be embarrassed or proud as shit, but I'm willing to find out.

Zara disappears, saying she's hungry, and she returns not long after with some hot dogs and what looks to be a calendar. She takes her seat and instantly breaks into the calendar, making me crack into laughter at what I see. The calendar is filled with half-naked images of the hockey team. "Apparently, it's a new tradition that some chick started last year," Zara tells me, relaying the information the girl at the stand gave her.

She continues to flick through the pages, and I stop her when I recognize one hell of a sexy body. "Wait," I say a little too loudly. "That's Xander."

"That's your boyfriend?" she asks wide-eyed. "Holy shit, woman. That man is hot."

"I know," I grin as I practically drool over the calendar. "I'm going to have to buy my own calendar."

"Indeed you will," she agrees as she turns to the next page. "Who the hell is this guy?"

"That would be Aaron," I tell her. "He's sorta become Xander's new bestie over the last week."

"Is he single?" she asks with interest.

"I, umm . . . I actually have no idea," I say, realizing that's probably something I should know about the guy by this point. After all, he welcomed himself over three nights this week.

"Well, that settles it," she declares, practically drooling over the pages. "You're introducing me after the game."

"Deal," I laugh.

Twenty minutes later, Zara and I have downed some pretty questionable hot dogs, and the stands are at capacity. The atmosphere blows me away with the number of fans that have shown up tonight.

It's insane. There are hardly any fans here for the opposition, not that I've really taken notice of who the opposition is. All that matters to me is that I get to see Xander play.

Music blasts through the arena, and the crowd begins to roar as they start the Dragon's war cry. My eyes flick to the hallway with a massive Dragon's banner above it, watching for the moment the team emerges.

As if on cue, Jaxon appears in the hallway during the war cry, leading the boys out to the ice. Two girls a few rows down are going nuts, and I recognize one of them as his girlfriend. I'm pretty sure her name is Cassie, but I don't really get a chance to think about it as Xander flies out of the hallway looking like a fucking god.

Zara and I jump to our feet, cheering and waving our foam fingers in the air. I scream out his name and grin wide as he somehow hears my voice over the massive crowd. His dark eyes fly up to the grandstand, and within seconds, he's found me. His whole face lights up, and goddamn, I don't think I've ever seen him so happy. I cup my hands around my mouth and scream out, "I love you."

His eyes dance with mischief, almost as though he's picturing all the ways he's going to show his appreciation for me coming tonight. Not a moment later, he mouths it back to me, making those pesky butterflies swarm through my stomach.

Zara groans next to me. "You two are going to make me nauseous, aren't you?"

I can't help but laugh. "Yeah, probably."

We watch as the Dragons step onto the ice, and it's obvious that

Xander belongs there. He's only warming up, and yet he's already dominating. The way he so effortlessly moves across the ice is incredible. I've never been ice skating, but I know I'd be terrible at it.

Someone skates past Xander, and my eyes follow along. "Ahh, there's Aaron," I tell Zara, but when I look over at her, it's clear she's already spotted him.

The game gets started, and I watch in awe as Xander, Jaxon, and Bobby seem to work as a unit, scoring one goal after another and wiping the ice with the other team. I hardly understand what it is I'm watching, but I know what I'm witnessing is something amazing. Hell, just like when I'm watching Xander in the ring, I can't seem to tear my eyes away.

By the end of the game, I can honestly say that tonight has been one of the best nights of my life, and the beauty of it is that it's only just begun.

Zara and I head downstairs after the final buzzer sounds, and we wait for Xander to come out of the locker room as we rave about the game. To Zara's pleasure, Xander comes out with Aaron right by his side. I should have known they would be together. After Aaron busted him at the fight, they've been tied at the hip. As much as I hate sharing my time with Xander, it's actually really nice knowing Xander can finally be himself.

"Hey, babe," Xander says as he makes his way over to me. He drops his bag at our feet and pulls me right up off the ground as he wraps his arms around me. "You look so fucking sexy in my jersey," he murmurs into my ear. "The things I'm going to do to you in this . . ."

"You want me to wear it for you later?" I reply with a grin, both of us with a one-track mind.

"Fuck, yeah," he says before narrowing his eyes in suspicion. "Don't get me wrong, I loved having you in the stands and watching me skate, but what are you doing here? Did Micky finally force you to have a night off?"

"He wishes," I scoff. "The bar flooded, so I'm all yours for the next few nights." A groan travels up his throat as his eyes become hooded, and I have no doubt he's thinking about all the things we could get up to. "You were amazing," I add, my voice filled with pride.

Without another word, he crushes his lips to mine, kissing me deeply and making me melt in his arms.

Not wanting to be rude to our audience, Xander pulls back and reluctantly places me back on my feet. "This is Zara," I say to Xander and Aaron, who are probably wondering why some random girl is standing beside us and watching me and Xander make out. "She works at the salon with me. Zara, this is Xander and Aaron."

"It's a pleasure to meet you," Aaron says, instantly stepping forward and taking her petite hand in his. He brings it up to his face and gingerly places a kiss just above her knuckles, laying on the charm. And goddamn, she eats it up.

"The pleasure's all mine," Zara says with a sultry tone as her eyes travel up and down his strong body, probably remembering exactly what's underneath those clothes from his page in the calendar—a calendar that she's still clutching tightly.

Aaron's eyes light up with interest, and I know my great night is about to get even better. "What are you guys up to?" I ask, knowing they always end up somewhere after a game.

"Jaxon's having a party at his place," Xander says, "And you're coming."

I grin at his assumption as I turn to Zara. "Are you up for a party?"

She turns toward Aaron, looking at him like a lioness about to strike. "That depends if Aaron's going."

A cocky grin crosses Aaron's face, and I know there's no chance in hell he's missing this party tonight. "Fuck yeah, baby. I'll be there."

Xander rolls his eyes at their display. "We'll take my truck," he says, and without another word, Aaron's hand falls to the small of Zara's back as he leads the way out the door.

Xander and I follow behind, and he pulls me into his arms as we head out to his truck. "She seems nice," Xander comments, watching the two of them up ahead of us. "You like this one?"

"Yeah," I say as I look up at him with a fond smile. "I think I do."

Xander gives my side a gentle squeeze. "Good. I'm happy for you."

A thought strikes me. "Do you have a fight tonight?" I ask.

He cringes as he looks down at me. "I do," he says cautiously, clearly knowing where I'm going with this.

"Can we come?" I ask.

"I don't know, babe," he says. "It's dangerous. You remember what happened last time."

"What if Aaron came along?" I suggest, buttering him up, knowing just how much he loves it when my eyes are on him during a fight. "I mean, it's not like he isn't going to go anyway."

Xander's thoughtful for a moment, and I know the idea of taking me anywhere like that kills him. But he's my man, and I want to support him. "Fine," he grunts, finally giving in. Though, it's damn clear he isn't happy about it.

I grin up at him in victory, and he rolls his eyes in surrender. Score one for me.

We all pile into his truck, and we're halfway there when Aaron and Zara start making out in the backseat. Tonight is going to be amazing.

It's almost midnight when we pull up at an abandoned warehouse, and Zara looks around, confused why we've brought her to a place like this in the middle of the night. "I knew it," she says. "You fuckers are gonna kill me."

"Trust me, that's what I thought when I first came to one of these," I laugh as we hop out of Xander's truck. "But I swear, I have a feeling you'll love it in here. If you don't, we can leave."

She looks at me with a wary stare as she walks around the building, following Xander's lead to the back entrance. We head in and find Cole, and by the way Zara latches onto Aaron's hand, it's clear she's beginning to work out what kind of place this is.

There are people everywhere, and I have to admit, it's pretty cool seeing behind the scenes of a night like this. There are big, bulky men all around, and the sound of fists pummeling into punching bags echoes through the hallways. Just by looking at them, I have no doubt these are the contenders for tonight.

We pass one guy whose ferocious stare instantly locks on mine, making a shiver sail down my spine. I don't know who this guy is, but there's no doubt in my mind that he's dangerous.

We pass him, but I can't shake the feeling that his eyes are still on me. As I glance back over my shoulder, sure enough, his stare is piercing right into me, following my every step. "Who is that guy?" I ask Xander.

"That's Pitbull," Xander says, putting his arm around me and pulling me closer. "He's on top of the leaderboard, and he's fucking pissed that I'm right up there with him."

"He looks dangerous," I murmur.

"He is," Xander grunts.

The shivers shoot down my body once again. "Are you against him?" I ask nervously.

He shakes his head, and a wave of relief pulses through my veins. "Not tonight," he clarifies. "But I will be eventually. He has a . . . unique style."

My gaze narrows on him, not liking his tone. "What's that supposed to mean?"

"You'll see. He's fighting tonight," he says, then stops in the hallway to glance back at Aaron. "I don't like the way Pitbull keeps looking at my girl. Can you take the girls out to the ring?"

Aaron nods, but Zara cuts off his reply, her eyes wide. "Ring? As in a fighting ring?"

I grin at her reaction. "Yeah," I clarify with a laugh. "Exactly that."

"Shit," she says, wide-eyed. "This is illegal, isn't it?"

"Umm, sort of."

"Sort of," Xander scoffs. "There is no *sort of* about it."

"Seriously?" she shrieks, her wide gaze swiveling back to me before muttering something about there being rules of fight club and that I'm not allowed to talk about fight club. But I have no idea what she's talking about. Seeing the blank expression on my face, she knows it, too.

Xander shakes his head at me as though whatever I just missed is some kind of big deal, and I have a feeling he won't rest until I completely understand the reference. Needing to get a move on, he nods to Aaron, gesturing for him to get us out to the ring. Pushing up on my tippy-toes, I wish Xander luck, give him a kiss, then scurry out of there. I want to be as far away from Pitbull as possible.

We head out to the ring, and just as expected, the place is packed. This time around, I feel a lot safer than I had last time. Though, that has everything to do with the company I'm keeping.

The drinks are flowing, and after having our fair share, Zara and I are positively wasted, but Aaron seems to have a handle on us. At least, I hope he does.

The crowd cheers as The Widow Maker is announced, and I jump up and down as Zara chokes back a laugh, almost spitting her drink across the back of Aaron's neck when she hears Xander's ridiculous name.

She seems to have fallen right in with this crowd and even admitted that she was secretly impressed to find out I was sitting on a bomb like this. I was nervous that she might have turned out to be more like Lex than I initially thought, but I quickly dismissed that notion. She's definitely a good girl at heart, just a little wild when she lets loose, which Aaron seems to really like.

Xander steps out into the crowded room with Cole on his heels, and from where I'm standing, it looks like he's giving him a few motivational words. Though something tells me Xander's got all the motivation he needs tonight.

Xander steps out into the ring and puts on his little show, making the girls drool. They wolf whistle and call out crass comments, but it's me he is looking at.

"Shit, that's hot," Zara comments, fanning her face.

"Tell me about it," I mutter breathlessly.

The announcer calls Xander's opponent to the ring, and this guy looks big. Nervousness flutters through me, even though I know Xander can handle himself. He's told me a million times, it's not about size or strength, but how you use it to your advantage. I can't help worrying about my man, though. His ribs are finally starting to improve, but they've still got a long way to go, and I don't want to see him get hurt again. It's one thing to hear about it, but to see it go down . . . it'd kill me.

The fight gets started and the noise around me turns into a distant whir. My eyes follow each and every movement, cringing with every blow the other guy lands on Xander. Though for every blow, Xander returns it twofold.

This fight seems more intense than the last one I saw, and it's obvious that Xander is making his way up the ranks. He's already taken out the easy fighters, and now this shit is starting to get serious.

The fight carries on, and the other guy starts to wear down, but looking at Xander, it's clear he could do this all night. The man is a machine.

The minutes tick by before Xander finally puts me out of my misery and takes the big guy out. He crumbles to the blood-soaked ground and his team rushes in to check on him as some other guy races in and shoves Xander's hand high in the air, declaring him the winner. The crowd roars for The Widow Maker, and I let out a heavy breath, both hating and loving the adrenaline of these fights.

Zara raves about the fight, while Aaron hangs on her every word, mesmerized by this woman before him. But I don't hear a bit of their conversation. My eyes remain locked on the door leading to the back area, waiting for Xander to come out.

He doesn't make me wait long before he shows his gorgeous face. The moment his eyes lock onto mine, a cheeky grin takes over his features, and I can't help but laugh. He's such a dork. Xander quickly weaves through the crowd, and soon I'm wrapped in his arms and being swept right off my feet, lost in his kiss.

We watch the rest of the fights together, Xander's arms holding me close, and I make sure to pay extra careful attention to Pitbull. Within seconds of his fight, the cautiousness around him becomes ruthlessly clear. The guy is brutal, and he doesn't hold back. This isn't just fighting for the win; this is fighting for vicious dominance. His opponent comes out of the ring with a fractured eye socket, a split lip, and a massive gouge through his thigh that barely missed the artery. Hell, the guy is lucky to be alive. This fight was one step away from a murder scene.

I turn in Xander's arms and look up at him, and I know he sees the fear in my eyes before I even get a word out. "You really have to go against that guy?" I ask, more than ready to chain him to my bed to keep him safe.

"Yeah, babe," he says with a tight smile, trying to keep things positive. But after what I just witnessed, I'm going to be shitting myself when the time comes. "I've got a game plan. It's okay."

I press my lips together, unsure if that's enough to satisfy me, but it will have to do. There really isn't anything I can do about it. "He's a monster."

"I know. He fights dirty," Xander confirms. I nod, not sure what to say when he leans down and presses his lips to mine. "Come on," he murmurs against my mouth. "Let me take you home."

"Okay," I whisper, knowing we can have the Pitbull conversation another time. For now, I need to finish this night off right.

CHAPTER 16

XANDER

The sound of Charli stirring on Saturday morning wakes me, and I pull her into my arms, not ready for this sexy she-devil to leave my bed. "Good morning," I grumble into her hair as I inhale deeply, breathing her in.

"Morning," she murmurs against her pillow, turning in my arms so she can plant a kiss on my lips. "How'd you sleep?"

"Like a fucking baby with you beside me," I say as I roll us over so I hover above her, letting her feel me everywhere.

"Hmm," she groans as she closes her eyes and opens her legs. She reaches down between us and wraps her tight fist around my cock, pumping twice before guiding me to her sweet cunt.

"Ready for me?" I smirk as I push inside her, feeling the way her tight walls stretch around me, gently clenching as she lets out a satisfied moan.

"I was hoping for it," she whispers as she looks up at me with those blazing blue eyes, her arms locking around my neck as I start to move, so fucking slowly it has us both desperate for more.

I keep moving, right up until I've got Charli right on the edge, ready to detonate. Only then do I reach down between us, grazing my fingers over her sensitive clit and picking up my pace. She gasps, her body jolting beneath me, and I watch as she explodes around me. Her walls clench and spasm as her orgasm tears through her. She digs her nails into my back and screams out my name, and the sound has me coming right along with her.

I press my forehead to hers as we both pant, trying to catch our breaths after the best fucking wake-up call a man could ask for. "I could get used to waking up like that," she murmurs, before catching my lips in hers.

"Music to my ears." Her lips lift in a soft smile against mine as those beautiful blue eyes shimmer with happiness. "Got any plans today?"

"No," she says, a hint of suspicion in her tone.

"Good. I'm taking you out for breakfast," I say, looking over at my clock. "Fuck. Make that lunch."

"You've got yourself a date."

An hour later, we're sitting in a café, finishing lunch when my phone vibrates in my pocket. I pull it out, hating the feeling of being rude on our date, and consider silencing it when I realize it's Coach

Harris calling.

My stomach drops, and I lose my appetite. "Shit," I murmur. Charli notices the change, and her brows crease with concern as I hit accept.

"Hello," I say into the phone, my gaze locked on Charli's.

"Xander, it's Coach Harris. I need to see you in my office. Now."

Fuck.

I press my lips together, knowing exactly what this is about. Though, I thought I might have had a little more time. Well . . . I'd hoped, at least. There aren't that many rounds left in the Underground, so I thought I could complete the competition before my world exploded and burned to ashes around me.

"Yes, Coach," I sigh, preparing for the worst. "I'm around the corner."

"Good," he grunts, ending the call without so much as a goodbye.

"Is everything alright?" Charli asks as she reaches across the table and takes my hand in hers.

I let out a sigh before shaking my head. "That was Coach Harris. He needs to see me in his office, and judging by his tone, it's not good."

She cringes, sympathy in her sweet stare. "Does he know?"

"He didn't say, but there's no other reason he would drag me in on a weekend," I explain, dropping some cash on the table and double-checking Charli's finished with her lunch. "Did you want me to drop you at my place first?"

"No, it's okay," she says, forcing an encouraging smile across her face. "The rink is around the corner. It'd be silly to go home first. I can come. I mean . . . if you want me to," she says, practically stuttering over her words as she tries to backtrack.

A small smile comes over my lips. "Sure, babe," I say, realizing I'll never tire of her quirky ways. "Though, there's no chance in hell Coach will let you in his office. He'll make you wait outside."

"That's fine," she says, grabbing her bag and pushing out of her chair. She reaches for my hand and we walk out to my truck. "Come on," she says, trying to perk me up. "He might let you stay on the team. You never know."

"Thanks, babe," I say as we climb up into the truck. "But if he knows about the Underground, he has no choice but to take me off the team. A player participating in illegal activities is grounds for immediate dismissal. My hockey career is over."

She lets out a sigh as she presses her lips together, clearly deep in thought. The drive is short and within a few minutes, we're stepping through the doors of the rink. I find Coach leaning up against the barrier, talking schedules with the head figure skating coach.

The Figure Fairies skate around the ice, and for the millionth time, I'm absolutely stumped with how the hell they do that shit. I mean, fuck. They have toe picks to think about. It's a suicide mission.

Coach's eyes flick to me the second he notices someone approaching, and as he takes me in, a furious scowl settles over his features. Seeing Charli beside me, he narrows his gaze on her, and I see the question in his eyes. He's probably wondering if this is her influence, and honestly, the idea infuriates me. "You," Coach says, pointing at me. "With me. You," he adds, turning his finger toward Charli. "Sit."

Charli swallows hard, her eyes wide as if she's just been caught drawing dicks on the librarian's car by the school principal. She lets go of my hand, and I give Coach a nod as he turns his back and storms in the direction of his office. "You'll be okay out here?" I ask Charli as she promptly drops her ass onto the bench.

"Yeah, I'm fine," she says. "I love watching ice skating. It's beautiful and terrifying at the same time."

"You've got that right," I murmur as I step away.

She latches onto my hand, and I turn back. "Whatever happens in there, just remember. I love you."

My chest fills with emotion as I look down at my future. "Love you, too, babe."

Charli gives me an encouraging smile and releases my hand, her wide eyes giving me the courage to go on. I head down the hallway leading to Coach Harris' office with an awful feeling inside my gut. I hesitate for a moment before knocking on the open door, despite him knowing I'm already here.

"Take a seat," he grunts as he looks up from his computer, his emotions radiating from his vicious stare.

I do as I'm told and make it quick, not wanting to fuck around. After all, a quick game is a good game. "What can I do for you, Coach?" I ask.

His eyes shoot daggers at me, and it's clear he's mightily pissed off. "Don't bullshit me, Phillips. You know exactly why you're here."

"Yes, sir," I say. I may as well own it. "I do."

"Underground fighting?" he confirms, his voice raising a notch in disbelief. I give a curt nod, letting him know we're on the same page. "How could you be so fucking stupid? You realize I have no choice but to expel you from the team? There'll be a fucking investigation. Fuck your career, what about the boys? They could go down for this bullshit too. Do you understand that? Everything they've worked for. Their whole fucking careers are on the line. *My* career is on the line."

Fuck. Hit me right where it hurts.

"Yes, sir," I say, giving him the respect he deserves.

He stands, slamming his hands down on his desk as he hangs his head, needing a moment to calm down. He breathes. Slow inhale. Slow exhale. Repeat. Straightening up, he runs a hand down his face, staring at me as though he doesn't even recognize me. "What were you thinking getting involved in fighting? And an Underground tournament at that."

"Honestly, Coach, I was thinking that professional fighting is what I want to do. The NHL is my father's dream, not mine," I tell him, giving it to him straight. "I was taking a step in my own direction."

He lets out a scoff, shaking his head. "If this isn't what you want, then why the hell did you transfer here and spend half a season on my team?" he questions. "Do you know how many fucking applications I have? How many other kids would have killed for your position? Those kids wanted to be here. They deserved to be here."

"I know. It's a poor excuse, and I apologize for wasting your time. However, I was given no choice. You've met my father, you know what he's like," I explain. "My whole life, he's made it clear that my future is the NHL. I've never wanted that, Coach. I never wanted to live in his shadow." Letting out a heavy breath, I meet his eyes. "I started MMA when I was eleven and knew after my very first session that's what I wanted to do. My father practically kicked my ass when he learned I'd been training in fighting, and he made it clear that if I ever strayed from the plan, I'd lose everything."

His brows furrow in question. "How so?"

"Anything with monetary value would be taken to teach me a lesson, and I'd be disowned. My father has set up my life so that I am constantly depending on him. College fees are paid month by month, my trust account has a daily limit, and even my home and truck are in his name, all so he can use it as leverage against me," I scoff, almost embarrassed to be admitting this. "His plan has always been the same. Come the end of next season, if I don't sign on the dotted line and get into the NHL, I can kiss it all goodbye. I'll be out on the streets with nothing."

"Go on," Coach instructs.

I take a deep breath and continue my explanation. "I sought out a gym early in the season so I could continue my MMA training. I met with a trainer, and he incorporated my hockey training with his. We got to talking and he asked me what I wanted, and we found a solution that would allow me to live in both worlds. And honestly, Coach, I'm fucking good. Great, even. With my skills, I can win this thing."

"How is winning the Underground supposed to help?" he asks. "Sounds like an excuse to me."

I shake my head. "Each fight, the winner takes home a sum of money, and as you progress up the leaderboard, that sum increases. So, with the winnings I've already earned, I can put a deposit on my own home and be out from under my father's hold. However, if I were to take out the competition, I could put myself through college, build my own gym, and afford to train for the professional circuit," I tell him. "I know illegal fighting is not ideal, but it's all I've got to keep myself afloat."

He lets out a sigh, looking at me while deep in thought. "You're one of my best players, Xander. I wanted to offer you the place of captain next season. So, understand me when I tell you it kills me that this is the situation you're in, but my back is up against the wall. I have to let you go."

"I understand, Coach," I nod. "I thought this could happen, and I was prepared for it. I just hoped I'd be able to see the season out first."

"What am I going to tell the boys?" he murmurs to himself.

I look down at my hands, unsure how to answer that, but I go on anyway. "Coach, it may not seem like it, but hockey has been a part of my life for a long time, and I'm devastated that I can no longer be a part of this team. The team you've got here . . . fuck, they're the best I've ever skated with. It's a family here, but despite all of that, hockey just isn't my passion, and I hope you can understand that I need to do what's right for me."

"Kid, you need to know that if the professional circuit is what you want to do, then you have my full support, even though I don't support the Underground bullshit. It's dangerous, and you're a fucking idiot for getting yourself involved in it. Let me be clear, I'm pissed as hell at you for not being forthcoming. Had news of this spread to the media, the team would have been fucked."

"I know, Coach, and I apologize."

He lets out a heavy sigh while shaking his head, probably still wondering how he's going to get around this. "Alright, kid," he says, accepting my apology. "Get out of here. I need to figure out what the hell I'm going to tell the press."

"Shit," I groan. "You won't say anything about the Underground, right?"

He gives me a blank stare like that's the stupidest question he has ever been asked, and honestly, it is. I should know Coach wouldn't throw me under the bus like that. "No," he says, "I'll probably say that you have decided to put a hold on your hockey career while you pursue other avenues."

"Hmm," I grunt. "Not bad."

"Not my first rodeo," he explains.

"Got it," I say, getting up from my chair and making my way out of his office.

"Xander," he calls after me. I turn back to meet his stare, only this time, it doesn't look quite so ruthless. "Be careful," he says. "I've witnessed a few of those fights and it never ends well. I don't want to be walking into your hospital room, finding you attached to life support."

"I know, Coach," I say with a nod. "I'm careful. I should warn you though, the moment my father hears about this, he's going to be busting down your door."

"Let him. I have a few choice words for bastards like him."

I hold his stare, something aching in my chest. "Thanks, Coach," I say with a smile, feeling as though I've just been handed my future on a silver platter. It's bittersweet, though. One door closes as another opens. It doesn't change my disappointment about not seeing the season through. I wanted to be there for my boys.

I walk back out to the rink with a strange sadness filling me. I knew this day was coming, but for it to actually happen is a whole other thing. There has never been a time in my life when I've not been on a team, and suddenly, I'm free to take my own path. I don't know whether to be nervous or excited. Maybe both?

The moment I walk out of this ice rink, I won't be looking back. I have a new future before me, and I'm going to do whatever it takes to succeed. I'll train harder and faster, be stricter on my diet, and study each and every match I can get my hands on. But no matter what, I will not fail.

I come to the end of the hallway and find Charli deep in conversation with a figure skater, talking about all the crazy shit she's able to do. Charli is beaming at her in awe while the girl is sucking up as much attention as possible.

"Hey," I say, stealing Charli's attention.

"Oh, hey," she says quickly, eyeing me, probably trying to gauge my mood. She quickly says goodbye to the girl and heads over to me. "How'd it go?" she murmurs, keeping her voice low to not draw unwanted attention.

"It could have been worse," I tell her with a shrug as I lead her out of the rink. "Coach was pissed as fuck. But at the end of the day, he supports me pursuing a career in MMA. Well, as long as it's got nothing to do with the Underground."

"Smart man," she mutters before glancing up and meeting my stare. "What does that mean for the team?"

"Means I no longer have one," I tell her.

Her face falls, and I see the way she hurts for me, which only makes me want to comfort her and tell her that it's all going to be okay. "Shit, I'm sorry," she whispers, her hand tightly clutching mine.

Taking our joined hands, I loop them over her shoulder and pull her in close. "Don't be sorry," I tell her. "It means that I can focus on fighting, and I can be honest with the guys so they can stop looking at me like I'm hiding something."

"A bit like Aaron?" she smirks.

"Exactly like Aaron."

"So what now?"

"Now we head home and look for a place of our own."

Charli sputters, stopping in the middle of the athlete parking lot as she gapes at me. "Um, what?"

"You heard me," I say, a grin tearing across my face. "I give my father at least three days before he finds out. And when he does, I want to be prepared."

"Okay," she says, trying to wrap her head around it. "But you mean *your* own place."

"No," I correct her. "*Our* own place. I hate to drop a bomb on you, but now that I've got you, I'm not letting you go. And fortunately for me, that means you'll be coming with me to wherever that new place may be."

Her eyes light up with excitement, but I also see regret there. "Don't get me wrong," she says, "I really want to move in with you, but there's no way I can afford that. Not yet. I'm barely just getting on my feet, and you know my traineeship doesn't exactly pay that well. I mean, I make plenty in tips at Micky's, but not enough to buy a house."

"Babe," I say, taking her shoulders and holding her stare, making sure she truly hears me. "I don't want you to worry about money. I've got us covered. I just want you to go to the salon every day, then go to Micky's if you want to. I honestly don't care what you want to do as long as you're happy, and you're the person I come home to at the end of the day."

She shakes her head. "You're crazy," she tells me. "You can't be serious."

"Dead serious."

"Holy shit," she breathes, tears welling in those soft blue eyes. "We're going to do this. You and me? Living together? Buying a house?"

I nod. "You better fucking believe it."

She shakes her head, barely able to wrap her head around it, but she knows this is happening. Though after dropping a bomb like that, there's no way she's about to make it easy for me.

Pressing her lips into a tight line, she schools her features and gives a noncommittal shrug of her shoulders. "I don't know, Xander. I'll have to think about it."

Before she breaks, she quickly turns and scurries toward my truck, but there's no mistaking the wide grin that takes over her face, her cheeks pushing right up and scrunching her eyes.

Yeah, she definitely knows it's happening. And the second I get the chance, I'll have her barefoot and pregnant, dancing around our kitchen.

CHAPTER 17

CHARLI

It's barely seven in the morning when a loud pounding sounds at the door, and I practically spring out of bed. Who the hell would be banging on the door at this ungodly hour?

Grabbing Xander's shirt off the floor, I throw it over my naked body and scurry out the bedroom door.

I dash down the stairs and come to a standstill, my hand hovering over the handle as I realize I could be walking right into a trap. What if it's my stepmom or her boyfriend coming for round two, or is it three? Have they found me?

No. Of course not . . . right? It's Xander's place, so it's probably the boys from the hockey team coming to bust his balls about the whole illegal fighting thing. I'm sure Coach Harris has let them all in on the secret by now.

Feeling a little more confident, I double-check myself, making sure none of my lady bits are hanging out, and I step forward to answer the door.

The loud pounding starts up again just as I pull the door open, and I nearly get punched in the head by some older man. I jump back out of the way, and the guy at least has the decency to lower his hand. A small woman stands beside him, looking down at me. Though, I don't know how that's even possible since I'm taller than her by at least a foot.

"Who the hell are you?" the man demands.

"Excuse me?" I ask, completely on edge. I mean, who are these people to come here so early on a Sunday morning, nearly breaking down the door, and throwing out demands? Nuh-uh, I don't think so. "I could ask the same question," I say, but I'm quickly starting to realize who they are. It's no wonder Xander prefers to stay as far away from them as possible.

They ignore my question, just as I had theirs. "Where's my son?" the man demands.

Realizing there really isn't much I can do in this situation, I decide to be a little helpful. I mean, the sooner they get their answers, the sooner they'll be gone, right? "It's seven in the morning. He's in bed," I inform them. Not that they need so much information. "I'll go wake him."

His mother scoffs at me, but I turn my back and leave them standing in the open doorway, not bothering with an invitation to come in. Though from what I've heard from Xander, that probably would have brought along snarky comments about how it's their house, and they don't need to be invited in. I'm sure they think they can come and go as they please.

We only started looking for a place to live together last night, but I suddenly can't get out of this house fast enough.

I dash up the stairs and back into the bedroom before striding over to Xander's side of the bed. I bend to wake him, only his hand snakes out and grabs me around the waist, pulling me to him. "What the hell are you doing out of bed? The sun has hardly risen," he grumbles as he rolls us until he's hovered over me, my legs wrapped around his waist and his morning wood grinding against my clit. Though, he's probably going to need to get that shit sorted out . . . and fast.

"Stop," I laugh, gently pushing against his chest to keep him from kissing me. Because the second those lips touch mine, all hope will be lost. "First of all, it's just after seven and the sun certainly has risen. And secondly, your parents nearly broke down the door trying to let themselves in."

His body stiffens. "What?" he asks, wide-eyed, staring at me like I'm playing some fucked-up game. "My parents are here?"

"Yep," I confirm, popping the *p*. "And let me tell you, they are the most pleasant people I have ever met. I don't know why you haven't introduced us earlier."

"Shit, babe." He sighs as he hops off the bed and pulls on a pair of jeans, his morning wood long gone. "I'm sorry. I thought we had a few days before this would happen."

"Apparently not," I say, also getting up and pulling on some clothes.

Xander heads to the stairs, but I detour to the bathroom to make sure I look decent. After all, these are his parents, no matter how much Xander despises them.

I head back down the stairs to find Xander's parents have most certainly invited themselves in. Xander's father stands in the center of the living room, arms folded across his chest as he scowls at his son, while his mother potters about in the kitchen, making herself a coffee.

I'm hardly down the stairs by the time Xander's father is tearing into him. "What the fuck is this shit I hear about you being kicked off the team?" he demands.

"Dad," Xander starts, but his father isn't hearing him and cuts him off.

"Did you get yourself in trouble?" he questions. "What is it? Drugs? Partying? Or you just couldn't cut it in training? You've always been useless. Do you know what kind of strings I had to pull to get you on this team? I should have known you'd screw up like this. You don't have the drive that I had."

Xander leans back against the railing of the stairs, and I slip my hand through the gap to rest it on his shoulder. His body is shaking with rage, and I sense him trying to hold himself back, but fuck, if he doesn't say something, then I will. How dare this asshole speak to Xander like that.

Xander shoots daggers at his father. "I've been a better player than you ever were for years. Always have been, always will be. I train my ass off every day, so don't come storming in here telling me I have no drive. And drugs? Are you fucking kidding me? If you knew a damn thing about me, you'd know I don't fuck around with shit like that."

"Then what the hell happened?" his father cuts in again.

"I was fighting," he says.

"What?" his mother cuts in. "You got kicked off the team for fighting? That seems a bit harsh now, doesn't it?"

"No, Mom. It doesn't," Xander says with annoyance in his tone.

"Don't you speak to your mother like that," his father scolds, earning himself a groan from Xander. "Now, what are you talking about?" he questions, finally starting to calm down. "Fights have always been excused, especially in hockey. Everyone knows you boys like to get rowdy. I'll go down there and speak to Coach Harris. He's just trying to make an example out of you, the damn fool."

Fucking hell. His dad's mood swings are giving me whiplash. They're worse than my stepmom's. First, he has a problem with Xander, and now Coach Harris? How is it possible for one man to be so blind?

"Would you shut the fuck up?" Xander snaps. "I didn't get kicked out for getting into a fucking fistfight. I've been fighting in an underground ring."

Oh, shit.

His father turns bright red, and his hands ball into fists at his side. Xander immediately adjusts himself, his exceptional training kicking into gear. "Just fucking try it. I dare you," Xander insists, practically begging his father to come at him, giving him the perfect excuse to retaliate.

His dad takes a step forward, making my hand squeeze down into the flesh of Xander's strong shoulder. "Underground ring?" he roars. "You're throwing away your future for shit like that?"

"How many times do I need to tell you before you will listen? I don't want to be in the NHL. I never have. That's your dream, not mine. My future is MMA," Xander says, and it's clear this is an old argument. One they've had a million times before.

"The hell it is. This ends now. You march your sorry ass back to that ice rink and tell Coach the fighting is finished. You're going to beg for your position back, and I don't care if you look like a fool doing it. You're not throwing it all away like this. Everything we have worked for."

"Are you serious?" Xander scoffs. "I'm not playing hockey. I'm not going to the NHL, and I'm sure are fuck not going to have this conversation again. It's over, Dad. Hockey is over. Get it through that thick head of yours. "

His father is beyond furious. "You ungrateful piece of shit," he yells.

That's it. My fuse is blown. "Hey," I yell, as I storm down the rest of the stairs and come to a standstill in front of Xander's father, painfully aware of the fact his hand is still balled into a fist. "Don't you talk to him like that. If you had even the tiniest bit of decency, you would notice that your son is amazing and could easily make it in the professional circuit, probably earning twice the amount of a skater in the NHL. But you're so damn self-absorbed that you can't see anything past your own damn nose."

My whole body shakes, but it instantly relaxes when Xander

threads his arm around my waist and pulls me into his chest.

"It's this little hussy, isn't it?" his father says to Xander, ignoring my outburst. "She's the one who has corrupted your mind, has turned you into this pathetic excuse of a man."

In the blink of an eye, I find myself behind Xander while his fist strikes out a devastating blow. He nails his father in the jaw, and my mouth hangs open in shock. Resting my hands on Xander's naked back, I feel the vibrations of his rage through his skin as he roars at his father. "Get the fuck out. No one talks about my girl like that."

"You're going to regret that," his father scolds as he spits a mouthful of blood onto the cold tiles.

"Fucking try it, Dad. I'm done with you. I don't need your bribery or your damn money," he says before leaning over to the hallway stand and grabbing the keys to his truck. "Here," he says, tossing them at his father as his mother begins sobbing. "Take that, too. I'm finished with you. With both of you."

"You're going to regret this," his father repeats as he storms toward the door with his wife on his heels.

"No," Xander says, as confident as ever. "I'm not."

His father turns back around, just before slamming the door. "You have one week to vacate this property."

"Consider me already gone."

The door slams with a shattering bang, and we stand in silence for a moment. "They seem nice," I say, trying to hold back my tears.

Xander scoffs but pulls me against him once again. "I'm sorry you had to witness that," he says as he leans his head down to my shoulder.

"Don't worry," I tell him, brushing my fingers up his strong back before running my nails through his hair. "Are you okay?"

He pulls back ever so slightly so he can look me in the eye. "You know, I think I am. I feel free," he says with a heavy breath that contradicts what he just said. "I never have to worry about them again. I can pursue MMA, join the professional circuit, and make whatever career choices I want."

I smile up at him, hoping he really is okay. He seems full of confidence, like nothing can stop him from getting what he wants, and the more I watch him, the more I start to believe it. Honestly, I've never been so proud.

"Alright, babe," he says, pulling me toward the couch and flopping down. He pulls his iPad out of the coffee table drawer and puts it on my lap. "Get searching. We have a week to find a new place."

"Okay," I say. "But you know Micky would let us stay at the bar. There's no reason to rush."

He becomes thoughtful, but I knew he wouldn't be too keen on the idea. "I don't know. I'd feel like I was taking advantage of his hospitality."

"He wouldn't feel that way," I tell him.

"I know, but I would," he explains.

"Fine," I say, swiping my finger across the screen to unlock it. I pull up a search and find hundreds of listings that I could only dream about before I narrow my search to places a little more in our realm of expectations. I point out a few, and less than an hour later, we're walking through properties and crossing them right off our list.

By the time night has fallen, we're both exhausted and curled up in bed, wrapped in each other's arms. "So, if the cat's out of the bag now, does that mean you can start training for the professional circuit?" I ask with a yawn.

"Technically I can, but I want to finish the competition first before I put my name out there. I can't have anything leading me back to the Underground once I go pro," he explains.

"Oh, really?" I ask, a little disappointed by the images of Pitbull flashing in my mind.

"Yeah, I can't give in now, especially after everything that's happened. It would mean it was all for nothing."

"Yeah," I agree, understanding where he's coming from. "I guess I'm just nervous about Pitbull."

"Don't be," he says, pulling me in tighter. "I'll be fine. There are only a few weeks left until this is over. I can handle him."

"I know," I sigh.

Xander rolls me over and presses his lips to mine. "Quit worrying so much," he tells me.

"I can't help it," I grin as another yawn takes over. I lay my head down on Xander's chest and listen to the steady beat of his heart.

Sleep takes over within moments, and before I know it, I'm waking up to start another day in the arms of the man I love.

CHAPTER 18

XANDER

It's been five days since my parent's intrusion, and life couldn't be better. Or at least, it will be the second we get out of that house. Even though it's over, it still pisses me off the way they barged into my home and spoke to my girl. I can handle the shit they give me. After all, I've gotten it from them my whole life. But for them to turn that bullshit on Charli, it was uncalled for, and completely sealed the deal for me.

From that moment, I swore to myself that I will never put myself or Charli through the ugliness of my parents again. They will never intrude on our future, never make demands of me, and sure as fuck never call my girl a hussy ever again.

I have no doubt that I will make it in the professional circuit, and

I know the moment my name starts spreading around, my parents will be right back, begging for a piece of the pie. But they've burned their bridges, and I'll never go back on my word. I'm finally done with them.

Cole and the boys at Rebels Advocate were thrilled when I walked in on Monday morning as a free agent. They always hated the hockey thing. Not the actual sport, but knowing it wasn't what I wanted and that I was wasting good energy that could have been dedicated to upcoming fights.

I spent the next few days the same—fucking my girl until she came. She would then go to the salon, and I would go to Rebels. We'd each spend our days doing what we did best before heading home, cooking dinner, and making sweet, sweet love.

Though, now that's all ruined because Micky called yesterday to tell Charli the bar has been reopened and her shifts are starting up again. Charli was thrilled, and of course, I was thrilled for her, but only because she loves the place so damn much. Otherwise, I would have kept her to myself.

So, here I am, Thursday after training all day. I've decided to wait to get a new truck until the end of the competition. That way, I'll know exactly how many extras I can afford to put on the big bastard. Which means I've been running to and from training, which isn't too bad in the mornings, but after a day of vigorous sessions with Cole, it really fucking sucks.

It starts to drizzle outside, which refreshes me and makes me feel brand new, so I push myself a little harder. I run through the back streets rather than sticking to the main roads as my headphones blast in my ears.

I get lost in my thoughts as I run, and when I realize I've taken a wrong turn, I stop and glance around, trying to catch my bearings, which is when I see it.

The perfect home.

A for sale sign is perched in the front yard, daring people to check it out with the realtor's details below, and as I look over it, I know this is the one. After working out where the hell I am, I save the details on my phone before taking a quick picture of the house for Charli.

I find myself hovering out front, picturing my whole life here. Carrying Charli over the threshold, starting a family, and growing old. There's space for a garden and a tire swing hanging from the tallest tree. It's fucking perfect.

Unable to wait another minute longer, I break into a sprint, racing back home. I quickly clean myself up before heading down to Micky's to find my girl. I was going to go down there to walk her home later, so what if I'm a few hours early?

The place is packed, and I have to boot some drunken idiot off my favorite stool before I can sit down and enjoy a beer. Charli's face lights up the second she sees me, and I can't wait a second longer. I pull my phone out and slide it across the bar, watching her intently, waiting for her reaction.

Her eyes widen, and I know she sees it like I had. Our whole future, right there on the screen. "Holy shit, it's everything," she breathes, looking up at me, her eyes brimming with emotion. "Are you sure about this?"

"I've never been so sure in my life," I tell her.

Her eyes flick back to the picture on my screen one more time before she leans across the bar and fuses her lips to mine in a deep kiss. "Do it," she tells me, grinning wide against my lips. "Call the realtor."

I stand in my new living room with Aaron as we wait for Charli and Zara to hurry up and get ready. I swear, the moment Charli discovered makeup, she went crazy about the shit. She's fallen in love with it so much that she wants to study cosmetics too and offer that as a service in her salon. You know, when she gets one. But if that's what my girl wants, then I'll make my way through the darkest pits of hell to make it happen.

Glancing around the living room, I can't help but take it all in, thinking of all the different ways Charli and I can make this house a home. We've been here for a week now, and while it's incredible and everything we wanted, neither of us came equipped with many possessions. We have a couch and a table, and that's about it. The rest is a work in progress.

Aaron ducks into the kitchen and grabs two beers from the fridge and offers me one as he takes a seat. "Nah, man," I say, shaking my head. "Not with the fight tonight. I need a clear head."

"Yeah, sorry, man," he says, retracting his outstretched arm. "I should have known."

"No dramas," I say, flopping down on the couch, realizing the girls could be a while longer.

"Who are you up against tonight?"

"Some kid called *The Dark Shadow*. He's pretty good," I tell him.

"Oh, yeah. I caught him last week. The kid is fast."

"I know," I laugh. "Hence why I need a clear head tonight. The guys I'm up against are getting better. Stronger. Their hits are starting to fucking hurt."

"Yeah, but they don't have anything on you," he says, acting as my number one fan. Right after Charli, of course.

"True," I say, adding to the ever-growing giant which is better known as my ego. "But all it takes is one punch. If I miss even the smallest move, they could take me out."

"I guess," he agrees, putting the empty beer down and reaching for a second already. "But I got bets on you, so you better not fuck up."

"Really?" I laugh. "That might just be enough incentive to throw the match."

"Fuck off," he grumbles, as the girls finally emerge from the bathroom.

Charli comes out in a gold sequined dress that hugs her perfect body just right, and I get up off the couch and go straight for her, unable to resist. I grab her wrists and hold them up over her head before slamming her up against the wall.

My lips come down on her neck, and I press my body against hers as she stifles a needy moan. She lifts her legs around my waist, and I grind myself into her, knowing she's fucking wet for me. Pinning her against the wall with my body, I release her wrists so I can begin exploring.

A throat clears behind us, and I groan into her neck. "Do you think they'll go away if we pretend they aren't here?" I murmur.

Charli giggles. "It's worth a try."

"Seriously, dude? I know you love your girl and all, but I'm sure tonight's forty grand will look pretty good in your bank account," Aaron comments.

"Would you shut up," Zara scolds Aaron. "This shit is hot. Please go about your business. Just pretend we're not here."

I let out a sigh as I grind myself against her again. "This isn't over," I warn her.

"I'm counting on it," Charli grins as she untwines her legs from my waist.

We lock up and head for Aaron's truck, and as he pulls the keys from his pocket, I snatch them from his hand before making my way to the driver's seat.

"Hey," he demands, spreading his arms out. "What gives?"

"You just had two beers in the space of five minutes. I'm not letting you drive, especially with my girl in the truck."

"Fine," he sulks as he climbs up into the passenger's seat, knowing I'm damn right. The girls get in the back, and soon enough, I'm pulling up at tonight's location.

We make our way in, and just like the few times before, they come in through the back with me until it's time to get ready.

Cole wraps my hands, and I'm pleased to find my match is second in line. I'll be in and out in no time, then I can get back home and bury myself deep inside my girl until she screams.

Half an hour later, I stand in the middle of the ring with the crowd cheering my name, waiting for my opponent to emerge.

The kid who's better known as *The Dark Shadow* struts out into the ring, too fucking cocky for his own good. He's roughly the same size as me, and from watching him the week before, he's just as quick, which means tonight comes down to pure skill.

Luke blurts out his stats while Jace helps me warm up, and apparently, while he's fast with his punches, his footwork is lacking. He also favors his right side, which is just enough information to give me a good boost into the match.

The fight gets started, and just as I expected, we're equally matched. As I land a blow, he gets one on me in return. I know watching this must be killing Charli's nerves, so I do my best to get the job done without being touched.

Just as I had told Aaron, I need a clear mind with this one. I keep my stare focused on the guy, forgetting Charli in the crowd, forgetting the eager fans, forgetting Aaron's bet. All that matters is taking him down. I watch, waiting for every little movement he makes, and I quickly realize that I'm so deep in concentration that I'm almost his mirror image. When he moves, I move.

The fight goes on and the crowd screams for an ending. Comments like *finish him* fly around, and I have to admit, the crass nature sort of spurs me on.

I could go on forever, but at the same time, I want to get back to my girl and enjoy the night, so I push myself a little harder. My punches come out stronger and faster, and my reflexes sharpen.

I get the guy down to his knees with a kick, and I hear him gasping for breath, even though I could have just kept going until exhaustion claimed him. I get him down, but he isn't ready to forfeit that forty grand just yet.

The Dark Shadow punches and kicks up at me in desperation, so I drop down on top of him, locking his arms at his side. He squirms beneath me, and I see the realization in his eyes. He knows I've got him. Putting him out of his misery, I bring my fist down against the side of his head.

His eyes roll back, and just like that, it's light's out.

I hate winning by knockout, but I'm so fucking good at it. I've always felt it was cheating, but in the Underground, you do what you got to do to make it to the next round and keep your name on the leaderboard.

Once I'm declared the winner, I make my way back to the fighter's area with Cole, who scolds me for each mistake I made. As I get myself dressed, Cole grabs a first aid kit to clean up all the little cuts marring my skin.

I head back out to the ring and find Charli in her sexy little dress. It doesn't take me long to realize she isn't alone. In fact, she has quite the crowd surrounding her, and a wide grin stretches across my face.

All of the Denver Dragons stand with my girl, and I wonder how the hell I didn't notice these bastards while I was in the ring. Hell, even Coach Harris stands among them, and man am I happy I didn't fuck up that fight. I would have never lived it down.

Charli throws herself into my arms and kisses me with pride. "Do you have any idea how turned on I get watching you fight?" she murmurs into my ear.

I grin down at the little minx. "Don't you forget it."

"Fuck," Jaxon says as I make my way over to the guys. "You've got skill, man," he says as he pulls me in and claps me on the back. "I'm not even pissed you kept it from me anymore."

"Thanks," I say with a grin. "And sorry. I wanted to tell you, but I couldn't."

"Nah," he says, shaking it off. "Don't worry about it. I get it."

Relief washes over me. I hated the feeling that I was betraying the boys, especially Jaxon. I had really come to respect him, but hearing that we're good makes everything feel right again.

One by one, the boys come around and bitch me out while also offering their compliments on the fight. I introduce Charli to the guys properly even though she's apparently already done it. The next fight gets started when the boys settle in for another show, and it appears we're making a night of it.

Countless drinks trade hands until the boys are wasted, and it's not long before Coach starts looking like he'd rather be anywhere else. When he finally takes off, a few of the more well-behaved boys follow his lead and get going.

There's just a small group of us left, and we all move in to watch the last fight when someone barges past me and knocks me in the shoulder, spilling my drink all over Charli. She gasps as the cold liquid splashes across her body.

On instinct, my arm snaps out to grab the culprit. I instantly recognize Pitbull, a sickening smirk across his face. I realize pretty damn quickly that he did it on purpose and rage fills me, easily getting the rise out of me he came looking for. "You owe my girl an apology," I spit as Charli stares at him, half hidden behind me and looking more than uncomfortable around this asshole.

Pitbull looks Charli up and down with a sick kind of interest that has me right on edge. "Your girl don't need no apology," he says with a smirk. "Bitch looks like she needs a good, thorough fucking, though."

My jaw clenches, and I have to restrain myself from lashing out in the middle of this crowd. All that's going to do is invoke a reckless panic that will quickly turn into a brawl. "You better fucking watch it, asshole," I warn.

"Or what?" he laughs, shrugging me off as though I'm not the biggest threat in the room. "You've got no fucking chance against me. You're nothing, just some random scum standing in between me and my fucking payday. You better watch your back because I'm coming for you."

I smirk back at the loser, knowing he's talking shit. He wouldn't have said a word if he wasn't worried I could beat his ass. "Bring it, fucker. The only place you're coming is in second after I wipe the floor with you."

He lets out a growl and shoves me right into the rest of my group. I can't help but lose my shit. No one disrespects my girl and then my boys. I push him back and suddenly it's on. He goes flying over the back of a table, chairs spilling out around him. I pin the fucker to the ground and pummel his face with my fists. With every strike, I'm distantly aware of Aaron grabbing Charli and yanking her out of the way.

Cole is on me in seconds, desperately trying to pull me off him, and after Luke and Jace join in, they eventually get us separated. "Deal with it in the ring," Cole scolds us both, giving Pitbull a hard shove when he tries to come for me, barely blinking an eye at the asshole. "It's only a fucking week away. I'm sure you dickheads can rein it in until then."

Pitbull scoffs before spitting a mouthful of blood at my feet, then he finally turns and disappears through the thick crowd.

"You," Cole says, pointing an angry finger at me, forcing my attention back to him. "Get your ass out of here before I fucking take you down myself."

Shit. I'm going to pay for that.

CHAPTER 19

CHARLI

I stand in the salon, working on a new client's hair. As soon as she sat down, she couldn't wait to tell me that her name is Bri and that her twin brother, Bobby, plays for the Dragons and is good friends with Xander. I'm pretty sure I met the guy the other night at the fight, but there were a lot of people and a shitload more alcohol. The girl seems nice and has been telling me all about some guy, Carter, who apparently is dynamite in bed. Although, I'm sure she doesn't truly understand the meaning of a man being dynamite in bed, unless she's ever been with Xander Phillips. But that's never going to happen now.

The last few days have been blissful. Living with Xander and starting our lives together, loving life at the salon and Micky's, it feels surreal. Xander is a whole new person since getting out from under his parents' hold. He isn't so broody anymore, which, don't get me wrong, his broody side was damn sexy. But the playful, carefree one is even better.

After finishing a wash and blow dry on Brianna's hair, I send her off feeling as fresh as a daisy with a clubbing date scheduled for Saturday night with her best friend Cassie, who apparently is Jaxon's girlfriend. Come to think of it, I think I've seen them at Micky's, and they were most likely at that game I went to. Though, I was a bit preoccupied with the sexy slice of heaven down on the ice.

Xander has his final fight in two days, and I have to admit, I'm a wreck. I know he'll do great. He's mentally and physically ready. Without a doubt, I know he could take it out, but I can't help but wonder how far Pitbull is going to take it before Xander gets through with the winning hit.

I've watched as many of Pitbull's recent fights as possible to find out what areas he's lacking in, but to be honest, I really don't know what I'm looking for. I'm sure the boys at Rebels Advocate have been studying up on Pitbull to give Xander his best chance, but when it comes down to it, Pitbull fights dirty. He's brutal and terrifying, and that scares the living shit out of me and leaves me wondering if Xander is going to be quick enough to evade Pitbull's advances. Or, is Pitbull going to play dirty and beat Xander to a pulp before he has a chance to come through? All I know is that there's a lot of money on the line, and when money comes into play, people change.

I know Xander has the skill and the will to beat him, but I hope he can stay true to himself. Win the fight without getting dirty, and leave the competition with his head held high. He'll never forgive himself if he played by Pitbull's rules and left him permanently injured.

I head out toward the break room when Gina comes striding out of her office, looking down at her iPad, and accidentally walking straight into me. The iPad goes flying, and I stumble around, desperately trying to catch it before it cracks on the tiles.

"Oh, my goodness," Gina exclaims as I finally get purchase on the iPad. "I'm so sorry, Charli. I've been so caught up doing this order."

"It's fine," I say, handing the iPad back with a smile.

Gina glances out to the salon, looking over her stylists and what they're doing. "How's it going out there?" she questions.

"Good," I say. "Zara's in the middle of a color. There are two style cuts, and I just finished my wash and blow dry."

"Oh, excellent. What's your schedule like now?"

"My next client isn't due for thirty minutes, so I was just going to get some cleaning done," I explain.

"Don't be silly," she says. "Go take your lunch break. I'll get Steph to clean after her client. You've been working off your feet."

I give her a grateful smile just as my stomach starts to growl. Excellent timing. "Thanks," I say, ducking into the break room and grabbing my bag. "I'm gonna head down to the café. Can I get you anything?"

Her eyes light up, and I already know what she's going to say. "A coffee would be great."

"No problem," I laugh as I sling my bag over my shoulder. I make my way out of the salon and down the road to fill my stomach. I order a sandwich and Gina's coffee before playing a game on my phone while I wait.

My order is ready in record time, and I sit out in the sun to annihilate my lunch.

Not wanting Gina's coffee to get cold, I head back a little early. The streets are quiet, but there's a nice breeze, so I enjoy the walk and work on relaxing my body and arms for my afternoon filled with clients. They never tell you about all the negative things that go along with your dream job. For me, it's the arms. After doing blow-drys all day, my arms feel like they're about to fall off.

I'm completely lost in my own world as I make my way back to the salon when a black van screeches to a stop beside me. My eyes widen in shock before my body starts to react. What the hell is going on? The door slides open, and I gape as Pitbull barges out onto the street before me, a sickening smirk across his face.

He runs at me and fear pounds through my body.

I throw Gina's scalding coffee at his face and start to run, a ferocious scream tearing from my throat. I hardly make it two steps before he's on me, his hand slamming down over my mouth, stifling my screams. A vise-like grip locks around my waist, and he lifts me off the ground with ease.

Pitbull rushes back to the van as I claw at his arms, desperately trying to get free. He climbs in the side door and throws me down on the hard floor, slamming the sliding door as he goes.

My heart races as I try to get myself up, but he's on me once again, pressing a foot against my chest and shoving me back to the ground. "Nice to see you again," he says with a wicked grin as the driver takes off, making me slide to the back of the van. My arms fling out, trying to save myself, but it's no use. My balance is completely thrown, and I slam into the metal doors with a heavy thud.

Pitbull is on his feet, crouching in the small space and making his way to me. I scream while kicking out at him, trying to keep the bastard away. What does he want from me? Am I supposed to be his leverage to use against Xander in the fight? Is this his big plan to make Xander throw the fight or forfeit?

He continues toward me, which doesn't take him long in this cramped space, and reaches out for my bag. I hold onto it with everything I've got, and as he yanks it up, I dangle from the straps. He kicks me in the ribs, and I scream out as I drop back to the van's floor and latch onto my aching ribs with tears of agony in my eyes.

Pitbull smirks at my display but quickly disregards me as he pours the contents of my bag out on the floor to find my phone. He laughs like this is some kind of game before stomping on my phone and smashing it to pieces. He collects it from the ground and shoves it at the driver, who instantly tosses it out the window.

What the fuck?

I manage to get myself into a sitting position, but still have to hold onto the side of my ribs. "He's going to kill you for this," I say, not needing to clarify who *he* is.

"Let the fucker come," he scoffs.

It becomes clear that he's scared of Xander. If he thought he could win, he wouldn't have gone to these lengths. He would have just shown up to the fight and taken him out. But no, here I am, being held as leverage so he can get what he wants.

I don't know what possesses me to do it, but the rage and fury circling my body have my tongue loosening up. "You're fucking chicken shit," I laugh.

Pitbull storms forward and grabs me by the collar of my shirt, hoisting me up before slamming the back of my head against the blacked-out windows. "The fuck did you say?" he roars.

"You heard me," I spit. "You're nothing but chicken shit. You're a loser. You're scared he's going to kick your ass, and you'd be right. He will. Maybe before you might have stood a chance, but not now."

He lets out a terrifying growl and slams me against the window once again, this time making my head spin. If there ever was a time to thank my stepmom, it'd be now. If not for her regular beatings, I probably would have passed out on the first hit. Hell, I probably would have already pissed my pants as well. But not now. Not with this bastard.

"I ain't scared of shit," he says, lowering his tone, trying to invoke fear in me, but I'm too angry. Too riled up.

"Bullshit," I yell back at him. "If you weren't scared, you would have faced him like a man. But instead, you're pulling this shit."

His hand flinches at his side, and not a second later, I feel his fingers at my throat, closing around my windpipe and squeezing hard.

Holy shit. Bad move. Bad fucking move. I can't breathe.

I try desperately to gasp for air, but his hold is too tight, and my eyes widen, the fear like nothing I've ever known. He grins at me for long, painful seconds before clenching harder around my throat and using his hold to throw me across the van. I gasp for sweet oxygen as my body crashes into the opposite side of the van, hitting it so fucking hard I dent the panel.

Pain shoots through my body, but at least this time I have the sense to stay still and quiet.

"Still think I'm scared?" Pitbull taunts as he presses his heavy boot against my wrist and crushes the bones with ease.

Yes, in fact, I do.

I scream in agony, tears instantly springing to my eyes as intense pain rocks through my wrist and shoots up my arm. He doesn't release me, and I claw at his boot, desperate for relief.

He waits until most of my screams have been swallowed by my sobs before finally removing his foot from my shattered wrist. He crouches down, pushing right into my personal space, a twisted smirk on his face that has me choking back vomit. "That fucker is going to be annihilated in the ring, and I'm going to make sure of it," he says with a promise in his eyes. With that, his hand closes into a tight fist and comes hurtling toward my face.

The last thing I see is that twisted smirk before my world disappears.

CHAPTER 20

XANDER

"Faster," Cole demands as I punch the boxing pads he holds in front of his chest. I push myself harder. I only have two more days before I face Pitbull, and not a damn thing is going to stop me from taking that fucker down. Not after his bullshit last week. And certainly not with two hundred thousand dollars on the line.

Cole moves the pads, and my eyes follow each of his movements, not missing a beat.

My phone ringing in the background cuts into my concentration, but I ignore it. I've got shit to do. I continue with the punches, kicking and evading, while I hear Jace in the background answering the call. "Roadkill grill. You kill 'em, we grill 'em."

I roll my eyes, but can't help the grin that cuts across my face. "Shit, yeah. I'll grab him," Jace says before jogging over to me.

Cole instantly puts his pads down, and I turn to Jace who has a strange look on his face. "Sorry, dude," he says, handing the phone over, knowing not to interrupt my sessions unless it's important. "It's some guy, Micky. He says there's a problem."

I take the phone. If it's Micky that means it's got something to do with Charli. My heart rate increases, despite the workout Cole's been putting me through. "Micky," I say. "What's up?"

"Have you heard from Charli?" he demands, not beating around the bush.

"No," I tell him, my back stiffening. "Is she okay?"

"I don't know, kid," he says, the concern clear in his voice. "Just had a call from Gina. Charli never returned from her lunch break."

"What?" I question. Charli has never ditched work before. It's just not something she's capable of. Even on her deathbed, she'd still try to work. Something must have happened. I can't help but wonder if her stepmom finally came for her again, and fuck, the image of my girl laying in a gutter somewhere has me doubling over.

My heart races as I end the call, not even bothering with a goodbye. I find her name in my contact list and hit call, waiting the few painful seconds for the call to connect, but it beeps at me, saying call failed. I give it a second try then a third. "Fuck," I roar.

"What's wrong?" Cole rushes out, alarmed.

"It's Charli. Something's wrong," I tell him as I rush to the back and grab my shit. Cole throws me the keys to his truck, and I've never been so grateful. It's times like this I wish I still had my own fucking truck.

I'm out the door in seconds, rushing home and hoping like fuck she just wasn't feeling well and I'm going to walk through the door to find her curled up in bed, pleased to see me.

I make it home in no time and push through the door, narrowly escaping having to break it down. "Charli?" I call as I make my way through the house, but I know in my gut that she isn't here. "Babe? You here?"

I double-check every room of the house before I head over to Micky's and bolt straight up the stairs to check the apartment, hearing Micky call after me that he's already checked up here. But I'm not taking any risks. I'll check her apartment a million times over.

Running back down to the bar, I find Micky standing at the bottom of the stairs waiting for me. "You haven't heard from her yet?" he questions, panic lacing his tone, his eyes just as wide as mine.

"No," I roar in frustration, shaking my head as I try to work out where the hell she could be, and where the hell I'm supposed to go from here.

Micky tells me he's going to do a drive around the city and leaves me to check the more serious places. I'm halfway to her stepmother's place when a text comes through on my phone. I pull it out of my pocket and open the text before coming to a screeching halt in the middle of the road, other cars whipping around me, horns blaring as they narrowly avoid rear-ending me.

There's a picture of Charli on a wet concrete floor in what looks like some kind of basement. She's bloodied and bruised with her hands and feet bound. Her clothes are torn, and a thick piece of duct tape covers her mouth. But what fucking kills me is the terror in her eyes.

My gaze snaps down to the message below the image.

Unknown - Throw the match or you'll never see this bitch again.

"Fuck," I roar.

I should have known.

Pitbull has my fucking woman. How stupid could I have been to assume this was about Charli, that it was her stepmother? But of course, it's about me. The moment I'm finally in control, someone has to come and fuck it up. But this dickhead is finally going to learn his lesson. No one fucks with what's mine.

Come for my throat, my home, my career. But my girl is off limits.

The thought crosses my mind that I should do as he says and throw the fight. It's the easiest way to get Charli back, but the fight is still two days away, and who knows what could happen to her in that time. He's an unpredictable bastard and probably wouldn't stand by his word. Fuck, she's already bloodied and bruised and she's been gone an hour, maybe two. Who knows what kind of damage he could inflict in two days.

I pull Cole's truck around and hit the gas, flooring it back to Rebels before bursting through the door. Cole and Jace are already standing, and before they get a word out, I thrust my phone toward them. Cole looks it over with wide eyes before they quickly narrow and become full of rage.

"How the hell am I supposed to find her?" I ask.

I see the answer behind his eyes. "Let's go," he says.

We pile into his truck while Jace gets on his phone and gives Luke a call, asking if he can get a friend to track the phone number before telling him to meet us at Mario's. He calls Caden next and relays the same message, telling him to get a move on.

"Who the fuck is Mario?" I demand, my hands balled in tight fists.

Jace looks toward Cole before finally telling me what I need to know. "He's the asshole who does the paperwork for the Underground. He's dodgy as fuck, but he'll know where I can find Pitbull."

I nod, knowing this could be my only lead to Charli.

We come to a stop in front of some old restaurant, and find Luke and Caden already waiting. We catch up with them, the five of us storming through the doors. I follow Cole's lead, and the way they handle themselves suggests that maybe they're more than used to dealing with shit like this.

We walk straight past the gawking diners and through the kitchen before Cole busts down a door to an office that has some guy sitting behind a desk. I can only assume this is Mario. He doesn't startle, and I realize it's because he knew we were coming. The whole side wall of his office is covered in monitors and surveillance equipment, making me wonder just how dodgy this motherfucker is.

He stands from his expensive chair, placing his hands on his desk and fixing us with an intimidating stare. This guy must have something special up his sleeve, because he stands with confidence before five guys who are all twice his size. "Gentlemen," he says. "I'd love to say what a pleasure it is to see you again, but that would be a lie."

Cole lets out a grunt. "We need everything you've got on Pitbull."

Mario laughs. "No can do. You know the rules of the game."

"The game just changed," Cole says, his tone enough to turn my blood cold. "You know how this is going to end. You can either give us what we need or we'll find it ourselves." Mario's eyes narrow dangerously on Cole before flicking to the rest of us. He lets out a sigh and sits back in his chair before going through some paperwork in his desk drawer. "Good choice," Cole mutters, sarcasm lacing his tone.

"Well, the last time you idiots ransacked this joint, it cost me nearly ten grand in damages," he informs us.

"Lesson well learned then," Jace grunts, earning himself a nasty glare from Mario.

The seconds tick by painfully slow when he finally finds what he's looking for and silently hands it to Luke. "This is all I've got," he says. "Now get out of my restaurant. It's bad for business."

Luke looks over the papers and he clearly doesn't seem happy about it, but he grunts anyway. "It's going to have to do."

He hands the paper to me, and all I see is the name and address of a gym. Without hesitation, I turn on my heel. "Let's go."

We get back in the truck, and Cole navigates to the gym. We pull up, the truck flying up over the curb and stopping on the sidewalk in front of the building. I'm out the door before the truck has even come to a stop.

Pushing on the door, it doesn't budge, and I clench my jaw, giving the bastard a good shake just to be sure. "Fuck. It's locked."

Luke and Jace appear behind me. "We'll check around back," Luke says before they take off at a run. They're gone for all of thirty seconds before they come tearing back around the corner. "No luck."

I shrug my shoulders. If we can't get in the right way, then we're doing it my way. I take a few steps back to Cole's truck and search the back, coming back a moment later with a crowbar in my hand. Then without hesitation, I smash through the thick glass doors.

The alarm screeches to life, and the five of us hastily make our way inside. Breaking and entering is not my best idea, particularly in broad daylight, but my options are slim. "We don't have long before the cops are here," Caden says, making us all move a little faster.

I head straight for the office with Cole on my heels, kicking in the door and instantly heading for the filing cabinets.

Cole hacks into the computer, and we spend the next few minutes searching. Each minute is another one that Charli is in the hands of that bastard, doing who knows what to her. The thought has another spurt of anger coming on, and I search faster, finishing the cabinet before moving to another, but still coming up blank.

I'm two seconds away from ripping the cabinets off the fucking wall when Jace comes darting into the office with a picture frame. He slams it down on the table, sending a big crack right through the center of the glass, but that's not what catches my eye. Pitbull stares straight back at me, with the text below stating he was last year's most promising fighter, his name printed clear as day right next to it.

Jackson fucking Delaney.

Cole wastes no time getting started searching through the gym's records, and he pulls up the fucker's file not two seconds later, finding every bit of information we could possibly need and more.

We're out the door with moments to spare and turn onto the main road when we see the cops heading in the opposite direction.

"Which property are we heading to?" Cole asks, hitting the gas and sending us soaring down the main road as the cops speed past us, flying into the gym parking lot.

I look over the paper once again and find two addresses. One is a residential address and the other seems to be a warehouse. I give Cole the details of the warehouse and he hits it, with Luke and Caden following in the truck behind.

It's just past nightfall when we finally get to the place we've been looking for, and I feel like it's taken us way too fucking long to get to this point. The warehouse is old and abandoned with dim lights coming from inside. The place reminds me of the locations where the underground fights have been, and I don't doubt that this place would probably be used in the future.

Bailing out of the trucks, we make our way toward the doors, and I prepare myself for the fight of my life.

Nobody touches my girl and gets away with it.

CHAPTER 21

CHARLI

Consciousness comes back to me and my eyes spring open to a cold, concrete room. My head is groggy and pounding, but it's nothing compared to the fierce agony of my shattered wrist. My heart races, as it all comes back to me. The street, the van . . . Pitbull.

Adjusting myself on the cold ground, I quickly realize just how much trouble I'm in. Both my ankles and wrists are bound with rope and there's a thick strip of duct tape across my mouth, making it impossible to scream. But what's the point? I have a feeling no one is coming for me here.

It's not like the dickhead who put me here is going to come down and help me out. My only hope is Xander, but how the hell would he know where to find me? Hell, I don't even know where I am. I have to trust he will work it out. I have no doubt he will come for me, but how long is it going to take? A day? Two?

Wanting to take note of my surroundings and start working out some kind of game plan, I look around the room, peering over my shoulder to the door and—Oh fuck.

A huge motherfucking dog sits at the door, his sharp gaze watching me like a hawk. My body starts to shake, my wrist screaming in protest as my heart races with fear. I love dogs, but not unpredictable ones that look as though they could tear my head clean off my body.

Shit. Shit. Shit.

Not liking my stare, the big bastard starts to growl and the fear that pulses through my body is like nothing I've ever felt. I drop my gaze as my heart rate peaks, knowing he'd be able to sense it. One wrong move from me and this giant asshole will eat me for dinner.

I shouldn't be surprised. Of course Pitbull put a fucking dog by the door. There isn't even a window for me to escape through. The room only has the one, dog-guarded door, that will no doubt lead me straight to my captor. Though it's not like I'd even attempt to get past the dog. He looks just as lethal as Pitbull, with sharp teeth that I'm sure could tear through my skin like a hot knife through butter.

Tears well in my eyes and as I blink, they fall down my cheeks, splashing against the cold concrete. Why did I have to go and tell the guy he was chicken shit? Maybe he would have been kinder had I not provoked him. Maybe I'd be sitting in a warm room with my hands and feet free. Maybe he would have let me go.

Wishful fucking thinking.

As the tears flow, so do the sobs, and with each heaving cry, my ribs protest, so fucking sore from Pitbull's booted kicks. The dog tilts his head, his slight movement sending waves of nervousness soaring through me, and I lock my gaze onto his, seeing a strange curiosity in his big eyes. He holds my stare and that curiosity starts to shift into something a little more sympathetic, and it's almost as though he senses my pain.

What the hell?

Keeping my eye on him, I awkwardly try to get myself up into a sitting position, while hoping like fuck he stays on his side of the room. Each movement sends searing pain through my body, my wrist burning from within, and I clench my jaw, keeping myself from screaming. It takes a lifetime, but when I finally sit up, I feel as though I've won some kind of small victory.

With my hands bound tightly behind my back and a shattered wrist, it makes it nearly impossible to lean against the wall, so I turn to the side and try to make myself somewhat comfortable against my shoulder.

Now in a better position, I can properly catalog my injuries. My wrist and the bump on my head are the most obvious, but my whole body is covered in scratches, bruises, and cuts, making me wonder exactly how I got into this room. I doubt I was carried, and judging by the grazes along my arms, I'm assuming that I was dragged.

Tears continue to fall and knowing I'll never get through this if I'm in a constant state of fear, I close my eyes and take deep, calming breaths, trusting the dog to remain by the door. I start to block out the pain, and I let my mind wander to Xander. The way he holds me in the night or the way I catch him looking at me when he thinks I'm busy. The sexy way he smirks when he's teasing me, and how the words *I love you* sound rolling off his lips.

I repeat the thoughts over again like an endless loop, just waiting for it to be over.

Please, Xander. Hurry.

The dog's ears suddenly prick, and he turns his big head in the direction of the door, a soft growl rumbling through his chest, sensing something outside the door. My heart races, having a sinking feeling that whoever is coming isn't Xander.

The door flies open and some guy stands before me with a sick, twisted grin on his face. I stare at him in horror, my body violently shaking, too fucking vulnerable to even fight back. He takes a step toward me and the dog stands before turning around, growling at the man.

I stare, wide-eyed as the dog's body seems to tense, looking as though he's preparing to attack. What is going on here? Is the dog protecting me? That couldn't be right. He's *their* guard dog, not mine.

The guy focuses his attention on the dog, and I see the hesitation in his eyes. He wants to take me. Wants to force my legs apart and take what isn't his, but he's too fucking pussy to take his chances against this beast of a dog. With a curse, he slowly backs out of the room and slams the door behind him, making it clear that the dog has no loyalty to him. He probably belongs to Pitbull.

A lock slides into place, and I let out a breath of relief, realizing just how close that was.

The dog relaxes as he turns back to face me, and I give him a small smile, wishing I could somehow express to him how grateful I am for his protection. Then realizing I'm trying to have a silent conversation with a dog, I let out a heavy sigh. I'm more than ready to go right back to my thoughts, when the dog slowly approaches me. He keeps his gaze on mine, watching me closely as though still unsure about me, but then in a swift movement, drops down beside me, making himself comfortable on the ground before placing his giant head on my lap.

I gape down at the dog, wondering what the hell I did to deserve his friendship. It's the strangest feeling. It's almost as though I share some sort of connection with this beast, and the need to reach out and give him a scratch pulses through my fingers. But that will have to wait until Xander gets here and my hands are free.

I briefly wonder just how badly the dickheads in the other room have treated this poor dog for him to turn on them the way he did, but one thing I know for sure is that the second I get out of here, he's coming with me.

With my protection detail right by my side, I let my mind take me back to the sweet memories of Xander, hoping that will be enough to make the pain of this reality sink away into the darkness.

CHAPTER 22

XANDER

I'm flying up the driveway that leads to the entrance of the warehouse, taking in the property with a sharp eye as the boys flank me. There's a big metal roller door with a normal wooden door beside it and I move in front of it, quickly surveying what I'm dealing with. I grip the handle and, finding it locked, I bring my foot up and with a heavy blow, the door splinters into pieces and comes crashing down.

The boys and I push through, knowing we just lost the element of surprise. We find a group of at least seven men waiting for us inside, all up and standing, facing the entryway as if they knew we were coming. Pitbull stands front and center, wielding a knife and a sick grin, and the need to end him burns through my veins.

Fuck. I guess we're about to get a little preview of fight night.

There's no way to know if these assholes are carrying weapons, but what I do know is that with just a quick glance, it's clear they haven't been keeping up with their training. Cole and the guys can handle them. As for Pitbull, he's the biggest threat here. And he's all mine.

Not wanting to prolong this a second longer, we rush forward, putting them on the defense.

My eyes remain locked on Pitbull, but some dickhead cuts in front of him. I raise my fist and send him flying with one punch, the crunch of his bones echoing through the old warehouse. With Pitbull back in my sights, I forge ahead without even a glance for my boys, knowing they can handle themselves just as well as I can.

I finally reach Pitbull, who scowls at me with the knife clenched in his fist. His arm strikes out, but I'm ready for him. I block him with ease, and I see the wariness in his eyes when he realizes the knife isn't going to stop me. I'm here for my girl and nothing is going to stand in my way.

"Where is she?" I growl as my fist comes up in an uppercut to his stomach while my eyes remain locked on any movement he makes, especially any movements which include the knife.

"Wouldn't you like to know," he spits before attempting a kick to knock me off balance. I easily duck out of the way, which only seems to infuriate him. He comes at me with both arms swinging. His moves are a mess, sloppy even, and I realize he's been drinking. Fucking stupid move on his part. This isn't the same brutal dickhead I've been watching at the Underground. This guy isn't thinking straight. He isn't clear in his mind, and every fighter knows you don't go into a fight without a clear head. Otherwise, you make mistakes. And today, he made the biggest mistake of his life.

The angrier he gets, the worse the taunts become. "You should have heard her scream when I fucked her," he smirks.

I stumble back, prepared to hear anything come out of his mouth but that.

No. No. There's no way. He's lying. I would feel it.

Whether he's lying or not, I see red and quickly recover, getting through with a devastating blow to his jaw, watching with satisfaction as a spray of blood splatters across the concrete. "You want to win with this shit? You can't even nick me with the fucking knife," I taunt him with a smirk as his skills become comical. In any other situation, I'd be laughing by now, but this fucker deserves everything that's coming his way, especially after claiming he laid his hands on my woman.

Pitbull lets out an angry growl before rushing me, just as I knew he would. So fucking predictable. The knife arches behind his head, and I have no doubt he's looking for a kill shot. My leg comes flying up in a spinning kick and smacks him right across the face.

He falls back and I take my chance. It's clear he only has formal training in boxing, which is no match for my extensive MMA skills, and it's obvious he's finally come to this realization. He wants the money, and he knows he doesn't have the skills to take me down.

All this time watching his fights, I thought he would be my hardest opponent, but what I'm seeing now is like facing off against a toddler.

Maybe I'm just that filled with rage and desperate to get to Charli that I don't notice his skills, or if he even has any at all, but it really doesn't matter to me. I'm gonna kick his ass now, and I'll kick his ass in the ring.

I push forward and lay into him, but I don't have time for bullshit. My fist rears back, and I nail him as hard as I can in the temple, once for Charli, once for me, and once for the rest of his opponents who never got the chance to see a fair fight. I follow it up with a punch to the jaw and a few to his eye for good measure.

The fucker goes down, the knife clattering to the concrete floor.

Grabbing the knife, I slide it into my back pocket before looking around to see that the guys are almost done with the rest of Pitbull's men. Since they don't need me, I push on to find my girl. There's only one other door in this place, and I rush to it as fast as I can.

A big lock blocks my entry, and I bring my foot up once again. The door takes a few tries, but it eventually gives way.

The first thing I see is Charli, and I start to rush forward before I notice the big fucking dog guarding her, ferocious growls tearing from deep in his chest. My hands instantly fly up, and I come to a standstill, showing the dog I mean no harm as I take in the scene. This dog isn't guarding her. He's protecting her.

My gaze roams over Charli, taking in every fucking bruise marring her skin. I'm desperate to get to her, but I need to get past this dog first. I go over all the ways to show the dog that he can trust me, but I'm coming up blank. All I can think about is Charli and how fucking broken she looks.

The dog must see something he likes as his growls begin to ease and he takes a step backward, his big-ass body pressed firmly at Charli's side. Keeping my eye on the dog, I slowly make my way toward Charli, not wanting to make any sudden movements.

Charli lies in a heap on the floor. Her precious face is streaked with tears, and those blue eyes that I love are clenched as tightly as possible. Her clothes are torn, but they're still on her body, so despite everything, I'm still confident he didn't touch her. "Charli?" I whisper gently, so that I don't freak her out. I place my hand on her shoulder and her eyes spring open.

Her eyes seek out mine, and she looks at me with fear, begging for me to take her away from this place as the tears stream down her face.

I reach for the duct tape across her mouth and try to slowly peel it off, but the shit must be industrial strength and won't budge. "Sorry," I say, leaving the duct tape and moving onto her hands and feet. I know she desperately wants it off, but if I ripped it, she'd probably lose half a lip.

I pull the knife from my back pocket and the dog instantly goes on guard again. I move ever so slightly so the dog can watch my every move as I take her hand in mine. Charli flinches and attempts to scream in pain, though the sound is muffled by her taped mouth, which only pisses the dog off more. I focus on her hand and realize that her wrist is broken. Fuck, it's not just broken, it's shattered.

"Fuck," I grunt, desperate to get back out there and end him for good. The only thing stopping me is how desperately Charli needs me right now.

I slip the knife through her bound hands as gently as I can, cringing as I try to cut the rope, sick to my fucking stomach that my touch causes her pain. "Sorry, babe. This is going to hurt," I tell her.

She lets out a pained sob, letting me know she understands, and I do what I can to make it quick for her.

Her arms come free, and she carefully brings her wrist around her body and cradles it to her chest while I work on releasing her ankles. This seems to cheer the dog up as he comes forward and starts looking her over, proving to me once again that he's protecting her.

Charli stretches out her good hand and gives the dog a gentle scratch behind his ears, making him rub his large head up against her, but that only has Charli cringing in pain.

I try my hardest not to look at the cuts and bruises on her body, to keep myself focused, but I can't help it. My heart breaks with every new scratch I find, but I need to know that she's okay.

She tries to reach for me to get to her feet, but I bend down and scoop her into my arms instead. I go to leave, but Charli looks back at the dog who sits on his ass pouting, clearly upset that I'm taking her away. Charli looks back at me, trying to convey some sort of message. "You want to bring him?"

She nods ever so gently. I look back at the dog, knowing damn well I could never deny her, especially right now. "Come on," I say, hoping the big guy understands what I'm asking of him.

To my surprise, he gets up and follows me as I take Charli out of the room and into the main warehouse where all three sets of our eyes dart around, searching for a threat.

I see the moment Charli's gaze lands on Pitbull, her whole body tensing with unease. A sigh of relief comes out of her as she takes in the damage I've done, though none of it will make up for what he's done to her. Not with the physical and mental scars he's left behind.

Cole, Luke, Jace, and Caden have finished taking out all of Pitbull's men and quickly look over Charli, assessing her injuries before dropping their curious gazes to the big-ass dog. Not one of them asks, just going with the flow as we hurry back out to the trucks, desperate to get Charli to the emergency room.

Jace opts to ride with Luke so I can lay Charli across the backseat of Cole's truck. With the dog seated in the tray and Cole in the driver's seat, we're gunning it to the hospital. Cole hands me a bottle of water to help unstick the duct tape from Charli's lips, and I get to work as her head rests in my lap.

I manage to get half of it off before Cole pulls up to the hospital.

"Thanks, man," I grunt as I help Charli out of the truck.

"No problem. Get your girl inside and checked out. I'll deal with the dog until you're finished here," he says, looking annoyed with the task, but I know he'll do the right thing.

I give him a grateful nod before I rush Charli inside and watch as the hospital staff immediately come to her aid, finally able to breathe for the first time in hours.

CHAPTER 23

CHARLI

I've spent the last two days in the hospital with a nasty concussion, and it's been driving me insane. The second Xander found me in that god-awful warehouse, all I wanted was for him to take me home to the place I feel safest. Instead, I ended up a prisoner at the hospital.

I mean, come on. I was kidnapped, beaten, and held hostage, and they wanted to hold me against my will again. Seriously? I get that I needed serious surgery on my wrist and all that, but staying in a place that wasn't my home just didn't sit right with me.

All I can say is that it sucked. Like, really bad. Xander stayed as long as he could before the hospital visiting hours kicked in and the nurses promptly threw him out, no matter how much he protested. Though I have to admit, it was a little comical to watch, and his persistence was admiral.

So, there I was, during every closed visiting hour, left alone with nothing but my own thoughts and memories to haunt me. Exactly what I needed. Not. I don't know how I would have survived the warehouse without my new dog Beast. When I asked what happened to him, Xander explained that Cole had taken care of him the last few days, made sure he'd seen a proper vet, bought him all the things dogs need, and then watched as he shit all over his backyard.

It's the afternoon of the final at the Underground and the fact that I'm still here is driving me insane. Xander sits in the chair opposite my hospital bed, fast asleep. I tried to get him to sleep in the bed with me, but he flat-out refused. Though I don't know what good that's going to do for tonight's fight. He promised me that with everything that's happened, he will have no problem taking the guy out again. After all, the last fight was won in seconds while Pitbull wielded a knife.

Xander tried to explain that Pitbull has only been trained in boxing, and doesn't stand a chance against his extensive MMA training, and apparently that means a slam dunk in Xander's eyes. He just has to use what he knows against him. But he also said that Pitbull had been drinking when they fought, so who knows what could happen.

When a knock sounds on the other side of the door, my eyes fly up to see the doctor hurrying into the room, bumping into a tray before stumbling the rest of the way in with my discharge papers in hand. Xander's eyes snap open at the sound of the commotion, and he's on his feet in seconds, prepared to beat the crap out of whoever just barged into my room.

In his sleepy state, it takes Xander a moment to realize it's just the doctor and not someone coming to snatch me out of my bed, and the poor guy narrowly avoids a nasty uppercut.

After receiving instructions on caring for my cast and confirming I know what I'm doing with my vast array of pain meds, I finally get to sign the discharge papers.

We quickly get our asses out of there and walk down to the parking lot, finding Cole's truck right by the door. Xander helps me up into it despite my objections. I'm more than capable of managing on my own. But, I'm not going to lie, if it means having his hands on my body, then I'm going to allow him to do it. "I can't believe Cole hasn't demanded his truck back yet," I say when Xander hops in the driver's seat.

"I know," he grunts. "I don't like putting him out like this. I'll go and buy one this weekend."

"Yeah?" I ask.

"Mmhmm," he murmurs as he pulls out of the parking lot and onto the main road. "I'll get you one, too."

"What?" I practically choke, my eyes wide. Are we sure it was me who took a hit to the head and not Xander?

"I'm thinking something big to keep you safe," he goes on as if I'm not having a mini heart attack right next to him.

I gape at him. "Hold it right there," I demand, putting my hand up. "Has it ever occurred to you that I don't drive?"

"Well, yeah. You don't have a car," he states flatly.

"No, you moron," I grin. "I don't drive because I don't know how.

You really think the evil stepmonster would have taken the time out of her busy drinking schedule to teach me? I mean, I could get from point A to point B if I had to, but it won't be pretty."

He considers this for a moment, sparing me a quick glance, those dark eyes of his sailing across my face as though he still can't believe I'm right here. "All the more reason to buy you one," he tells me. "I'll teach you."

Let's face it, the idea of having driving lessons from Xander is beyond ridiculous and will only end up in an argument. Maybe Micky will teach me. "You want to buy me a car just so I can destroy it while I learn."

"Yup," he announces proudly.

I know a losing battle when I see one.

Letting out a huff, I fold my arms over my chest, being careful not to bump my wrist, but it should be fine now. It's in a cast, a black one that reminds me of my black sheep boyfriend and my new guard dog.

We make it the rest of the way home, and the second I step through the threshold, that feeling of safety I've been longing for finally washes through me. I absolutely love that my home can offer me this because I've never felt safe at home before. Well, Micky's was kind of a safe haven, but there were always drunken losers hanging around downstairs. And despite the lock on the door, a woman's mind can't help but take her to some dark places.

After being in the warehouse, followed by the hospital for two days, the need to scrub myself silly is all I can think about. I make my way toward the bathroom, stripping as I go and adding a little strut to my walk, knowing Xander's eyes are resting firmly on my ass. By the time I get to the door, I'm standing in nothing but a pair of panties.

Hooking my thumb into the waistband, I slowly drag them down my legs, giving Xander a perfect view at what he's been missing for the last few days. A ferocious groan tears from his chest, and a wicked grin shoots across my face.

Hook. Line. Sinker.

My panties have barely grazed the tiles before I feel his warm hands on my ass, one of which is quickly making its way between my legs. I straighten up and my back presses against his wide chest, his soft breath brushing across my skin. He winds a hand around my waist then trails it up over my ribs before cupping my tit, his thumb roaming over my nipple, feeling it pebble beneath his touch.

I let out a moan as my head tips back to his shoulder, not realizing how desperately I've been craving his touch. Xander's lips come down on my neck, sending electricity coursing through my body, heading straight for my core.

After turning in his arms, I start undressing him as his lips crash down on mine, claiming me just in case I'd forgotten that I belong whole heartedly to him. Clothes are tossed everywhere, and I'm pushed up against the wall of the shower, warm water streaming down around us as Xander buries that thick cock deep inside me.

He fucks me until I come, his fingers working my clit as his lips remain fused to mine. And only after my pussy shatters around his cock, does he do it all over again. All comments from the doctor about not getting my cast wet are completely forgotten, but desperate times call for desperate measures and if I have to get a new one, then so be it.

I'm barely finished getting dressed when I hear the sound of someone knocking at the door. Xander makes his way to the door as I drop down on the couch and not a moment later, a massive dog comes bolting through the house. He sniffs me out and jumps up beside me on the couch, his tail wagging as his tongue comes straight for my face.

"Hi, boy," I say with a smile as I give him a scratch behind the ears. He tries to climb into my lap, but I have far too many injuries for that, which means Xander is yelling at him from the door, demanding that he get off the couch. The dog practically gives him a death stare, and if he could, I'm sure he'd be flipping him off too. I realize this is going to be a love-hate relationship between the two males in my life.

Xander thanks Cole at the door, and on his way to join me on the couch, he takes a detour past the kitchen to bring in lunch. I'm about to compliment Xander on his cooking abilities when I see the familiar take-out bags from Micky's, and realize the old man must have popped over to check on me. Though considering we were in the shower since the second we got home and they weren't here before . . . ahh shit.

The old man has been checking in on me at least four times a day, whether it's a phone call or physically dropping everything to visit me. I have to admit, I kind of love it. Micky has taken over the role of a father figure in my life, and I couldn't be happier with that outcome. Even though it reminds me of how much I miss my own father every time I see him.

The afternoon and night fly by, and before I know it, I find myself getting up to get ready for Xander's fight.

"Uh, what the hell do you think you're doing?" Xander scolds as I pull on my jeans. Well, as I *try to* pull them on. It's a little harder with only one hand. He lays back on the bed, legs crossed with one arm carelessly thrown behind his head as Beast lounges at the end, despite Xander telling him to get off a million times. Xander looks damn sexy in his dark jeans and leather jacket, but right now, his attitude has me overlooking it all.

I look at him in confusion, my brows furrowed. "I'm getting ready," I clarify. "What does it look like I'm doing?"

"You're not coming," he scoffs from his position on the bed, looking at me as though I've lost my mind.

"Like hell I'm not," I say, facing him front on and making sure he knows just how serious I am right now. Beast raises his head at the tone of my voice, clearly ready to back me up if need be.

"No," Xander says, sitting up in bed. "You're not."

Fury takes over me in a flash. "I didn't just go through hell and back for this stupid fight to have my stubborn-ass boyfriend tell me I can't go right before the big ending. That's like pulling out right before I come."

He lets out a regretful sigh as he gets up off the bed and makes his way around to me, Beast's sharp gaze following his every step. He places his hands on my shoulders as if trying to calm me, but that only infuriates me more.

I deserve to go, especially after what I've been through. I want to watch him pummel the dickhead. In fact, I'm pretty sure I *need* to see it. "Babe," he says, softly. "It's too dangerous. What if he got his hands on you while I wasn't there? I'd be worrying about you the whole time rather than concentrating on the fight."

"That's not going to happen," I say. "I won't let him. I'll stay with someone the whole time."

"Charli," he says with pain behind his eyes, hating telling me no. "I just . . . I can't risk you."

"Please," I whisper, feeling as though I'm going to break.

He cups his hands around my face and gives me a gentle kiss before pulling back. "You know I would give you anything and everything I possibly could," he says. "But this . . . I won't risk your safety over a stupid fight. It's not worth it."

My head drops to his shoulder, and I'm pretty sure I start pouting. His arms wrap around me. "I'm sorry, babe," he murmurs as he holds me.

I give in as a plan starts forming. If he isn't going to take me, I'll find my own way there. I'm going to be fine, and he needs to learn that he can't treat me like a princess because of one bad situation. I need to be free and live my life. And right now, living my life consists of one thing—watching my boyfriend annihilate that asshole.

I make my way over to the bed and climb under the covers with a heavy sigh. The fight doesn't start for another two hours, so I have plenty of time. I watch as Xander goes about the room getting ready and pumping himself up, though every time he looks back at me and takes in the scars that Pitbull left behind, I know he's ready. He's got all the motivation he needs right here, and that's clear as he commits every last scar to memory.

I have absolutely no doubt that Xander will walk out of that ring tonight as the Underground champion.

Xander comes over to me half an hour later and gives me a kiss. "I better get going," he tells me. "I want to get a proper warm-up in before the match."

"Okay," I sigh, still not happy that he isn't willing to take me with him, but I know my plan will work. "Good luck," I say. "Maybe bring me back an eyeball or something."

"That's foul on so many levels," he says, shaking his head in disgust.

I shrug my shoulders, an innocent smile pulling at the corners of my lips. "Eh, you still love me."

"That I do," he says.

"Kick his ass, okay," I tell him, though this time, he knows it's more of an order than a simple request.

"Babe, I promise you, I will not leave that ring until I've thoroughly fucked him up."

"I really like the sound of that."

"I know you do," he says, getting to his feet. "Be safe, okay? I've programmed the boys' numbers into your new phone, so if anything happens and you can't get ahold of me, you call them, okay?"

"Okay," I say, hating the thought of being alone for even the smallest amount of time, but I know it won't be for long.

"I hate leaving you," he tells me.

"I'll be okay," I say, snuggling deeper into my bed. "Please don't mess up that face of yours. I'm quite fond of it."

I finally get him out of the door, and the second I hear the lock click into place, the covers come flying off. I grab my phone as I dash around the room looking for the clothes I had earlier as I search through the contacts on my phone, hitting call, and holding it up to my ear while trying to pull a shirt over my head.

"Hey, Slutbag," Zara yells into the phone over the sound of what I am assuming is either a house party or Micky's. Though, from the loud dance music, I'm going to go with the first option. Micky says he has no time for shit music like that, despite the objections from his drunk patrons.

"Hey, Whore," I grin. "What are you doing?"

"Hold on," she yells. I wait patiently as the background noise slowly fades to a dull buzz. "Okay, what did you say?"

"What are you doing?"

"Oh, we're at this frat party. The Dragons just won their game so everyone is pumped up, but this party stinks," she informs me.

"Were you guys going to Xander's fight tonight?" I ask hopefully, my fingers and toes crossed.

"Hell yeah, we're going. No way am I going to miss that fight," she says. "Hang on, shouldn't you already be there?"

"That's my problem. Xander is refusing to let me go. He says it's *too dangerous*," I say, mimicking his voice. "He's certain I'll end up kidnapped again, despite the hundreds of other people there."

"Ugh, that blows," she sighs.

"What do you mean that blows? I'm still going whether he likes it or not."

"Oh, dear. This isn't going to go down well," she murmurs, though

I hear the smile in her voice. "Tell me," she says. "How do you assume you're going to get there?"

"You're going to get that hot boyfriend of yours to pick me up on the way, of course."

She lets out a heavy breath. "There's no way he's going to go against Xander's wishes."

"Oh, please. Unbutton your top, push your tits up, grind against him, and that man will be putty in your hands," I tell her. "Besides, you guys are still in that stage where he's trying to impress you. You've got nothing to worry about. Now hurry up, I don't want to miss anything."

"Fine," she laughs. "We'll be there in twenty."

She hangs up the phone, and I use the time to get myself ready. Doing everything one-handed is a shitload harder than I ever thought possible.

A knock sounds at the door twenty minutes later, and I rush through the house with Beast by my side before subtly peeping through the window to confirm it's Zara and Aaron. When I'm certain I'm not about to be kidnapped again, I fling the door open and have Zara crashing into my arms.

"How are you feeling?" she questions straight away as I hold my breath, not wanting to let on just how much that hurt. "Are you sure you should be going out tonight?"

"I'm fine," I groan. "Now, help me do up my pants. The button is too hard with one hand."

She smirks at me but does what she's told, only then giving Beast the attention he's begging for. I grab my bag off the front table and lock up the house before climbing into the back seat of Aaron's truck. "Thanks, Aaron," I grin as he turns in his seat and gives me a scathing stare.

"You girls are going to get me in so much trouble," he mutters before looking over the back seat. "Does the dog really have to come?"

"Don't stress. By the time I'm through with Xander, he won't even remember what he's pissed about," I inform him. "And yes, consider Beast my permanent guard dog. Where I go, he goes."

I watch with a grin as Aaron shakes his head and murmurs to himself. "Yeah, I'm fucked."

CHAPTER 24

XANDER

The place is packed as I make my way out to the ring with Cole heavy on my heels. He has just finished putting me through the warm-up of my life while Luke sputtered out every detail about Pitbull he could think of. Although I think it's pretty damn clear that we know his fighting style by now.

I've never been more pumped for a fight. The adrenaline pulses through my veins, making me desperate to get in the ring and feel my fists pounding into his flesh. It's strange, as for the first time in my life, I'm not fighting for myself. This is for Charli, and giving her the closure she deserves. Well, nailing this fucker in the face again is a little bit for me, too.

I stand at the entrance of the ring, and there's still no sight of

Pitbull. He wasn't in the fighter's room out back warming up, but I know with every ounce of my being that he isn't missing this match, especially after everything that's brought us to this point. Pitbull will want to go out with a bang, and I bet he's hoping the rush of adrenaline is what will help him over the line.

But I've got a scorned girlfriend on my side, and just like I said to Charli, I will not come out of this ring without making him pay.

"Are you ready for this, kid?" Cole asks from behind me as the announcer starts his spiel about me.

I turn to face Cole and look him in the eye. "Yeah, I'm ready."

"Alright," he says. "Remember, he would have regrouped after the other night. He will try anything to win this. You need to be prepared for whatever he throws at you."

I nod, acknowledging what he's saying, but it's not anything I haven't already considered. When my name is called, I slip through the ropes of the ring and strut into the center, putting on my usual show. The crowd is wild tonight. There isn't even standing room with so many bodies crammed in together.

I begin disrobing when I feel that familiar piercing stare right before a deep bark echoes over the crowd.

Fucking hell. I should have known she'd get Aaron to cave.

My gaze snaps up into the audience, searching for those familiar baby blues. It doesn't take long to find her. After all, she's standing among the rowdiest bunch in the whole place with a fucking horse-sized dog right beside her.

I narrow my stare on Charli and she reads me like a book, instantly understanding the meaning within my gaze. She is in deep shit, but from her returning grin, she doesn't have a single fuck to give.

My stare flicks toward Aaron, knowing he was the pussy-whipped boyfriend who allowed my girl to pull this off. I should have known she would pull something like this. "Sorry, man," he mouths, but I realize that even without Aaron's help, Charli would have eventually found her way here.

The announcer calls out the stats for Pitbull when I finally put faces on the rowdy people surrounding my girl. The whole fucking hockey team has shown up, and seeing as though they still remain undefeated after tonight's game, it's no wonder they're so rowdy. Knowing they're here and looking out for Charli makes me feel a lot better about her being here, but don't get me wrong. We're still having words tonight.

The announcer finally calls Pitbull to the ring, and I look over to the opposite side of the ring where the opposition would usually come from. Only he doesn't appear from there. My eyes snap to a commotion in the crowd and notice Pitbull literally pushing his way through the body of people to get to the ring.

I feel sorry for the pricks in his way. Judging by the look on his face and the crowd's reaction, he isn't pushing them gently. He's here to inflict as much harm as possible. I hope he enjoys this little show he's putting on, because it's the only one he'll get tonight.

My gaze flicks up to Charli, making sure she's okay after seeing him again, but all I see is that angry little line between her eyebrows giving her away. Her stare moves from Pitbull to me, and that line smooths out. "Destroy him," she mouths.

I nod my head. No chance in hell that I'll be letting her down tonight.

Pitbull makes it to the center of the ring and faces me with a vicious scowl and a face full of cuts and bruises. I can't help but smirk at the asshole, knowing those marks are a sign of what he did to my girl. Those marks stand as a reminder for me which, unlucky for him, only spurs me on.

"Thought you were too *chicken shit* to show," I say, using the phrase Charli had used against him.

His eyes narrow, filled with venom. "You better fucking watch it," he growls before cracking his knuckles, trying to appear tough.

"I better watch it?" I question. "You took my girl off the street and beat her. You'll be fucking lucky if I let you out of this ring alive."

I'm usually the silent, broody type before a match, but I know the more I frustrate him, the deeper inside his head I'll get and the easier this takedown will be. And right now, by the way his eyes are shooting daggers at me, I'm already there, deep inside his head.

The ref calls a start to the match before he has a chance to reply and I jump straight into action, moving as fast as lightning. Pitbull is too wound up in his own anger that he doesn't even see me coming, and I land a devastating blow just below his chest, winding him.

The hit knocks him off balance, but it's not enough to do any damage. The crowd roars, but he quickly shakes it off and comes right for me. He throws his arm around my body, attempting to hold me while his other arm comes around in a quick short arc, taking a cheap shot at my ribs. The blow is devastating, but nothing I can't handle.

Had he hit me just an inch higher, I would have been fucked.

We scramble around as he attempts to land a blow while I try to hold onto the upper hand. I manage to duck under his arm and lean back into the ropes. I quickly push myself back before letting myself fly forward with the momentum of the ropes. I come at him with fists flying and a kick combination.

His boxing skills can hardly keep up, and it doesn't take long until he's fumbling around, looking like a damn fool. Blood drips from his lip while the rest of his body is covered in red marks. My knuckles are bleeding, but most of it is held back by tape.

My fist comes up and I nail him in the jaw. The crowd roars and the sound of Beast's bark is heard over the top as Pitbull's head is thrown backward. He quickly shuffles back, giving himself a moment to find his footing and spits a mouthful of blood onto the concrete floor.

Pitbull lets out a growl as he rushes me, trying to get me to the ground, but the move is predictable. It's the same one he has used in each and every match he has been in. He overpowers his opponent, gets them to the ground, and beats them senseless.

But I'm ready for him. I watch his movements closely and duck out of the way while grabbing his left wrist. Giving it a twist, I land directly behind him with his wrist firmly in my grasp, but come to think of it, it's the same wrist he crushed of Charli's . . . Wouldn't it be a shame if I accidentally shattered it?

His howls of pain only drive me to pull tighter, and I push him into the ropes, hold him there before nailing him in the back of the ribs. Before allowing him a chance to recover, I kick the back of his knee while pushing him to the side. He goes down to the ground with the weight of my body coming down on top of him.

Pitbull struggles under my weight, but now that he's down, I want this shit over with. Charli's voice carries over the top of the crowd, or maybe I'm just listening out for it. "Finish him," she screams.

There's one thing I know for sure. What my woman wants, she gets.

I release his wrist and grab him by the back of his hair, all too aware that this shit is getting scrappy now. Then just as he did to Charli, I slam his face down against the concrete. I hate the feeling of being so brutal, but in the end, he touched Charli. He slammed her head into the side of a van, twice, then shattered her fucking wrist. Consider it karma.

Pitbull manages to adjust himself beneath me, but all that does is put him on his back.

Bad move, dickhead.

He puts his hands down on the ground, trying to find purchase on the concrete to buck me off. I consider how easily I could get up and shatter his wrist, the same way he'd done to Charli. But I don't have that nature within me, no matter how badly I want to do it.

Instead, I finish it.

Before he has a chance to get me off him, my fists come down to his ribs and chest in rapid movements. My knuckles protest in pain, but I will them to hold on for a few more seconds.

As his hands move down to protect his ribs from my blows, I shift myself forward and deliver my final punch. With everything I've got, I let the fucker have it. I nail him in the temple, and this time, it's lights out.

The crowd cheers, and an announcement rattles the speakers as some guy comes into the ring and pulls my aching, bloodied hand up toward the ceiling. "Winner by KO. The Widow Maker."

The crowd continues roaring, but I only have eyes for Charli.

I hate that she witnessed how I nearly just lost myself during that fight, but in the end, I know she will find some sort of peace after seeing him go down.

The guy has hardly let go of my hand before Cole and Luke burst into the ring and tackle me to the ground. Jace and Caden come in close behind them and land right on top of the pile of muscle. "Two hundred fucking grand," Cole shouts in excitement.

"Hell yeah, motherfucker," Jace exclaims.

In all the time since Charli's attack, the money never once entered my mind. But now it's over, I can't help the grin that tears over my face.

"Get off me, fuckers," I demand. "I have a girl to see."

"Fuck, you're pussy whipped," Cole murmurs.

"You would be too if you had a girl like Charli to go home to every night. Too bad all you have is your hand and PornHub," I say as the boys start getting off me. Luke holds out his hand and helps me to my feet before we start making our way out of the ring.

"Get fucked," Cole laughs as he knocks my shoulder.

"Dude, he's fucking right," Jace scoffs, making the rest of us crack into laughter.

I notice some big guy come into the ring and check on Pitbull with a scowl, realizing that must be his trainer, but I don't give it a second thought as he hauls the dickhead over his shoulder and struggles to make his way out of the ring. That's not my problem.

We head out to the fighters' room, and Cole instantly jumps on the first aid. It hurts as he peels the tape off my bloodied hands, then slathers them in antiseptic cream. He's almost done when a guy in a suit comes in and delivers a few envelopes filled with my winnings. Clearly just one wasn't going to do the trick.

"Hopefully we'll see you in the next round," he says.

I give him a nod, but there's no way I'm putting myself through this shit again. Besides, now that the Underground is over, I'll start training for the professional circuit.

We finish up in the fighters' room, and I head back out to the main warehouse. The majority of the crowd has disappeared, though all my boys are still here. More importantly, Charli stands front and center with the dog glued to her side, waiting anxiously to get her hands on me.

The moment I come through the door, she's flying toward me. With barely enough time to brace myself, she's airborne, and I throw my hands out just in time to catch her. Her arms wrap around me, her cast smacking me in the back of the head in the process, but I honestly don't give a shit.

Her lips crash down on mine, and I welcome them like fucking oxygen, kissing her deeply. The boys all crowd around, ready to give their congratulations, but I'm not finished with my girl yet. She pulls back from me with a massive grin. "You were amazing."

"Were you expecting anything different?" I question with a raised brow.

"Oh, yeah," she teases. "I knew you could do it, but honestly, I could have fallen asleep waiting for the big finale."

I can't help but crack a grin at her smart mouth. "Yeah, well I was kind of expecting you to be at home, fast asleep."

She arches a brow, looking at me as though I'm a fool for thinking she would have stayed at home with her horse. "You seriously thought I was going to miss this?"

"I was hoping," I tell her.

Charli scrunches her face and shakes her head before pressing her lips into a hard line, a look of complete seriousness coming over her face. She leans forward and murmurs into my ear. "Thank you," she says before pressing a gentle kiss to the side of my face.

I turn my face into hers and catch her soft lips in a kiss. "Always," I promise.

Aaron grows tired of our display and steps forward. His arms come around Charli's waist and he literally pulls her off me while she bursts into laughter with Zara. The second I'm free, the boys start up with their own versions of congratulations, which consists of back slaps and fist bumps, though I try my best to avoid those.

A few guys begin to lock up the warehouse, and we take the hint to get out of here. We all pile into different vehicles and eventually end up back at Micky's for a night of wild celebrations.

CHAPTER 25

CHARLI

My life is ah-mazing. I swear I have it all.

I stand at Micky's as a customer rather than the bartender, enjoying my night out. Zara stands by my side as Micky whips us up a few cocktails, though I had to sit through some extensive questioning first, like why the hell I was out partying rather than asleep in bed and taking care of myself. But he eventually let me off the hook.

We lean back against the bar, watching the boys get smashed, and I can't stop thinking about how my life has completely turned around. Only a few short months ago, I was beaten and torn down, an empty version of myself. But here I am, now strong and confident with the most amazing man, who I can honestly say is the love of my life. Hell,

I even own a house now, and apparently we're going car shopping tomorrow.

I'm working toward my dream job and can happily say I now have a real friend. Well, I guess I have to include all the hockey boys in that equation. The moment they found out I was with Xander, I was welcomed into the family, despite Xander's current status with them. I guess once a Dragon, always a Dragon.

That Dragons' family also includes Cassie and Brianna, who are here tonight. And by the way, they are definitely letting loose on the dance floor.

Never in a million years would I have thought my life would turn out this way. I have everything I could ever have dreamed of, and it's all thanks to Xander. I honestly have no idea how I will ever repay him for the way he's managed to turn me into this new person. Or at least, the person I used to be back when my father was still around.

Micky hands us our drinks, and we're halfway back to our table when a girl bumps in front of me with a nasty scowl. "Well, if it isn't the little prude," she says with a smirk.

"Oh, Lex. How great it is to see you," I comment, though the sarcasm lacing my voice is pretty damn thick. I don't need someone like her ruining my night.

"Heard your boyfriend got kicked off the team," she says with a knowing grin. "It's a real shame the coach was let in on his little secret," she adds, letting me know that it was her who came forward and spilled about the Underground.

"Yeah," I say. "It was a shame. But you know what, leaving the

Dragons was the best thing to ever happen to him," I smile as I look over her shoulder. "I mean, can't you see how happy we are?"

Her face drops and anger quickly takes over. She lets out a huff, throws her drink all over me, and turns to storm off. I let out a gasp as the cold liquid drips all over my body, but Zara doesn't plan on letting her get away with it. She grabs a fistful of her oily hair and yanks her back. "What the fuck is your problem, bitch?" Zara demands, releasing her.

"My fucking problem is that this whore goes around acting like she's too fucking good for the rest of us. She needed to be brought down a few notches," Lex spits.

"Are you serious?" I ask, getting in her face. "You have a problem with me because I didn't want to waste my time hanging out with you and getting raped by your lowlife friends? Get a fucking life, Lex," I say. "And while you're at it, you may as well pull your shit together, too."

She lets out a growl, but she's got nothing. The other girls crowd around, and seeing that I'm not an easy target anymore, she storms off. Though, at least she's smart enough to go in a different direction to avoid getting her hair pulled again.

"What the hell was that about?" Cassie asks as she grabs a few napkins off the closest table and tries to mop up the mess.

"Not really sure, but my guess is that she's upset I don't want to be her bestie."

"Are you serious?" Brianna scoffs.

"Apparently," I smirk before the girls and I steal the keys to

Micky's apartment and head up so I can get rid of the now sticky liquid covering my body.

I quickly rinse off in the shower while the girls attempt to salvage my dress. They go hard cleaning it off, even going as far as blow-drying it before shoving the dress back over my head. Cassie and Bri stop to touch up their makeup as Zara starts going into details about her sexcapades with Aaron.

Once everyone is sorted out, we stumble our way out the door and get our asses back down to the bar, more than ready to continue the party.

I'm sitting on my man's lap, feasting on the soft skin of his neck, while his hand begins traveling up my skirt. "Hey, man," Jaxon says, dropping into the seat beside us with Coach Harris falling into the seat next to him, putting a stop to any funny business.

"Hey," Xander says, slightly surprised to see Coach Harris. After all, he wasn't at the fight, but I hardly expected him to be. It's not like it's his scene. He would be risking his career just being seen at a place like that.

"Xander," Coach says with a nod of his head. "Or should I call you *The Widow Maker?*"

I scoff, rolling my eyes. "That shit's over," Xander says as his finger draws little circles on my thigh.

"Over?" Coach questions with a strange tone in his voice that makes me pay a little more attention.

"Definitely," Xander confirms.

Coach looks at Jaxon for a brief moment and gives him a slight nod. "So, the boys and I were talking," Jaxon starts. "Now that the Underground is over, we'd like you to finish off the season as a Dragon."

My eyes bug out of my head, my gaze snapping to Xander's, who looks at Jaxon like he's gone nuts. "Are you serious?" he asks, his gaze flicking between Jaxon and Coach Harris.

"Yeah, man," Jaxon grins.

"How is that even possible?" Xander questions, clearly very deep in thought as he tries to work it out.

"I think you're underestimating the kind of strings I can pull, kid," Coach Harris says with a smug tone.

"But what about the fighting?"

"Look, as far as we're concerned, you were known as *The Widow Maker* in the Underground. That person no longer exists. Here, you're Xander Phillips, a hockey player who would like to pursue a career in professional fighting next season. Nothing to draw any red flags," Coach says.

"So, I can skate until the end of the season?" Xander clarifies, his hand frozen against my thigh.

"You know the rules, kid. Every team member needs to attend classes, and as long as there's no illegal fighting, then I don't have a problem with it. Though I would like to oversee the training program you're doing at Rebels Advocate."

"The college would let me resume my classes?"

"It's already sorted out. You just need to accept the offer," Coach grins.

Xander looks at me, a question behind those dark eyes. "I think you'd regret it if you didn't," I tell him honestly. And besides, when would he ever have another opportunity like this?

He nods, and I see the excitement in his eyes. I know hockey isn't what he wants to do, but he loves being on the team, and no matter how much he loves fighting, hockey will always be part of his life.

I'd hate to hear later down the track that he regretted not playing the championship with the Dragons. It's an opportunity he will never get again, and he needs to take it with both hands and hold on tight.

Xander looks at Jaxon before turning to Coach Harris. "Alright, Coach. Count me in."

CHAPTER 26

XANDER

We're in New York for the Frozen Four, the ice hockey semifinals and finals.

We competed yesterday in the semifinals and won, which means today is it. The fucking championship game. The day we've all been waiting for. Miller Cain led our team to victory last year, and now it's Jaxon's turn. We all know he can do it, and he will most likely end up with a contract with the NHL by the end of the night. Hell, that goes for Bobby too.

But I'm doing this for myself. It will be the last game of ice hockey I ever play. Well, except when Charli gives me a beautiful little boy or girl who I can teach, but until then, this is it.

I managed to pull a few strings when it came to my business

degree, not that I really wanted it, but I had to study something while I was still playing. I managed to take a few extra classes to fast-track my degree, and now I'll also be graduating in a few weeks. That way, with school and hockey out of the way, nothing is stopping me from opening the gym I've always wanted and competing in the professional circuit as a fighter.

Everything is finally happening for me, and having Charli by my side supporting me has made all the difference.

I'll never forget this trip. It's been amazing so far. Well, the amazing bits have all been because Charli has never set foot on a plane before. She completely freaked out. Her nails tore holes in my hand when the plane took off, and then she scratched the shit out of my arm on landing. If it had been anyone else but her, I would never have put myself through it. Hell, I would have kicked the person out of the seat beside me, but I'd do anything for Charli.

When we pulled up at one of the nicest hotels in New York, she was in awe. She couldn't believe her luck that she was going to spend the next few days in a place like this, and then she went on to tell me over and over again how the place has its own gym, day spa, and jacuzzi. I'm just lucky Zara is here to go and do all that girly shit so I don't have to go with her.

It's bad enough she begged to practice her makeup looks on me the other day. I know I tend to say whatever Charli wants, she gets, but I had to draw the line somewhere. So instead of giving up, she waited until I fell asleep. I woke up the prettiest damn drag queen you ever did see.

I stand in the locker room, all suited and ready to go. Skates are on, helmet is on, and stick is in my gloved hand.

Coach Harris comes forward, and I don't doubt he's preparing for one of his famous pep talks. He takes a deep breath and lets us have it. "Alright, boys. We're here defending our title. This is going to be the hardest game of hockey you'll ever play. Hell, for some of you, it might be the last," he says, his eyes briefly flashing to mine. "I want you to go out there and annihilate this game. Show that crowd that you deserve to reclaim the title, that we're the hardest working motherfuckers in this league."

Wow, he's really laying it on thick today.

The boys roar their excitement as the adrenaline pulses through our veins. "Are you ready?" Coach calls out.

"Yes," we respond in unison.

"I said, *are you ready?*" Coach says a little louder.

"Yes!" we all scream out.

"Then get out there and own that ice."

With one final shout, we break out into the Dragons' war cry before lining up by the door and shuffling out of the locker room. Coach stands at the front of the line, clapping each of us on the back as we pass him, then takes up the rear as we head out into the arena.

The place is packed, and considering we are so far away from home, I can't believe just how many of our supporters are in the crowd. The whole place is practically a sea of Dragons' jerseys.

The crowd roars and chants as they see us coming out of the hallway, and I take it all in. My eyes search the stands and come to a stop on Charli, needing to know exactly where she is. She's cheering her lungs out, surrounded by a group of the boys' girlfriends and families.

She's been to every game I've had since the Underground finished, and I must say, she's become quite a fan of the sport. She hardly knows what she's talking about, but I love it either way.

Charli blows me a kiss, and I send her a wink, making her cheeks flush red. There's always been something about the way her cheeks flush that drives me crazy. Even though she's not shy anymore, a wink from me always sends a flush her way.

We step onto the ice and have a quick warm-up before the referee blows his whistle and gets the game underway. Jaxon is center and takes off with the puck, Bobby keeping right up by him. I do what I can to get the opposition out of his way, but they're not making it easy. These fuckers are just as fast as we are.

Jaxon scores the first point of the game, and the crowd cheers right along with us.

On and on it goes. Just as Coach predicted, this is the hardest game we've ever had to play, but with the adrenaline pumping through our veins and the encouragement we're getting from the crowd, it's not that hard to stay ahead.

We're kicking ass, and the opposition already shows signs of fatigue, but we're ready and waiting for more. Minute by minute, we continue to prove that we are the mighty Dragons, the Kings of Denver, and the rightful owners of that big-ass trophy.

Half an hour later, we no longer have to prove it.

We *are* the undefeated, two-time reigning champions, and it feels incredible.

I glance up into the crowd and find my girl staring straight back at me, looking as proud as ever, but I don't get to look at her long before the boys are celebrating in the center. Looking up, I find Coach Harris has somehow made it over the ice and is been consumed by his rowdy team.

Too quickly, the officials are pulling us in for photos and a presentation of the trophy. Even though it's been sitting on a big table in its special glass case while we competed all season, it had to come back to receive a new inscription, and will now be heading right back home again.

The boys and I finally make it off the ice, and we rush through our after-game showers, anxious to get back to our families and friends. Jaxon and a few of the other seniors are called back, and I wonder if it's got something to do with their contracts for the NHL.

I wish them all luck as I make my way out to the ice rink to find Charli. The majority of the crowd has made their way out of the arena, but it's still pretty damn busy. I find Charli leaning up against a big concrete pillar, staring off into space, and I make my way to her when two people insert themselves right in my path.

"Xander," my father exclaims as he pulls me into a hug and claps me on the back a few times. "What a great game, son."

What the fuck?

I can't help the venomous scowl that crosses my face as I step out of his embrace, shoving him off me. "What the hell do you think you're doing?" I ask both my parents.

My father ignores my question. "Glad to see you came to your senses," he says with a grin, trying to look good for the press scattered around.

"Senses?" I scoff. "You need to come to your senses. This was my last game. As of now, I'm no longer a Dragon. I'm in training for the professional fighting circuit."

"Don't be ridiculous," he scolds.

"Get fucked," I scoff before shouldering past him. I don't have time for his bullshit. I hear my mother's outrage, but I don't give them a backward glance. I should have known they would try this shit on for size. Besides, I've got better things to do. Like kissing my girl.

Charli is still staring out into space when I reach her, a wide smile across my face. She gasps in shock when I grab her, but quickly realizes it's me and relaxes into my body. "You were great," she mumbles, her lips pressed against mine.

"I was pretty fucking good," I agree.

A beaming smile takes over her whole face. "You're so full of yourself."

"Would you like to be full of me?" I ask her.

"Xander," she shrieks with wide, frantic eyes, desperately looking around to make sure no one overheard me.

"Come on," I whisper into her ear. "I need to get you back to the hotel."

I do just that and take advantage of her willing body until I get a call from the boys, saying there's a celebratory dinner down in the hotel restaurant.

Charli gets dressed to the nines and looks stunning while she sips on champagne. I lead her down to the restaurant, and we take our seats among the rest of the team.

Jaxon appears with his girlfriend, Cassie, and it's not long before they are announcing their engagement, which is when the party really starts. Drinks are bought and handed around while smiles and laughter are heard from every corner of the room.

I take hold of Charli's hand on my thigh and give it a small squeeze. She turns those beautiful eyes toward me, absolute joy radiating out of them. "I love you," I tell her.

She gets up from her chair and takes a seat on my lap before kissing me gently with her arms around my neck. "Without you, I would still be lost. I'd be fighting with my inner demons and hating myself for it," she starts. "But you changed it all for me. You made me see that I was strong and turned me into this confident woman—a woman I never thought I'd get the chance to be. I love you so much, Xander Phillips, and one day," she says, her eyes flicking toward Jaxon and Cassie before settling back on mine. "That's going to be us."

I pull her in and kiss her one more time. "I can't fucking wait."

EPILOGUE

XANDER

2 YEARS LATER

I stand in my gym, looking around at this masterpiece before me. I can't believe I've done it. Three months ago, Charli and I opened the doors to Warrior's Paradise, and every single day I've had an influx of new members. I have to admit though, it's hard work owning your own business, but that doesn't make me love it any less.

Seeing kids coming in off the street with nowhere to go, feeling like Warrior's Paradise is a safe place for them, makes me feel more accomplished than any of my wins in the professional league last season.

Though, those wins are what's made all of this possible. I was able to buy this place and fix it up. It took a lot of hard work, but eventually we turned it into the best gym equipped for MMA. I made it so it functions as a regular gym as well because Charli wouldn't have it any other way. She demanded that women have a place to train as well, but with my name attached to it, it's damn clear this is a gym designed for serious fighters.

I still train with Cole every day, and we regularly have arguments about whose gym we're going to work out in. Though I find when I win that argument, my training session is usually brutal and has me wishing for sweet, sweet death.

I come home to find Charli dressed up in a sexy, black, knee-length dress with strappy heels, just as I had requested of her. She smiles at me the moment I walk through the door, those stunning blue eyes still managing to take my breath away. And as usual, that damn dog of hers is lying right by her feet.

"You look incredible," I tell her, seconds before I rush in and kiss her.

"You don't look too bad yourself," she teases, as I'm still in my training gear. Though, she often tells me just how much she appreciates this look. The need to strip her naked and take her on the kitchen counter pulses through me, but I have a plan to stick to.

"I'll be ready in five," I tell her before dashing into the bathroom and rushing through a quick shower. I come out precisely five minutes later wearing the cologne she loves and give her a big-ass cheesy grin.

"A suit?" she asks as her eyes rake up and down my body, appreciating the view. "Where the hell are we going?"

"You'll see," I tell her as I take her hand and lead her out to my truck. I help her up and quickly dash around to the driver's side, anxious to get tonight started.

I drive in the direction of the gym, but take a few different turns and watch as her brows furrow in confusion. She has absolutely no idea where we are or where we're going. I find a park and cut the engine, then lean across and give Charli a quick kiss before hopping out of the truck and helping her down in her heels.

We walk down a street lined with stores, and I watch as her confusion sinks further. "Xander," she says, scanning the names of the stores. "There are no restaurants down here. Are you sure we're in the right place?"

"Positive," I tell her.

We walk for a few more minutes until I stop in front of a storefront and pull a key out of my pocket before handing it to her. "Open it," I tell her.

She looks around, searching for a sign to tell her where we are, but so far, there isn't one. Her eyes go wide with alarm as she shoots a funny look at me. "No," she hisses, trying to keep her voice low. "Where the hell are we? I'm not breaking into someone's store. I'm too innocent to go to jail. I'd never survive."

"Babe," I tell her calmly, trying to hold back my grin at her comments because she couldn't be more wrong. She's the furthest thing from innocent. "Open the damn door."

She lets out a huff but does as she's told, after looking up and down the street twice more. She pushes the door open, and I turn the lights on behind her. The store instantly comes to life as she takes it all in.

"What the hell is this?" she asks as her eyes flick from the right to left, then top to bottom.

"This is your salon, Charli," I tell her.

Her eyes go wide as she turns back to me, sucking in a loud gasp. "Are you serious?"

"Yeah, babe," I smile. "I've been working on it for a few months with Micky. There's still some more work to do, but I wanted you to choose all the finishing touches so everything is how you want it."

"Thank you," she whispers with a lump in her throat as tears of happiness flow from her gorgeous blue eyes and drop down her cheeks. "This is . . . I don't know, I have no words for how amazing this is. It's my dream to have my own salon."

I step forward and wipe the tears away. "I know," I tell her. "Now, there's no time for tears. You need to see the place first."

She gives an excited nod as she wipes the rest of the tears on the back of her arms—she's classy like that. "Okay," she murmurs, taking hold of my hand and allowing me to lead her around the salon. I point out all the work that's been done and what still needs her final say. I show her where the register will go and where she can have shelves of products for sale.

"You're going to have to come up with a name," I tell her.

"Shit," she laughs. "But I swore after all the drama of picking a name for the gym that I'd never do it again."

"Tough shit, babe," I grin, remembering the hell of a time we had narrowing down the list of names for Warrior's Paradise. I couldn't have been happier with the outcome, but it was a long journey. "Why don't you keep it simple? Charli's Salon."

She stops in her tracks and looks around fondly. "Charli's Salon," she says, trying it out. "I like it."

"Well, that was easy," I murmur.

We come to a door, and she pushes her way through. "What's up here?" she asks, taking in the stairs.

"Go up and see," I tell her as the nerves start taking over.

I follow her as we head up the stairs and she pushes through the door. She lets out a surprised gasp as she finds the rooftop terrace completely overtaken with flowers and fairy lights that twinkle against the night's backdrop. "Oh. My. God," she whispers to herself as she takes it in. "This place is amazing."

I close the door behind me and drop down to one knee. I wait patiently as she takes it all in before slowly turning back to me with tears in her eyes. The second she realizes what I'm doing and takes in the big diamond ring sitting in the velvet box I'm holding out to her, she lets out another gasp and looks at me with wide eyes.

"Charli," I start. "Since the day I saw you working behind the bar at Micky's, I knew you were going to be mine. I've watched you grow into this beautiful, strong woman, and still to this day, you continue to surprise me with how far you've come. I'm pretty sure I fell in love with you that very first day, and since then, that feeling has only grown. I no longer know how to live my life without you, and what's more, I don't ever want to," I say, letting that sink in before I continue.

She wipes a stray tear, and I make sure she's hearing every single word I'm saying. "Charli, will you do me the greatest honor of becoming my wife?"

She drops to her knees in front of me, "Yes," she cries, throwing her arms around me and crushing her lips to mine as she continues. "Nothing in this world would make me happier. I love you so much."

"I love you, too," I say, taking the ring out of the box and sliding it onto her finger before pulling her back into me.

Our bodies crash together as she reaches for my suit jacket, slipping it straight off my shoulders before grabbing my shirt and ripping the buttons right off in her desperation to feel my skin on hers.

Her hands find purchase on my chest and begin roaming over the rest of my torso, while I grab the hem of her dress and pull it up before tearing her lace panties from her body. She undoes my pants and pushes them down just enough to let my erection spring free.

Taking her by the waist, I shuffle us around until I can bring her down on top of me, and she lets out a groan as she sinks down, allowing me to fill her completely. Fuck, I will never get used to the feeling of being inside her.

Charli begins to move, gripping me tight as she rolls her hips, and in record time, she's exploding around me with tears of joy in those beautiful blue eyes. I come with her, and we ride out our high together, her lips fused to mine.

I lean back against the door with Charli in my lap, trying to catch our breath. She comes forward and rests her forehead against mine while her fingernails run through my hair. "That was amazing," she whispers, her lips softly brushing over mine.

"You're amazing," I counter. "I can't wait to spend the rest of my life with you."

"Yeah, well let's just hope you don't need a hip replacement and you can still rock my world when we're ninety," she smirks.

"No matter what," I tell her. "I will always rock your world."

Sheridan Anne

Kiss My Pucking Bass

THANKS FOR READING

If you enjoyed reading this book as much as I enjoyed writing it, please consider leaving an Amazon review to let me know.
https://www.amazon.com/dp/B0BSDGWW49

For more information on the Kings of Denver, find me on Facebook –
www.facebook.com/sheridansbookishbabes

STALK ME!

Join me online with the rest of the stalkers!!
I swear, I don't bite. Not unless you say please!

Facebook Reader Group
www.facebook.com/SheridansBookishBabes

Facebook Page
www.facebook.com/sheridan.anne.author1

Instagram
www.instagram.com/Sheridan.Anne.Author

TikTok
www.tiktok.com/@Sheridan.Anne.Author

Subscribe to my Newsletter
https://landing.mailerlite.com/webforms/landing/a8q0y0

MORE BY SHERIDAN ANNE

www.amazon.com/Sheridan-Anne/e/B079TLXN6K

DARK CONTEMPORARY ROMANCE - M/F

Broken Hill High | Haven Falls | Broken Hill Boys | Aston Creek High | Rejects Paradise | Bradford Bastard

DARK CONTEMPORARY ROMANCE - REVERSE HAREM

Boys of Winter | Depraved Sinners | Empire

NEW ADULT SPORTS ROMANCE

Kings of Denver | Denver Royalty | Rebels Advocate

CONTEMPORARY ROMANCE (standalones)

Play With Fire | Until Autumn (Happily Eva Alpha World)

PARANORMAL ROMANCE

Slayer Academy [Pen name - Cassidy Summers]

Sheridan Anne